THE STREETS OF SEATTLE

~A NOVEL~

Loretta Miles Tollefson

Palo Flechado Press

ISBN-10: 0-9983498-2-8
ISBN-13: 978-0-9983498-2-4

Palo Flechado Press, Eagle Nest, New Mexico

Other Books by Loretta Miles Tollefson

Fiction
The Pain and The Sorrow
Moreno Valley Sketches II
Moreno Valley Sketches I
The Ticket

Poetry
But Still My Child
Mary at the Cross, Voices from the New Testament
And Then Moses Was There, Voices from the Old Testament

THE STREETS OF SEATTLE

1

The Seattle bus depot was always busy on Monday mornings. Inside, lines snaked away from the ticket counter toward the restrooms and from the candy machines to the street door.

The yard outside was only a large shed with steel fences for walls. The passengers were uncomfortably aware of the city around them. They huddled at the closed doors of outbound buses or pawed hurriedly through the piles of luggage near the midsections of the buses just in.

There was only one person left of the group which had come via the stopping places of Dungeness and Maynard from the Olympic Peninsula. This was a girl who looked as if she was just out of high school. Her shoulder length brown hair and fair skin looked fresh even in the grimy light filtering through the greenish plastic overhead. She was asking the bus driver for directions.

He, of course, had no idea how far the Arctic Building was from the depot.

The girl thanked him and moved toward the bus depot. She had no luggage except her white fabric purse. The Portland bus had driven in behind hers. As she passed it, a tall slim young man in a dark overcoat pulled an old-fashioned black suitcase from the pile of cases beside it.

"Excuse me, miss?"

She turned.

"Could you tell me how to get to—" He looked at the piece of paper in his hand. "Nine oh nine Fourth Avenue?"

She shook her head. "I'm trying to figure out where I'm supposed to be going." She dug into her purse. "I've got a map though, if that will help."

He looked around the dingy yard. "I think there are benches inside."

She followed him through the thick wooden double doors. The benches were crowded with people. She found a bit of space at the end of one and perched on it. He put his suitcase down and balanced on it while he looked over her shoulder.

She opened the map. "The question is, where are we?"

He pulled his ticket stub out of his pocket. "You'd think this would say."

She looked at it. "No such luck." She looked around the room. "What's that sign over the door? Stewart Street? Let's see—"

"Right here." His finger ran along the line carefully. "The question is, where on Stewart? Ah hah, right on the map. Greyhound Bus Depot."

She laughed. "I didn't think of that." She ran an unpainted fingernail along Eighth. "It looks like all the numbered streets run parallel with the water. Well, that will help."

"Help?"

She grinned at him. "To know east from west. West is the water."

"W and W."

She ran her finger down Stewart. "And here's Fourth. Now the Arctic Building—" She reached into her purse. "Third and Cherry. It's not very far from where you're going."

"Well, a few blocks. Nine oh nine should be just about here." He stubbed a finger down at a street called Marion.

She reached for a corner of the map. "Do you think you'll be able to find it without this?"

"Oh sure, I'll be okay now. I just needed a general idea."

She looked up. His eyes were so blue. She hadn't expected that color with the black curliness of his hair. It gave his face an intense look. So very different from Andrew's.

She suddenly realized what she was doing.

"Are you uh— Do you live here?" he asked.

"No. I'm just here for the day, for a job interview."

"Oh. My name's Lawrence. Lawrence Anderson."

She began to fold the map. "I'm Deborah Brownell."

"That's pretty."

She smoothed the map. He watched her. She put the map in her purse. She was suddenly aware of how much the old depot echoed. The doors to the street banged open and closed and feet shuffled endlessly on the scuffed floor. All these people, but no one had paid any attention when she and this stranger had come in from the bus area.

"If you're going to be here all day, maybe I can take you to lunch—"

She caught the hesitation. She looked up at him, then quickly down. The piece of paper with her interview address on it lay in her lap. She slipped it into her pocket.

His mouth opened and then closed. He was being foolish and he knew it. He didn't have time for girls. More importantly, money. If he was going to make it in this city, he'd have to spend every penny on living, not eating. Eating out with girls, anyway.

Deborah glanced at her watch. Maybe it would be okay. If no one was watching, maybe it meant this was normal. After all, she had to learn to take care of herself in the city sometime. Today was for beginning, wasn't it? And he seemed nice. She looked at her watch again. She had an hour before she had to start searching for the Arctic Building.

"I don't have much time—" she began.

"Well in that case— Maybe some other time," he said. He smiled at her, their eyes not connecting. He picked up his suitcase. "It was nice meeting you. Thanks for the directions."

He was already edging away and she watched him go with the smile she'd been going to accept his invitation with still hovering around her lips.

Out on the sidewalk, Lawrence shifted into a near run, his cheeks suddenly warm. He couldn't afford to give himself away to the people he met here in Seattle. Portland was different. The people he knew there were friends from school. They knew his situation. That he'd just gotten his History B.A., but only with the help of his father's Social Security funds. That there hadn't been much left from the sale of the household stuff when his mother had entered the nursing home two months ago.

If he expected to manage here, he'd have to go it alone. It cost money to get to know people. Especially girls. And money was one thing he wasn't going to have much of. Not right yet, anyway. He slowed down, looking at the buildings around him, then stepped out firmly, his jaw tense.

Deborah's face relaxed and she looked around the waiting room. No one seemed to have noticed. A benefit of being in the city which she hadn't thought of. Make a mistake, no one sees. She stood up, smoothed her skirt and moved toward the door labeled "Stewart."

Nothing like a rejection your first time around. Not that it was really rejection. Not like Andrew's sudden change of face after that night in the back of his car. She tightened her lips, then her face relaxed. These young dandies lounging outside the door of the depot might be making her feet want to move faster but the things they were saying were meant to be compliments. They at least told her she was attractive.

She breathed in a mouthful of city air and let it out again. She looked up at the buildings. So this was Seattle. Seattle on her own. Not the same as Seattle with parents and brother. She looked around again, then down at her jacket and skirt and back into the shop window she was passing. She touched a hand to her hair and studied the windows lining the street, looking for a place to eat. She really didn't have much time.

Though if a man suggested lunch again, she'd try to make it clear that "not much time" didn't mean "no," she promised herself as she pushed open the door of the nearest cafe.

2

The Arctic Building was actually easy to find. Deborah was at the office where she was to be interviewed ten minutes ahead of time. She breathed a sigh of relief as she sat down to wait.

She looked around, her mind carefully blank. Relax. That was the main thing she'd learned from all the magazine and newspaper articles she'd been reading about interviews. Above all, don't project an image of tension.

Her lips twitched. She looked at her watch. One thirty exactly. She looked at the doorway leading from the reception area. No one came out of it. The receptionist ignored her.

She studied the framed poster on the opposite wall. One thing her high school art classes had given her was an awareness of painting. Even if she didn't have any talent herself, she could appreciate the work of someone who did. The poster advertised a local art gallery. She wondered if it was nearby.

The door behind the receptionist opened. A slim, artfully dressed young black woman led Deborah down a carpeted hallway to a door at the end. A large woman in a flowered dress sat behind a desk surrounded by plants and filing cabinets.

The woman pushed at a piece of hair which had escaped the mousey-brown bun at the back of her neck. She waved Deborah to a seat and opened a manila folder lying in front of her. She began asking questions about classes Deb had taken in high school and the office work she'd done after hours. Finally, she closed the file with a bored look and folded her hands over it. "And you're interested in art?"

"Very much."

She pushed back her hair. "What kind of interest do you have?"

"I'm not sure—"

"Is it—" she smiled. "Passionate, shall we say? Or casual? Maybe this is a better question: Is it a hobby?"

"It's not really any of those, though I suppose it's all of them, too." Deborah's hands came out of their grip on each other for the first time in twenty minutes. "I really love art. I like to draw and to paint. But I know I'll never be famous or even really good, if I pursue it. Grants and galleries and stuff. I've done a lot of reading on my own and for classes, but I don't really know that much, growing up on the Peninsula and all." She waved a hand toward the file on the desk. "I would like to do something, though," she said.

The woman nodded. She pushed the piece of hair behind her ear again and reached for the phone.

"We usually don't do this," she said as she dialed a number. She spoke into the phone and looked at Deborah again. "Usually we make you wait. Send you a letter or call you. But since you're not actually living here yet and this position doesn't need to be filled for another couple of weeks—"

She turned her mouth toward the receiver. "Sue, I've got someone here for your Assistant position. Yeah, I guess that would make the last one, wouldn't it? When would be good? This afternoon. And Clarissa is leaving next week? All right."

She put the receiver down without saying goodbye and picked up a pencil. She opened the file again and made a note on the top sheet.

"We have a position open right now in our Arts Support area. It's a small department but it does quite a bit with the community. The opening I'm sending you on actually works with the applications which artists fill out when they apply for money from the County. It's mostly paperwork, but if you want the inside story of what the art world looks like, it may be as good a place as any to begin."

She looked at Deb. "This isn't exactly a glamour job. You'll be pushing a pencil, mostly."

"Oh, that's—"

"Here's the information. You need to be there at two thirty."

Deborah stood up and took the file. She opened it. Name, room number and time, and a telephone number if she needed it. She flashed a big smile. "Thank you."

The woman smiled back at her. "Good luck. If this doesn't work out, we'll be letting you know as other positions become available. Actually, I have something else right now, but it's in the Bookkeeping department."

"Oh, that would—"

She waved her toward the door. "We'll talk about it if this doesn't work." The girl who looked like a model was putting her head in the room. "Yes, June. Whenever you're ready."

"Thank you again," Deborah said.

The waiting area for the two thirty appointment was very different from that of the one thirty one. The art department seemed to be all in one very large room, rather than spread among different offices. The reception area was in the center. Hallways led from it at odd angles. The office areas were open-doored cubicles formed by short walls of a heavy cardboard covered with cloth. The cloth was a greenish tan color.

Around her, voices were talking, papers rattling and desk drawers banging open and closed. Somewhere a computer beeped and its printer began clattering.

Deborah sat there a long time.

The receptionist had her head bent over several strips of shiny white paper with all the print on them scrunched to one side in a long narrow row. From time to time she made a mark on the white part with a blue pencil.

Suddenly a short, lumpy man came barreling out of one of the hallways. He was wearing a bright purple cardigan pulled haphazardly over a sky blue Seattle Symphony tee shirt. He glanced at Deborah and hurried toward the hall opposite. He reached it and then he stopped with a jerk and turned to the receptionist.

"I suppose this isn't Susan's appointment?"

Deb turned her head, startled by the crisp British accent coming out of his mouth.

The receptionist looked up. "I called and said she was here."

"And Sue never showed?"

She shook her head and looked down at her papers. She made a mark with the blue pencil.

The man jerked around to face Deborah. "Hi. My name's Peter. I'll take you back. Looks like Susan got busy and forgot."

Deborah looked at the receptionist, but her head was bent over her papers. Deb followed the cardigan down a hall. The blue jeans he wore were ragged at the hem.

Just as she had lost all sense of direction, Peter stopped short. He flourished a hand at the doorway of a cubicle, then knocked on the plastic edge of the board.

A skinny blond woman looked up from the desk. "Just a sec." She made a note on a piece of paper, added it to a pile and reached for something buried under another stack. "Yes?" She pulled a pack of cigarettes from a drawer.

"Your appointment, madam," he said.

The woman jerked her head toward Deborah. "Oh! Sorry. I was in the middle of things." Her hands moved over the papers scattered several layers deep on the desk. "We need help."

"Well, that's what I'm here for." Deborah flashed her a bright, interviewing smile. She smiled at the man named Peter, too. "Thank you."

"Anytime. Cheerio."

Deborah handed Susan her file and sat down. The phone rang and Susan began speaking into it without saying hello.

Deb looked around the room, trying to think about something besides the way her stomach was churning.

Susan was listening to the phone and looking at Deb's file at the same time. Deborah tried not to stare at the short chopped haircut and chewed fingers and nails. They made her look skinnier than she already was.

Susan hung up the phone without saying good-by and turned intensely pale blue eyes onto Deborah. "Credentials look good," she said. "Interested in art?"

Deborah nodded. She opened her mouth to begin repeating what she'd said to the woman downstairs, but the blue eyes were looking at the wall, then at the file again.

Susan stood up. "Let's introduce you. To the guys you'd be working with. See if you can put up with them." Her smile was only in her lips. "May not be easy."

"One is Peter. He showed you my office," she said as they walked down the hall. "Other's Al. Does liaison with artists. Basically P.R."

She stopped in front of another open doorway and pointed at a large wooden desk in the corner. "That's the desk." She pointed at the desk catty corner from it. "Peter's there. He'd train you." Deb followed her into the office next door. "This is Al. Al, Deborah—"

"Brownell," Deb said.

A small, thin, dark man, thirtyish, looked around from the file drawer he'd been searching through. "Pleased to meet you. Sue, where is that damned Exempt file?"

"You put up with his mouth." She smiled again.

He looked around again. "Oh, you're applying for Clarissa's position. What kind of experience have you had?"

"Well, some secretarial." She glanced at Susan, who was rummaging through the papers on Al's desk. "Not much in the way of working with grants or anything like that."

He nodded. "That's the best type. You're forthright, too." He took the papers Sue had been going through from under her hands and began shuffling them into a pile. "Hire her," he said.

Susan reached for the papers. She looked at the top one. "I see these," she said. "Before they go."

"You usually do."

"Always," she said. "All of them." She turned and Deborah followed her back down the hall.

Susan dropped into her chair, rattled some papers together, made a note on another sheet, and again answered the telephone without saying hello.

She put the receiver down without saying good-by and swung her chair around. She looked at Deborah. "Well?"

"Well, it sounds interesting—"

"Want it?"

"Of course, if—"

"Pay's nine hundred." She scrabbled through some more papers. "Raise of fifty in six months. No union. No parking. Discount on bus passes. Saves about five."

"That sounds great."

"When can you start?"

Deborah tried to keep her voice casual. "When do you need me?"

"Clarissa leaves end of this week. First part of next?"

Deborah stared at her, then choked her voice into existence again. "Yes," she said. She smiled at her, trying to keep the ringing noise out of her head. "Yes," she said again.

But it wasn't until the Greyhound bus was rattling down the hill toward the ferry dock late that afternoon that it began to sink in. A real job. In the arts. Not exactly an art gallery, but— Wait until she told her parents!

Suddenly she was sitting straight and tall in her seat. She'd done it. She really had. Let's just see them try to stop her moving now!

~~~

Lawrence stood outside the big double doors of the YMCA and looked around. City library across the street. That could be nice. A bank, too. It was on the same side of the street, down a ways.

But first a place to sleep. And eat, possibly. He eyed the restaurant next door and his stomach growled. What he really needed was a grocery store and things he could cook in his room. The "souvenirs" that he carried from his childhood were all of them practical, from the biggest and sharpest of the kitchen knives to the frying pan and the dishes. They'd been scrounged from his mother's apartment before the tag sale. After it, the leftovers had been hauled off to the Salvation Army. That was after the nursing home people had come for her.

"You've got to live," he told himself firmly. He took a last look around and picked up his suitcase again.

A few minutes at their front desk and he knew the YMCA would never work. No cooking allowed in the rooms and you paid by the week. In advance. His money would be gone in a month, living like that. He bought a paper and crossed the street to the library. He sat down in a corner and read the housing section.

The cheapest places advertised were studio apartments on Capitol Hill. He tried to remember if he'd seen anything on that girl's map labeled "Capitol Hill." East, behind the downtown area. Not west, west was the water. He smiled, then forced himself back to business. No time for girls. Though Deborah was a nice name.
~~~

He marked a few more advertisements. There were pay telephones in the lobby. He straddled his suitcase and punched in the number for the first listing. The phone at the other end buzzed softly over and over. Finally he gave up and made a small check mark beside the ad.

He punched in the number for the second ad. The ring at the opposite end was lengthy and harsh. No one there either. He looked down at the number and dialed again. The same long harsh ring. He hadn't gotten it wrong.

The third number was busy. He put the receiver on the hook, fished his quarter out of the change compartment and dialed again. He did this three times. Maybe he'd ring through as soon as the connection was broken. It was busy each time. He took the quarter out of the compartment and looked at it.

He knew it was foolish, but he tried another coin, just for luck. Somebody answered.

"Hello?"

"Yes. Hello. You have an apartment for rent?"

It was an elderly voice. "No, I do not have an apartment for rent! I'm not planning on going anywhere and I like it where I am. Now you stop calling me, hear?" The line clicked off. He looked at the receiver and checked the number. He hesitated, then tried again. He kept his hand over the silver lever at the top of the phone box. "Hello?" It was the quavering voice. He pressed the lever down gently.

Two quarters wasted on the newspaper people. He dialed the next number. It was probably wrong, too. Or no one there, or the phone off the hook. At this rate, he'd never get a place to stay. At least, not tonight. He peered out the window. He could see a corner of the YMCA building across the street from where he stood. He hated paying twenty dollars a night just for a place to sleep. That wouldn't get him off to a very good start.

But there actually was someone at the other end. A sharp male voice that softened when Lawrence asked if the furnished studio was still available.

He got directions by bus and promised to be there in thirty minutes. But he hadn't reckoned with the bus system. By the time he actually stood in front of the place, it had been almost fifty minutes. Still, he hesitated.

It looked clean, he had to say that much for it. But there were baby buggies on the porch and most of the windows had vividly colored curtains at them. A lot of the windows were open. There were loud voices coming out of them. But considering what they were asking, he couldn't be too picky. A hundred and eighty a month for a furnished studio was damn cheap.

"Wonder what it's furnished with," he muttered as he went up the steps. Two small Asian children came scrambling over the doorsill and he moved out of the way. He looked for a "Manager" sign. The scratched up door to the nearest apartment opened and a middle-aged man with a dark mustache leaned against the doorjamb. His white tee shirt stretched over his stomach and didn't quite meet his blue jeans. He was pinching a cigarette between his thumb and forefinger.

"Excuse me?"

"Yeah?" He put the cigarette in his mouth.

"I'm looking for the Manager."

"That's me."

"I called about an apartment."

"Oh yeah! Come in, come in. Studio, furnished, one eighty a month, that the one? Let me get the key." He went back into the apartment, leaving the door open. He rummaged through a drawer in the desk in the dark entry hall. "Hey, Mart, I got a customer. Back in a minute." He pulled a key out and led Lawrence up the stairs.

"This ain't nothin' fancy, but it's clean, like I told you on the phone. Furnishings is a stove and a frig and a couple of chairs. Hide-a-bed, too. There's built-in drawers in the closet. Bathroom doesn't have a tub. Just a shower."

Lawrence looked around the dark hall. He sniffed.

"We got a lot of boat people living here," the man said as he unlocked the door. "That's what you're smelling. Their food tastes good but smells rotten." He led the way in. "Table, too," he said. "And end tables for the couch. You gotta television?"

"Just this." Lawrence lifted the suitcase an inch higher. He put it down on the brown carpet.

He nodded. "You wanta get a TV, there's a hookup over by the window. Cable's about fifteen a month. Guy comes around and leaves his stuff on your doorknob every few weeks." There was an old fashioned radiator in the corner. "Steam heat, so you only got to pay 'lectricity for lights and the kitchen stuff. That's not in the rent." He pointed to one corner of the room. "There's your kitchen."

It looked like someone had taken the doors off a closet. There was a camper-size refrigerator, a sink and a row of cupboards where the closet shelf would have been. The stove was camper-size too.

Lawrence opened the door of the refrigerator, then closed it and went into the bathroom. There was only enough room to turn around in, with the shower, toilet and sink. But it did seem clean. "One eighty a month, right?" he asked as he came out.

"Yeah, it's real cheap, too, 'cause we don't ask for a first and last. Just the first and a hundred deposit for cleaning."

"So you want two hundred and eighty dollars before I move in." He knew exactly how much his wallet would deflate with that amount taken out of it.

"Yeah, that's standard. Only usually you gotta pay the last month's rent, too."

Lawrence nodded and looked around again. "Okay," he said. He reached for his wallet. "Do you want the money now or do I have to sign a lease or something?"

"No, we just got a rental agreement that says things like you won't have no pets or waterbed, stuff like that." He put out his right hand. "By the way, my name's Cal."

Lawrence gripped his hand firmly. "I'm Lawrence," he said. He looked around. "Always feels good to have a roof over your head."

"I'll go down and get the agreement and stuff and let you get settled in," Cal said. "Be back in a bit."

The door shut behind him and Lawrence nudged the side of the suitcase with his toe. First step accomplished. It hadn't taken that long, though the anxiety it had produced was enough for a week.

He picked up the suitcase and carried it to the table. He still had the newspaper he'd gotten earlier. He'd go through it for job possibilities tomorrow. For now, he'd unpack and find someplace nearby to get a few groceries. Relax a little.

"Home sweet home," he said aloud. He grinned. "At least there's nobody sleeping in the bed across the room!"

~~~

By the time her bus reached Hood Canal Bridge, Deborah had decided that she wanted to move without her family's help. It would spoil everything to have Mom poking her nose into corners looking for dirt. And Dad worrying about the number of locks on the door. As for Bobby, he was always a nuisance.

She sat very straight as the bus pulled into the yard of the combined tavern and grocery store at Maynard. Bobby was already there, lounging in the driver's seat of the family truck. He made no move to open the door from the inside, much less get out and help her in.
~~~

"Bus was late," he said as he started the engine.

She looked at her watch. "Only five minutes. It was fifteen this morning. Though the driver made up for it on the road, because we got to the ferry on time."

He grunted. She looked at him. "You're full of life."

The truck pulled out onto the highway. "I got better things to do than meet buses."

"Well, I didn't ask you to."

"Don't know who else could of done it. Andy's not around anymore. And Mom's baking pies for the church potluck."

Bobby's mouth was another thing she'd be leaving behind. Thank heaven.

"Dad's down helping the Braddocks with their hay," he said. "My job is fetching and carrying you."

"You won't have to do it much longer. Maybe not ever again."

He didn't answer. Her lips tightened. He knew she wanted to tell what had happened. She jerked her purse into her lap. It wouldn't break her heart to get away from him, that was for sure.

The sun had set by the time they reached the farm. The moon hung low in the fruit trees east of the house. Deborah stood a minute, breathing the cool air.

The farm backed into the hills. When you looked up and beyond the immediate line of trees, the Olympic Mountains glowered down at you benignly. She took another deep breath and shivered. It was so cold. But beautiful, too.

"Deborah? Deb? Come in, silly girl, you'll catch pneumonia." Her mother was on the back porch, peering into the gloom of the outbuildings and bushes where Bobby had parked the truck. "How'd it go?" she asked sympathetically as Deb neared the porch.

"Wonderful!" Deb took the steps in one jump and hugged her mother, flour and all. "I got it!"

"What?"

"I got the job. I got it."

"Oh Deb!"

"I start next Monday."

"Next week?"

"A week from today. At this time a week from today I'll have been on the job one full day!" She whirled into the kitchen and sat down at the table. She laughed. "Is there any tea? I'm dying of thirst!"

Her mother moved to the stove. Her back was to the table. "So, when do you want us to start looking for a place for you to live?" Her shoulders were tight under the house dress but Deb didn't look at her. Her mother brought her the tea.

Deb stirred her cup. "I thought I'd go over Thursday. I won't have all that much stuff. Only a couple suitcases. They've got lockers at the bus station I can leave them in and after I find a place I'll go down and pick them up. I can take Metro there and back if they're too heavy."

"They've got a really good bus system!" she rushed on. "Lots of routes going all over the place. But my job's right in the center of Downtown. It's in a really old-fashioned building, Mom. You'd love it. So anyway, I thought I'd try to find something close to it. Just a studio or something so I won't need much furniture."

"You have a bed and dresser already," her mother said. "You shouldn't need a whole lot."

"I couldn't put a bed in a studio," Deb said. "They look tacky. But I've seen pictures of things that are like great big pillows that fold into a couch during the day but at night you lay them out and they're a bed. That's what I want to get. They're pretty cheap too, so I can do it with the money Dad's letting me have."

"You have to live on that money, too, until you get paid." Her mother rattled the dishes in the sink. "And you'll need some set aside in case the job doesn't work out."

"How would it not work? I told you, I've got it. They gave me all sorts of information about what I'll be doing and brochures about the bus system and stuff."

"Did you meet the people you would be working with?"

"Uh huh. Two men. Though my actual boss is a woman."

"Well, that'd be nice. You'll have to invite them here for a weekend."

Deb took a sip of tea. "Um, that feels good. Why would I want to do that?"

"Well, so you can get to know them better. You can't tell much about a man by only seeing him on the job."

"Mother, I'm going to be working with them, not dating them."

"And why can't the two go together?"

"I don't believe in that kind of thing."

"How else do you expect to meet young men?"

"I don't know. I'll get to know people. In my apartment building and at art things I go to, I guess. But I'm not going there to find a man, anyway. I don't know why you keep pestering me about it."

Her mother went to the window and leaned toward the glass. She shaded her eyes with her hand. "That must be your father. I wouldn't tell him about the men you're working with if I were you. He'll just start worrying about you being in the right kind of environment."

Deb looked into her tea cup.

Her father came in the door. "Hi Dad!" she said. "Guess what? I start next week at nine hundred a month."

Her mother put the coffee pot down and then picked it up again. Her father nodded as he hung up his hat.

"And you think that's going to be enough to live on? Seattle's a big city. It's not like here, where your food is in the ground waiting for you."

"It'll be more than enough," she said. "I can make the move and furnish my place with what you're giving me and live on what I'm earning."

"You'll want to take your sewing machine," her mother said. "It's awfully heavy, even if you don't take the cabinet for it."

"Maybe later," Deborah said. Good, the nine hundred had shocked them. It was almost as much as he made in a month at the mill. That would show them what she was worth.

"Starting next week, then?"

"Monday morning. I have to be there at nine o'clock."

"Don't see how you're gonna do it. I've got that cow to butcher for the Camerons on Saturday. Been planning it for the last couple months." He went to the sink and began rubbing his hands with the Lava soap beside the faucet.

"I'm not expecting you to cart me back and forth," she said. "I've only got a couple suitcases of clothes. I'll take them over on the bus, if you can get me to the tavern Thursday morning to catch it. Then I'll leave them in a locker at the depot and look for a place to live."

"You're going to find an apartment in that city in one day?" Her mother was bumping things onto the counter from the refrigerator. "Isn't that asking a bit much?"

"It's a big city. There ought to be something."

"And what—"

"And if there's not I'll stay at the YWCA. They rent rooms by the night and it's cheap and safe."

"Speaking of safe—" her father said.

"I'll be careful while I'm hunting and sensible about what I rent," she told him. "I've been reading articles about how to keep yourself from being attacked and what to look for when you're apartment hunting." She met his eyes squarely.

His lips twitched. He turned back to the sink and began scrubbing his hands again. "You call us as soon as you get something," he said.

"Oh, of course!" she said. "Mom, is there any more tea? It's been a long day."

3

It took Lawrence's eyes a minute to adjust the next morning. Where— Oh yeah, Capitol Hill. Apartment. Furnished. He saw his black, boxy suitcase laying open on a chair on the other side of the room and swung his legs off the couch. He shook out his overcoat and looked at it. Using it as a blanket hadn't been a good idea, though he'd had no choice. He'd have to find some other kind of covering today.

He had to play with the dials on the shower a bit before the water began to flow sullenly. Afterward he fried a couple eggs, ate some bread and butter and then piled the dishes into the sink and sat down with the newspaper.

The want ad section wasn't long. He doodled through the list, marking a couple of them, then sat back to stare at the smudged print. The problem was, he didn't know what kind of job he wanted.

Anything, he'd said. That wasn't really true though. Anything in the way of a career was what he meant. The things he'd marked were just jobs. A way to put food on the table. Security guards. Cashiers in all-night stores. Janitors. And even most of those required experience. The one thing he didn't have. Last year's teaching job at that summer camp and selling books door to door the summer before. That was it as far as experience went.

And that eliminated two careers right there. Teaching and selling. Doing them had convinced him he wanted nothing to do with them. He looked at the paper in front of him. He probably should rethink the no selling decision. He hadn't marked any of the "salesperson wanted" ads, but they were just about the only openings not requiring experience. Though even most of those required some kind of knowledge or experience of the product.

He pushed the paper away, filled his single pan with water and put it on the stove. Coffee might help.

How was a person supposed to get experience if everyone required it? Wouldn't do any good to complain, though. He studied the ads again. Most of them gave a number to telephone.

He'd have to get one. That would be another expense. There was only a thousand left in his wallet.

He looked at the paper again, folded his wallet and put it away. It seemed like so much but it wouldn't go very far if he couldn't get a job right away. Not having a phone would complicate things. He had enough against him. No experience. No local driver's license. It was surprising the number of ads which listed that as a qualification.

Ah, but here was something. "Young Executives Wanted," it read. The ad was bordered in black and announced that several different companies were looking for outstanding young people with B.A. degrees in any field to train as executives in their organizations.

Lawrence read it again. A cautious warmth began to spread through him.

He got up and laid out his job hunting suit. Blue slacks, white shirt and blue tie. A blue and brown tweed jacket he'd lucked into for five fifty at the second hand place near campus the week he'd been in Portland before coming here. He looked out the window, saw a clear sky, and hung his overcoat in the closet to shake out its wrinkles.

It was eleven o'clock and he wasn't dressed yet. He'd need to get a telephone first, he decided. Then he'd have a number to give them. It wouldn't be good if they thought he was desperate. No job and no phone, one step away from the street. He'd have to look decent, seem prosperous, to get anywhere.

It took a while to locate a bus that would take him to the telephone place. He arranged for his number and bought the cheapest phone they had. By the time he'd purchased a blanket too, he was buried under packages and it was almost four o'clock. Now he'd worn the slacks and jacket a day they didn't need to be used.

He stayed in his robe Wednesday morning, looking at ads, writing down the numbers he wanted to call and what he wanted to say.

It was two o'clock before he could hear a dial tone on the telephone line.

He went through his list once more, deciding who to call first. There weren't very many. There wasn't much to any of them except the executive one. Just paying the rent kinds of things. Though would this executive job really be what he wanted? But he did want something more than eight hours of emptiness in order to pay for long evenings of nothing to do.

But then again, maybe that's what he needed. A job that would allow him to come home and just think. Read. Whatever. Nothing that would demand too much emotional and even too much mental involvement. Clerking at an all-night store, maybe. The executive thing was bound to be more demanding.

And then again, maybe that's what he needed. Something to get him busy and going and doing. Anything but just waiting and wondering what to do with himself. He studied the ad. It certainly sounded better than maintenance and security work. He reached for the phone and a few minutes later had an appointment to see someone named Steven at three on Friday afternoon. Well, if he wanted to have time to think he'd have tomorrow and Friday morning to do it in. He ran his hand through his hair. There wasn't a whole lot else he could do between now and then.

~~~

Deb paused in the hazy sun of a foggy Seattle morning and looked for a newspaper stand. A hot cup of coffee and a doughnut would be good too. It was chilly out here and she was hungry.

She soon had three studio apartment listings near Pioneer Square. That was the place to be if you were going to live Downtown. It was about the only information she'd gotten from the Sunday papers she'd been reading so thoroughly for the past several months.

When she reached Pioneer Square, she wandered for a few minutes, trying to believe she was really going to be part of this city, really live here. Even here away from the main business area, there was a busyness she wasn't used to. And a beauty. The streets were lined with buildings in mellow red-brown brick and there were hanging plants dripping from the old-fashioned lampposts on the sidewalks.

She recognized the name of a cross street as being in one of the ads she had marked and crossed at the light. But the numbers were wrong. She re-crossed the street and an old man leaning against a lamppost looked at her.

She smiled at him. "The numbers are backward!" she said. He grinned toothlessly. He mumbled something she didn't hear and waved the paper sack he was holding in her direction.

She looked at the building in front of her. Seven ten? Yes, this was it. She eyed the tall arched windows on the second floor. There were broad brick sills below them. She found the narrow black-grilled entrance and pushed at an old-fashioned buzzer. She watched the old man out of the corner of her eye. He was still talking in her direction.

A slim, gray-haired man with a goatee and wearing a wrinkled brown shirt came down the steps. "Hi," he said as he swung the gate open. "You want the studio?"
~~~

She nodded. She looked over her shoulder at the man at the lamppost.

"Hi Sam!" the man with the goatee called. "How's life?"

The old man blinked. "Heh? What's that?"

He pushed the gate farther open. "Come on in. Sam's kind of deaf. He's harmless. Just likes his booze a little too much."

The apartment was a single room with a huge window in the wall facing the street. In one of the back corners were unpainted pine cabinets and an old refrigerator and gas stove. The light from the window warmed the brick walls and softened the scratches in the wood floorboards.

"This is it," he said. "Two hundred fifteen a month, first and a deposit of a hundred. Heat paid." He pointed at a steam radiator next to the window. "You pay gas and electricity."

"How many feet is it?" she asked. It was kind of pretty, with the brick walls and wooden floors, but it seemed so big.

He named a figure that meant nothing to her and started talking about how he owned the building and there was a grocery nearby and the doors were safety bolted and there were only five other tenants. She looked around the room.

He stopped talking. "I have some other places to look at," she said. She looked at the window. "So I can't decide yet. Does the window open?"

He showed her the lever that swung it out over the sidewalk. She peered down. The old man was still leaning against the street light.

She nodded and moved away. "Well, I can't decide just yet, as I said." She wrote down his name, phone number and the amount of the rent and went back down the wooden staircase.

The door to the next place she was looking for was tucked into a dark entryway at one side of an old building. She climbed the musty-smelling stairs and knocked on a door labeled "101," as the ad had directed.

"Come in." She could barely hear the voice that said it. She turned the knob and pushed at the door.

Directly in front of her was an overstuffed green velvet couch with little pieces of crochet work laying at the top of each of its curves. Pillows covered with embroidery crowded its seat. The tables at either end were covered with small figurines and paperweights. The tables were protected with crocheted mats.

She heard the awkward clump of orthopedic shoes on linoleum and a tiny white haired lady in a large bibbed apron came through a door at one end of the couch.

"Yes?" she asked. "What is it, dear?"

"I— I've come about the apartment you have for rent."

"Oh yes. Yes, of course. Let me see." She pulled open a drawer in an elaborately carved desk and picked through its contents with a shaky finger. "Here we are. Come along, dear. It's right down this way."

"It's just a small room," she said as she clumped down the hall. Each shoe alone was probably bigger than her head. The awkward white squares moved steadily through the gloom.

Deb followed her into a large empty room with softly painted white walls and a row of small windows which faced the brick wall of a similar building. There were white frilly curtains at the windows. The bathroom held a huge claw-footed tub. The closet at the other end of the room was the walk-in type, with built in drawers and a scratched mirror. The rug was dull tan and rubbed-looking in places, but it covered every inch of the floor.

"I'd have to have a sweeper," Deb murmured as she went into the kitchen. She opened a cupboard. "My mother would like this," she said.

"You weren't looking for yourself, dear?"

"Oh no! I mean, yes I am. It just reminded me a little of home."

"Well, thank you! If you should decide you want it, it's two hundred and fifty dollars a month and everything's paid for.

There's a good strong bolt on the door and the little eye thing in it too, to see who is knocking."

Deborah nodded. She reached for her purse. "I have another place I'm supposed to look at," she said. She looked around, then back into the woman's bright eyes. "But I'll probably be back."

The old lady led the way out. Her shoes clumped on the floor. "This looking for a place to live is wearying, isn't it?" she said. "Would you like a cup of tea before you go on, dear?"

"Oh no, that's all right," Deb said. "I'm hoping to find a place today, so I need to keep moving." She smiled at her. "Thank you anyway."

The next place was a more modern building. It was made of brick which blended with its older neighbors and looked new at the same time. There was a smell of fresh paint in the foyer. She rang the manager's bell. Nobody answered.

She rang again and looked around. The foyer felt bright, even though the fog still hadn't lifted from the streets. She pushed the button a third time. A girl in blue jeans and a tight-fitting sweater with nothing beneath came down the honey-wood stairs. "If you're looking for the manager, he's in three oh one," she said. She unlocked a mail box in the rack on the other side of the hall. "Follow the paint smell and you'll find him."

The smell in three oh one was almost overwhelming. The young man in the white overalls didn't seem to notice it, though. He had a cheerful face and dark eyes. He waved a brush at her from the top of his ladder. "Be with you in a second, okay?"

He made a few more dabs at the ceiling, climbed down, and wiped his hands on a paint-covered cloth.

"I'm here about the studio you have for rent."

"This is it."

"Oh." She looked around. "I need something really quickly. Like tonight, if it's possible."

"I've got another one just like it downstairs."

It was exactly like the one upstairs, without the paint smell. Deborah walked through the rooms. A kitchen in a small separate room of its own. A bath with a tub and a shower. Even a Murphy bed springing out of the door of the big walk-in closet. The view was of a side street. Nothing very interesting, though better than brick walls.

"This is nice," she said. "How much is it?"

"Three fifty a month, first and deposit only," he said. "Deposit's four hundred."

Exactly half of the money her father had put into her checking account yesterday. And out of it had to come furniture, pots and pans and food.

"I don't know," she said. "It's more than I'd planned on. Does that include heat?"

"Heat's extra. It's electric, so you can control it yourself, instead of steam, where you don't have any say about whether you're going to cook like a lobster or freeze."

"It is awfully nice," she said.

He rocked back onto his heels. "If you're not sure, I've got a couple. You can let me know."

She smiled at him. "And you have painting to do." He smiled back at her and her cheeks grew warm. "I'll— I'll know this afternoon," she said.

When she reached the street she stopped and breathed in the fall air. He sure was good looking. And nice.

But it was too much money. She sighed, went over her budget in her head and sighed again. It really was too much.

She passed the building with the brick walled apartment while she was looking for a place to eat. She looked up. That window was beautiful.

She found the grocery store the manager had told her about and bought a packaged sandwich and can of soda. There was a park nearby, if you could call cobblestones and trees set in big concrete boxes a park. She settled onto a bench, watched the pigeons fighting over scraps of food, and tried to make a decision.

The apartment with the little old lady was awfully big. It looked comfortable.

Comfort wasn't the word for the one she'd just looked at. That was sheer luxury. The walk in closet. A Murphy bed. She could get a regular couch. It wouldn't take much for that place to be absolutely beautiful. Really glamorous.

She shook her head. It was too much. She could squeeze it out, she supposed. But it would be a pretty hard squeeze every month and there'd be nothing left for clothes or shoes and hardly enough for food, by the time the government had taken its taxes and she'd paid her rent and the heat bill. She'd never be able to afford a couch.

"You can't do it," she repeated firmly.

But what about the other place? The brick on those walls. There were lots of things you could do with those. She wasn't sure what, but they were intriguing. And that window.

She knew, of course, that her parents would choose the place with the old woman in it. She shook the last few drops of soda from her can and tossed it into a nearby garbage bin. Her mother would like her being there. And that was the best reason for not renting it. She squeezed the plastic her sandwich had been wrapped in. If she was the kind of daughter they deserved, she'd do what they wanted even if they weren't here to insist.

She stood up. Well, they weren't here and there was no law that said she had to do what they wanted and she didn't care if she felt guilty or not.

She grinned. The pigeons at her feet hopped away nervously. "Brick walls, you are about to be solved," she muttered as she turned out of the park.

Lawrence got to his appointment at two forty-five Friday afternoon. The receptionist was busy filing papers while she answered the phone and talked to employees rifling through the notes on the message board. It was several minutes before she noticed Lawrence.

He told her why he was there and she handed him a form to fill out and another to sign. He filled and signed without really reading them and went to the counter again.

She waved him away. "You give those to the person who interviews you." She reached for the phone. "Good afternoon Fully and Little. Who's calling please?" She punched a button and dialed another number. "Carl? There's a Mrs. Grant on six two." She stared at Lawrence. "You can wait over there."

He went back to his chair and picked up a three month old news magazine. There was an historical analysis of the Lebanese situation in it. He was absorbed in its details when he heard his name called.

He dropped the magazine and clutched at his papers.

"I'm Lawrence."

"Hi, I'm Steve. Pleased to meet you." Their handshake was brief. He was a short, dark haired young man in a three piece suit made of a shiny material. He led Lawrence to a desk in a corner of a room full of desks, people and ringing phones. "Have a seat. Now. You called about ad one one four five six. Is that it?"

"The one about executive trainees."

"That's the one." He picked up a pencil. He put it down again and straightened his tie. His eyes were dark and slightly protruding. He smiled at Lawrence. "Now," he said. "That advertisement was very general because we have several different companies we're working with. What particular field are you interested in?"

"I have a Bachelor of Arts in history, so there isn't any special field."

"No companies selling history today!" Steve grinned at him. "There were a couple looking for people with liberal arts educations, though. Let me see." He dug through a small file box. "No, I'm afraid we don't have them out anymore." He sat back. "There seem to be a lot of people with liberal arts who are looking for the same kind of work. Do you have any hobbies or other job experience that might lead into another field?"

"Nothing but reading."

"Well, we do have some sales jobs for books. They offer a pretty good commission."

"I've done that—"

"Well there! That's a beginning."

"It was an end."

"Oh?" He put down his pencil.

"I'm not a salesperson."

"Now, you can't tell from just one experience. Maybe it was a bad territory. And there are always openings in sales. Tell you what, it was just the wrong company for you."

"Maybe. But I wouldn't want to do it again."

"Now, if you're not interested in sales, I don't quite know what I can do for you. Other than the executive training programs— Do you type at all? Ever answer phones or anything like that?"

"Two finger typing. I answer the telephone at home, of course, but if you mean on the job—"

"Yeah. Well." He fingered his file cards. "I don't quite know what to tell you, but I don't know if we can really be of any help. I mean, we can try but if you're not interested in selling—"

"No."

He looked at Lawrence's sports coat and slacks. "No, I guess not." He stood up. "I'm sorry I couldn't be of more help to you."

Lawrence got up. "Could you keep my name, in case something comes in? Anything along the lines of the positions that were filled?"

"Now, to tell you the truth I don't know if that would do too much good. We pretty much place our people right away or they don't place at all. And we don't get that kind of requirement, for liberal arts I mean, very often. Even then, they're not requiring. It's a 'we'll take a look at them too' sort of thing. You know what I mean."

"Well, thank you anyway."

They shook hands even more briefly this time. Lawrence left, still holding the forms he'd filled out. There were no executive jobs, he thought dully. The ads were a kind of screen. What they were really after were sales people. There were always openings. Of course. It wasn't the kind of thing anyone would stay in very long if they had a choice.

Though did he have a choice? He pushed the elevator button and remembered the hundreds of doorbells he'd pushed that long dusty summer. The first job he'd had. It was worse than the teaching. And that had been unforgettably bad.

It was the humiliation of selling. The anxious twist of the stomach as they came to the door and the fear you had to keep from your eyes. The freezing look they'd get in their faces the minute they knew you were there for a reason. The ten thousands ways "no thank you" and "not interested" could be said. No thank you was right.

Though selling was really what executives did. Selling themselves to each other and to the public. At least they weren't knocking on doors. None of them wanted a history major, anyway. There was no point in thinking about executive stuff.

It would be a week on Monday that he'd been in Seattle. How long could he go before he had something, he wondered? He'd better figure it out. Even the thought was depressing. He'd thought it would be so easy to find something here. It was better in Seattle. That's what the rumors were. Places dying for lack of employees. Employees with experience and training, that is. He knew that now.

But it wouldn't do any good to be bitter. And it wasn't as if he was down to his last penny. He'd find something. It simply took time.

He pulled out his watch. Better go wait for the bus. The sooner he got out of these clothes the less wear they would get. And if he didn't stop walking aimlessly like this, he was going to wear out his shoes

.

4

Deborah woke early Monday morning. At five a.m. she was wandering around her apartment, touching the furniture. The fat cushioned couch which folded into a bed. The wicker table with a round sheet of glass as its top. On it was a shiny black vase she'd found yesterday in the antique shop around the corner.

She still couldn't believe she'd done it in only three and a half days. There were things to be added, of course. The dresser she'd bought wouldn't be delivered until tomorrow evening and she still didn't have any plants.

She looked around again, centered the vase on the small table, and tried to decide what to wear. The plaid skirt and dark vest looked so school girlish. She'd buy a fashion magazine at noon. She'd have to do some exploring then anyway, to find out what the shops were like near her office. What a nice sound that had!

There was a soft burring sound from the corner. She turned slowly and then dove for her phone. This could go on top of the new dresser, she decided as she picked it up.

"Hello?"

"My goodness, you sound all breathless and excited! Have you met a young man already?"

"Hi Mom."

"Just wanted to call and see how you were doing."

"It's a good thing I wasn't still sleeping."

"Why, it's six o'clock. Why would you be asleep?"

"I don't go to work until nine."

"So you're planning on sleeping 'til eight thirty?"

"If I feel like it."

"You know what they say, 'Early to bed, early to rise—'"

"Whoever 'they' are."

"Well, it's your parents for one thing, and I don't think it's very nice of you to go falanting off and then acting like you know everything."

"You were accusing me of knowing everything long before I decided to move."

"Well, you thought you did, didn't you? Simpson kid and all?"

"That's not what I meant."

"Deborah, I didn't call you to argue. I just wanted to see if you were okay and to tell you we're thinking of you. I've asked the prayer circle at church to pray for your safety and all while you're there."

"Where?"

"In the city."

"I see." Did she think it was going to be such a short period of time? She made it sound like the circle would only be praying for a couple weeks, like when the junior high kids went to summer camp. Anyway, she could take care of herself. "Thanks," she said.

"You're welcome. We do love you, you know."

"Ummm. I love you too. Look, I need to go. I've got stuff to do before I leave, and I don't want to be late."

"Okay. Call us if you need anything."

"Bye." Deb put the receiver down. Mothers. She looked at her watch. She could probably start her bath now. A long soak would be nice. Help her forget she was still being guarded.

The bath had been a good idea, she decided as she walked into the department later. She felt surprisingly confident, which was a lot better than being nervous, the first day on the job.

She asked for Peter, as she'd been instructed to do, and the receptionist gave her directions. She followed them carefully, trying to memorize the route, and eventually found the right cubicle. She knocked on the strip of plastic molding at the edge of the door.

Peter was wearing a snagged polo shirt and the same blue jeans he'd had on the previous Monday. He ran a hand through his hair and pushed his chair back. "Welcome!" he said.

Deborah blinked again at the incongruity of the accent and the clothes.

"I'm Peter, in case you've had other things to think about." He turned and banged an open palm on the partition behind the desk. "Hey Al! She's here!"

The small dark man who'd told Susan to hire her came around the corner. He held out his hand. "Hello. It's good to see you again."

Peter was rummaging through the desk in the corner. "Looks like you've got everything you need in here," he announced. "If you don't Al's probably got it. I can't keep track of stuff, myself."

"He loses it," Al told her. He grinned at Peter. "Wasteful Republicanism, operating per usual."

Peter sat down and kicked a tattered tennis shoe from his foot. It hit the wall and bounced onto the floor. It was followed by its mate. Al didn't seem to notice. Deb walked to her new desk and sat down.

"And what are your political leanings?" Peter asked her.

She wondered what to do with her purse. "I guess you could say I'm independent." she said.

"Undecided, huh? We'll fix that."

"Most of the women put their pocketbooks in the bottom desk drawers, I believe," Al told her. He jerked his thumb at Peter. "Simply don't listen to too much of his political theorizing and you'll be all right."

"Why is that?"

He grinned. "It's not conducive to one's mental well-being."

She opened the bottom desk drawer. When she looked up again, Al was standing in the door with an armful of forms. "After you're through proselytizing, you can start her on these," he said.

"Let her get settled first."

"That's the proselytizing part." He waved a hand at Deb and left again. "Just yell if he gets too obnoxious."

Peter knew what he was doing when it came to the forms she was to fill out. First a pencil draft to be checked by Al, then a typed version for Susan's review and signature. There were several forms for each artist's request.

Some of the information the artists gave wasn't too clear. You had to keep looking, maybe make a few phone calls. The details were going to be the most time consuming part of her job.

Then the forms went to the Council which made the final decisions and came back to be written on some more. After that, letters went out notifying the artists of the Council's decisions.

"Thankless task," Peter muttered as he explained the final part. He got up to retrieve his shoes. He pushed his hair from his face. "Got all that down?"

She smiled back at him and dug a pencil out of the drawer. "Guess there's only one way to find out," she said. She set to work. She chewed her thumbnail as she read the instructions at the top of the first form.

Lawrence's spirits had bounced back a little by Monday morning. He sat on the couch with the telephone beside him and listed the places he could call. There had been a few more things in the Sunday paper. Surely he could find a decent position out of these.

The first two ads he answered, the jobs had already been filled. In Sunday's paper and filled Monday morning at nine. He scratched them off his list and wondered why they'd bothered to advertise.

The next one was for a warehouse worker. The man on the other end wanted to know what experience he had.

"Well, none exactly," he said. "But I'm—"

"Sorry buddy. Experience is what we need. Don't have time to train nobody. With what we're paying, shouldn't have to, anyway."

"But I'm sure I could learn. And I'd be willing to start out for less."

"Sorry. Ain't interested." The phone line clicked. Lawrence ran his pen through the number. The ad hadn't said they wanted somebody with training.

The next one was for a manager trainee at some kind of electronics firm. No experience required, it said. Just your degree. He read it again before he dialed the number.

"Hello?"

"Yes. I'm calling about your ad in the paper?"

"You'll have to come down and fill out an application."

"Where are you located?"

He rattled an address off and Lawrence scribbled it down. He hoped he'd be able to read it later. "What exactly are your requirements?" he asked.

"A relevant B.A. Some selling is good. Any working with people. Or some kind of electronics background."

"My B.A.'s in history," Lawrence said. "Is that—"

"Don't bother."

"Pardon?" There must be someone at his end that he's talking to at the same time, Lawrence thought.

"Don't bother. History's not a relevant B.A. We wouldn't be interested."

"Oh. Well. Thanks."

"Yeah. Bye." Now he was talking to someone at the other end. Lawrence could hear his voice giving directions as the receiver went into its cradle.

He drew another line on the paper and wrote neatly beside it "not relevant." He drew a line under this. Then he drew a circle around the whole thing. He looked at it. Relevant. As in important. As in necessary.

He leaned over and looked at his books. They stood in a neat row on the lower shelf of the end table beside the couch. Tuchman and Toynbee. Tolstoy, Karnow and Shirer. He'd been reading one, then the other, all weekend. Waiting for the real business of looking for work to begin again. He ran a finger down the faded spine of the Tolstoy. Not relevant.

Not that that guy's electronics stuff would even be state-of-the-art by next week. His lips twisted. At least he knew a relevant phrase.

Meaning only "the latest thing." He touched the Tolstoy again. Not the most important. Of course, as Tolstoy would have pointed out, what we consider the most important at the time—men, events—may not be at all, if the truth were really known.

"All just pieces of driftwood on a mass of seawater, pushing across the sand toward the high water mark," Lawrence muttered. He was hardly aware he was talking out loud.

He got up. He moved around the room, stretching his legs, swinging his arms back and forth. "Though I feel sort of like a piece of driftwood. Beached, water-logged and no raison d'être." He ran his hand through his hair. "History not relevant. What little French I have of no use. Typing, two fingers. Telephone, only at home. No use, any of it."

He reached for the piece of paper he'd made his list on. He looked at the ads he'd copied out. There'd been seven and now there were three. They'd just say "not relevant" too. "Not what we want." What did they want, besides engineers? Wasn't there anything else in this world besides selling people things or being a technician? What about people who thought? Wasn't there a market for that?

But he knew the answer. The guy at the agency last Friday had said it. "Nobody selling history this week." What a smart ass. He hadn't had a chance there, from the beginning.

He was starting to wonder where he would have a chance. In three weeks the rent would be due again and in the meantime he'd have to have food. And there'd be the light bill to pay and the telephone too, with its deposits and all. He reached for his wallet. Only six hundred and fifty left. Wasn't much, with food and everything else.

He went to the window. He pulled at the string of the blind. The old paper was yellow. It was stained at the edges where someone had tried to clean it. Lawrence pulled again, sharply, until it spun all the way up, with the cord wrapped around the rod at the top. He looked out. Rain. No, not really rain. Drizzle. Good old Portland weather, only here in Seattle.

Well, at least he was used to getting wet. It wouldn't be a shock to his system. Because the only thing to do now was to hit the streets. Start knocking on doors. The three phone calls he still had to make wouldn't result in anything, he was sure.

They didn't. He hung up with a click on the last one. Even the security guard places considered him "not relevant." Over qualified, was what the guy had said. But it was the same thing. "Why don't you look for a teaching position?" he'd asked. Little he knew. Teaching was the reason he'd quit school. There was no point in going on if he wasn't going to teach. Besides, there was no money now to go back. He was living on it.

And he'd be living on it quite a while, he began to realize as the days rained themselves out one by one. Winter was coming and people were getting laid off, not hired. The papers he purchased so diligently were as depressing on their front pages as they were in the help wanted sections. And the "employment wanted" ads increased with each new layoff announced.

The people advertising their availability all had experience. In everything from managing apartments to making steel dies and working in print shops. They all wanted work and couldn't find it.

Stubbornly, he tried again. This time he walked into an industrial cleaning outfit. He took a form from the pile on the front counter and began filling it out. He was careful to leave out any mention of his years at school. "Caring for sick mother," he wrote. She'd been sick enough, though he'd only seen her on holidays and occasional weekends. It was better than telling them he was irrelevant.

The clerk barely glanced at the form as he handed it to her. "We don't have any openings," she said. She bent her head over her work.

"Nothing at all? There was an ad in the paper."

"Oh that. They'll be using those people, maybe, next spring when things pick up again. But in October, there's nothing going on that we can't handle with our normal staff."

He looked at the calendar behind her. It really was October already. He'd be paying his rent pretty soon. Another hundred and eighty out of his thinning wallet.

"What about temporary positions?" he asked.

She looked at him and picked up the form. "You can mark that down," she said. "But we won't have anything until Christmas and New Year's. There's always stuff then."

And why hadn't she said so before? But he bent his head and found the small box on the form beside the words "Temporary Employment?"

He filled it in and darkened the one for Permanent which he had already marked. He handed the form back.

"If you're looking for temporary or seasonal work, you might try the department stores," she said. "They should be looking for people to work during the Christmas rush."

He nodded and pushed on the double glass doors to go back out into the rain. He wouldn't make it to the Christmas rush at the rate he was going. He'd need something a lot sooner than that or he wouldn't be able to pay his December rent.

He walked through the damp mist of the rain. It was getting colder out too. He hugged his overcoat to his chest. He'd been wearing the coat almost every day for the last month. The wrinkles in the back were set in deeply now and the button he'd lost from the bottom hole made the cloth flap damply.

And he'd thought Portland was bad, going from class to class in the fog. This was worse, trudging block after block, crossing gray streets in gray traffic, dull buildings on every side. He shivered. He looked around for a department store to go into to get warm. Just pretend he was shopping and dry out a bit.

During the next few weeks Deborah's life fell into routine. Mornings getting dressed in her apartment, playing with different ways to use the silk scarf she'd found on sale. Then work and half-joking conversations with Al and Peter about the state of the arts and the world in general.

They were both married, she'd discovered in the first few days. She wrote to her mother quickly, to keep her from more speculation than she could help.

Deb spent her lunch hours browsing. She visited all the bargain basements and every designer boutique, but she bought little beyond magazines and a few accessories. "At least for the first few weeks," she would tell her reflection as she held a dress up to admire.

Evenings she spent with her magazines, unless she could offer to take an art showing ticket off Peter's hands. The office got their share, being representatives of the County, and there were more than enough to go around.

She daydreamed about what it would be like to turn to a good looking man beside her at a gallery opening and toss out observations which would make him start with surprise. Somewhere between that first meeting of eyes and final parting at her door, true love would set in. But the remarks never found their way to her lips while she was actually at the exhibits. At least, not when there was anyone around.

But then, to catch someone's eye you had to look as sharp as you were, she would tell herself the next morning.

That wasn't as easy as it sounded, she began to realize as the lunch hours of shopping walked by. Really nice clothes were expensive and a single paycheck could only be stretched so far. This was going to take some planning.

One night she sat down and made a list of what she needed. She sighed when she was through and went over the list again. If she was going to get everything she wanted, it looked like she'd have to sew them. Her lips tightened. That was one thing she was not going to do.

She hated the very thought of that stupid clanking machine. And all it symbolized. Pennies stretched painfully over the groceries to buy a yard and a half of plain muslin. And that stretched again and augmented with God only knew what from her mother's scrap basket to make one skimpy blouse. One "just like store bought," her mother would say proudly. One Deborah would cringe from wearing anywhere but at home.

Her parents had been right about one thing, though. It was more expensive to live in the city. She got up and went to the window. The long wooden bench below it was crowded with plants. They weren't very big yet, except for the fern she'd picked up so cheaply at that place in Northgate Mall.

Lugging it home on the bus had been crazy, but worth it. The big plant was perfect, set so firmly there at the end of the bench. It helped to keep the others from looking too scrawny and bare. She went back to the table.

If she made cookies here and took them to work instead of buying them at the stand outside the post office, that would save. She did some quick math. Enough for a new belt in a month. And she needed a belt for the suit she'd put on layaway at Lamont's. She doodled along the edge of her list, thinking about it.

She drew more circles. A little bit at a time, that's all she could do. And go carefully on food. That was one place she could save. At least she had just about everything for her apartment. She looked around. She'd spent every penny of her father's fifteen hundred on furniture and stuff. Maybe she'd been too extravagant, but it did look nice. It was good to come home to, after all day in that dreary cubbyhole at work.

"Poor Peter," she murmured. She looked at her plants. "To work in those walls and have to go home to a wife who's been sick all day long." His wife was pregnant and not having an easy time of it. She was sick so much that she'd had to quit her secretarial job. And the insurance company she'd work for had been so upset about it that they'd promised to make sure they never hired her back. And to give her bad references if she applied anywhere else.

Al had listened sympathetically, then said something about unions that had raised Peter's hair a couple of inches. She didn't remember now what he had said, but it was funny. Peter hadn't responded with a pro-Republican wisecrack the way he normally did.

But he'd cheered up afterward. He'd spent most of the afternoon interrupting Deb's work with stories about adventures he and his wife had had while they were dating. They'd spent a lot of time touring the country on foot or by bicycle.

She'd wanted to be interrupted though. The request she was working on was a real doozy. Unclear about background and incoherent about purpose. The kind which could either be someone onto something important but having trouble expressing it or just somebody looking for easy government money.

The trouble was, as Al put it, "They could also be one and the same individual. It becomes tremendously difficult to decipher motives. We can't really, and yet that is essentially our job."

Or part of it. There was still a lot about the department as a whole that she didn't understand. Al had given her a tour the first day she was there. And Susan had talked to her for fifteen minutes one afternoon about "purpose and reason for existing." Between phone calls and finding things in the piles on her desk, that is. Still, fifteen minutes was a long time for anyone to be in Susan's office.

But that had been several weeks ago and it all got sort of hazy after the fourth person explained the fifth thing.

It didn't matter. She'd figure it out eventually. A lot of it was just office politics, from what she'd heard Al and Peter talking about.

That was supposedly the reason Peter was a Republican among a department of Democrats. Al said it was simply a perverse need to be contrary. Peter insisted that he would not be connected in any way with "such goings on." "Goings on" had something to do with the way money was spent. Though there wasn't much being lavished on their office spaces. Or salaries.

But they were paying her enough to live on and buy clothes with. Slowly, but still clothes. She'd have enough next payday to get her gray suit out of layaway. The weather was getting colder. She'd need it. Wouldn't she look dressed! She'd have to find a white silky blouse to wear with it. Something like the one she'd seen in that last issue of Vogue.

She left her list on the table. She got an apple from the refrigerator and curled up on the couch with her latest fashion magazine. Actually, this other blouse would look good with her new suit, too.

5

The man in the dark blue wool suit stepped back and waved the young woman in the fashionable gray pinstripe onto the elevator. Deborah smiled a thank you at him as she glanced at the faces looking at her. She faced the door and fingered the batch of personnel records in her arms. It still wasn't clear why she'd been sent on this particular errand, but she didn't really mind. The looks she got when people saw her new outfit made her feel unbelievably efficient. She looked up at the elevator light. Second floor.

It seemed so long ago that she'd walked down this hall with a quivering stomach. She strode confidently now, round a corner. What a difference a job and the right clothes could make in the way one felt about— Whoops!

"Oh! Excuse me."

"I'm sorry. Are you all right?"

They stood back from each other. He wore a decent dull blue plaid suit and carried an overcoat over his arm. He ran a hand through his curly dark hair. "I'm really sorry."

She crouched to pick up her papers. "It's okay. I must have been daydreaming or something." She looked at the paper in her hand. "This isn't mine, though."

"If it's an application, it's mine." He knelt beside her. "Yes, that's it." He looked it over carefully. He didn't want it mangled. This was important. They really did have an opening and when he'd called, the woman had sounded enthusiastic about his background. He looked at the girl. "You must work here."

She reshuffled her papers into their original order and looked up at him. "I do when I'm not daydreaming myself around corners!"

"What were you dreaming about?"

A light pink flushed her cheeks. "I'm not sure, actually." Her eyes met his, then traveled to his hair. "Haven't I met you somewhere?" The pink deepened. "I mean, you look familiar."

He shook his head. "No, I don't— Wait a minute." He ran his hand through his hair.

"The bus station," she said as he snapped his fingers.

"Of course!"

"So how are things going?"

"Not bad." He held up the application. "Lots of leads."

"Oh, you're still looking?" She glanced at the carefully folded coat.

"Yes." His feet shuffled back, keeping the heels out of sight.

"Well, I've got to get going." She looked down at her forms and laughed. "I'll need to check these one more time to make sure they're all here."

He flipped a finger through the sheets of his application. "I don't think I have any of them."

"Oh, I didn't mean that! They need to be in the right order, is all." She took a hesitant step away from him.

"It's been nice seeing you. Deborah, right?"

She half paused. "Yes, that's right." She raised her free hand. "Nice seeing you. Good luck."

He nodded. "Bye."

She reached the far end of the hall and turned thankfully. Her cheeks were still burning. Talking about daydreaming, of all things. It was like telling him you were looking. She'd have to learn to watch what she said if she was ever going to meet anyone. He was good looking too.

But he wasn't working yet. How long had it been? Six weeks? Eight? She felt like she'd been here forever. She wondered idly what looking for work that long must be like and opened the door to the personnel section.

There was a dry feeling in his mouth. He watched her turn the corner. Not working. That settled it. He looked down at the application. His fingers twitched. He should just tear it up. That's what you can do with your job. I don't need you to make me a real person. His hands moved.

But he couldn't. One thing he'd been learning these past few weeks was how to take it. That's what looking for work was about. You lowered your shoulders and bent your head and pretended not to hear the tone in their voices when they said you weren't needed. The self-satisfied pity and the irritation that you'd wasted their time.

You were no good because you didn't already have a position and you weren't any use because you couldn't fill their exact requirements. Experience. He had begun to hate that word. He folded the application, tucked it into his jacket pocket and opened the door to the building's stairwell. He didn't want to look at another person right now.

He shouldn't do this. It would just wear his shoes out faster. His sole scratched against the side of the concrete stairwell. He was beginning to not care.

6

When Deb got back from Personnel she went to Susan's office. She paused in the doorway. Susan had the telephone receiver cradled on one bony shoulder and was pawing through a pile of papers.

"Just a sec," she said into the phone. She swiveled toward Deborah.

"I delivered the papers. Was there anything else?"

"They're here," she said into the telephone. "No." She waved at Deborah. "I'll call. That can't be right." She jerked her head at the receiver. "Here, I'll read. One three five point two zero. Four three point—"

Deborah hesitated, was convinced that Susan didn't need her, and went back to her desk.

She'd just gotten settled when she ran out of the forms that were kept in the cabinet in Al's office.

"Oh, there you are," he said as she opened the drawer. "Ran out of things to do, huh?"

"There's a whole pile of stuff on my desk." She pulled out a handful of papers. "They've been there since nine."

He nodded and looked at the sheets of figures in front of him. "Susan busy?"

"She was on the phone when I left."

"Only reason you aren't still there," Peter said from the door.

He moved around her and pulled at the handle of the top file drawer. It came out with a rusty squawk. He rummaged through the files and pushed the drawer shut. It squawked more loudly.

"Damned Democrat efficiency," he muttered. "You really ought to do something about this thing, Al."

"I thought the Republican motto was 'thou shalt worship thy boss, whence cometh thy food,'" Al said. "Meaning, don't ask for handouts."

He got up, opened the bottom drawer soundlessly and pulled out a small metal can of sewing machine oil. "I wonder what thoughts my wife will have on the subject when she discovers that this has disappeared."

He opened the drawer Peter had used and reached behind the files. He squeezed oil onto the metal track on each side. He moved the drawer back and forth a few times. It shut silently.

"Now Republican efficiency would have required that I wait three weeks to buy this can of oil through Supply. And that whoever Supply purchased it from would then charge us five bucks for a dollar and a quarter can."

"It would have been oil," Peter said. "And you wouldn't be paying for it."

"He's not, his wife is," Deborah said. "It's her oil."

"Ugh. Please don't try so hard." He waved a piece of paper at her. "I've got something that's top priority, if you're tired of running Susan's errands for her."

"Or if we're tired of having you do so, which may be more to the point," Al said. Suddenly his chair swiveled toward his desk. He shuffled a pile of papers into order. "Hello Susan! Anything we can do for you?"

"I need this right away," Peter said. He waved the paper at Deb again and disappeared around Susan's shoulder.

Susan stepped to one side and came further into the room. "Per capita figures," she said to Al.

Deborah slipped around her to her own desk. Susan looked so pale and tired. Maybe it was just her age showing. She had to be at least in her late thirties and she wore no makeup that Deb could tell. That would explain the oddly lifeless look.

It was a full ten minutes before the murmur of voices in the next office stopped. Peter's head lifted expectantly. Deb looked up. Al was in the doorway.

She saw them exchange knowing looks and put her pencil down. "Is it a secret or can I know about it?" she asked.

"No reason to get excited," Peter said. "Just normal office nonsense."

Al bounced forward onto his toes. He stretched his arms out to brace himself on the partitions.

"Don't push too hard," Deborah said.

He grinned at her. He glanced at Peter and then perched on the corner of his desk, facing Deb. "I think it's appropriate that she be aware of the situation, considering the possible repercussions," he said to Peter. He didn't take his eyes off her face.

"Situation as usual, in my opinion."

"It's not going to remain usual though, if your heroic Republicans have their way."

"That's federal, not county. It's a long way from L.A. to Denver—" His voice cracked off tune.

Deb laughed. "It's even farther from Seattle to Nashville, with that voice."

"Who'd want Nashville? I'm for Hollywood and the big tinsel time."

"Nashville's too democratic," Al said. He swung his leg and his heel knocked against Peter's desk.

"You're scuffing my desk," Peter said.

Al looked down. "How can you tell?" His leg stopped swinging and the foot on the floor began to jiggle.

"Now, if the truth were known—" he said to Deborah.

"It's all a Republican plot to deprive us of our homes and loved ones." Peter covered his mouth with his hand and yawned.

"You're beginning to understand."

"I hope not."

"Will you two please explain why this particular conversation keeps repeating itself?" Deborah asked. "I mean, I keep hearing the same things but I don't know why you keep saying them."

"It's like this," Al said. "The Republicans want to reform the government, right?"

"I understand that part."

"Are reforming it," Peter said.

"I'm giving the details of this story."

"And I'm keeping it from being a story."

Al's foot jiggled. "And they think they can make those reforms by eliminating what they define as the fat from the governmental system."

"Not think. They can. They're doing it."

"Peter here's partial to this particular system, as his mother country has a lady at the helm who's trying the same methodology."

"Is doing it."

"Whatever." He shot Peter a mock glare. "However, it's a very open question as to just how the bureaucratic fat-cutting is going to go into effect. Our associate here seems inclined to think that they can simply put the system on a diet. I'm of the opinion that our beloved leaders aren't aware of the subtleties of calorie counts. They're more likely to opt for elimination of what I personally consider very essential limbs."

"You get rid of the fatheads that way," Peter said to the ceiling.

"In my humble opinion, the party in question is being led by the fathead," Al said. "Be that as it may—" He looked at Deborah. "Our friends in Washington are doing their best to cut back by elimination. They've gotten especially excited by the fact that they've been voted in for a second round. One area they seem to think nonessential is the arts."

"That's not true," Peter said to the wall.

"The concept is valid enough. They want to eliminate the kind of graft that can shred paper into a trash can and call it art. I suppose you could say the plan is to return to 'high seriousness.' They think the way to do that is to withhold governmental financing of anything not fitting into their definition of the term."

"That sounds good to me," Deborah said. She pushed at the papers laying on her desk. "The applicant I'm working on now is trying to convince the city of Tacoma that they need more neon lights added to the stuff they already have decorating their sports dome."

Al didn't hear her. "The problem is that they don't know how to do it and aren't equipped to do it either. They think Louis L'Amour writes great literature."

"The cowboy writer?"

"One and the same."

"It's still a good idea," Peter said.

"But it won't work." Al's leg began swinging again. Peter looked at it. It stopped abruptly and the foot on the floor began to jiggle. "As I said, the concept of trimming leads to decapitation. Instead of streamlining guidelines, they simply stop the federal dollars from flowing."

"What's that got to do with us, though?" Deborah asked. "We're county."

"But we funnel a lot of federal money to artists. Those are federal forms you're working on at this very moment."

She grinned. "Well, not at this moment."

He waved a hand. "Current project. The thing is, that kind of attitude makes for a 'what's the point of funding arts?' feeling at the most basic level. And that's certainly dangerous because it could spell doom for the entire department."

Peter put a hand over his mouth. "You worry too much, Al my friend."

Al's foot jiggled. "I don't think so." He stuck out a finger. "I've got a strong suspicion that one of these days you're going to tell me I was right all along. I certainly hope not, but I've got a suspicion."

Peter twisted his chair around to face Deborah's desk. "And I've got a suspicion that if we don't get some work done, Ms. Susan is going to put us all out of a job long before Washington has a chance to start worrying about us."

"True." Al slid off the desk. Peter twisted his chair into its original position. "Forgive me. It wasn't my intention to harangue you."

Peter waved a hand at him and grinned over his shoulder at Deb. "We've all got our pet peeves. Yours is the Republicans and mine is Ms. Susan."

"In that case I've got two," Al said.

The telephone rang in the next office. Peter reached over a pile of papers, punched a button on his phone and lifted the receiver. "Peter Hawkes here," he said. "Hold on please." He covered the receiver with his palm and grinned at Al. "Speak of the devil," he said.

Deborah chuckled. Al hurried around the partition.

"Yes Susan?" she heard him ask briskly.

He'd fill out the application before he went home, Lawrence decided as he came out of the stairwell entrance on the ground floor. The girl Deborah was prettier now than she'd been at the bus depot. It was a self-possessed prettiness though and he wasn't sure that he liked it. Not that he had any business liking it anyway.

He avoided a puddle of water. Lately his shoes always seemed to be damp. More water wouldn't help.

He passed a drug store with a lunch counter near the front window. His stomach twisted. Maybe that was why he'd reacted so much to the girl. No lunch and not much of a breakfast. There'd been one slice of bread left this morning. He'd have to get more on his way home.

But the application came first. He put his hand into his pocket to touch it. This opening with the County sounded perfect. Someone to do research on historical buildings.

They weren't paying a lot so they couldn't be too choosy about what kind of experience the applicants had. Those were the exact words the woman on the telephone had used. At least there was someone besides himself who knew what a horrible word "experience" could be.

She'd said his education sounded excellent. Excellent. No one had applied that expression to him since he'd left school. Last spring. It seemed like a whole other life.

He breathed in the warmth of the library and found an empty table in a corner to spread his things on. When he'd finished he'd find a couple books to check out, he promised himself. He'd been doing that more and more lately. It was a way to keep his mind off his predicament. And his stomach. He'd been stretching his food as far as it would go, trying to make his money last.

But maybe this application would solve the problem. He unfolded it and dug his job hunting information from the other pocket. Why he bothered to carry this stuff with him, he didn't know. He had all of it memorized.

He filled in the blanks of the basic form swiftly, pausing only to resharpen his pencil. Then the three pages of specialized questions. This was always the hard part. They were designed to test whether you had experience doing exactly what the job they were hiring for involved.

But these seemed to want answers based on education. He was still in a basically hopeful mood when he finished forty-five minutes later. He sat back, retraced a word and erased and rewrote the last part of a sentence. He turned the pages. Yes, they were all answered. Everything filled in as well as he could.

He still had to sign it. He dug into his pocket for his only pen. It was cheaper to use pencil for the rest of the writing.

There was a paragraph of print above the line he was supposed to sign on. The usual certification that what he'd written was true and release of records for the employer's inquiries. He wrote in his name and the date.

Below the space where he'd signed was more print. This had been typed in as if in afterthought. "Please be advised that notification regarding eligibility for employment, and therefore interviews for positions, cannot be made prior to at least six weeks after the closing date for any particular position. Please do not contact this office before that time."

Six weeks? "Closing date" meant the last day the application could be turned in. That was tomorrow. Six weeks from tomorrow was mid-December.

He sat back in his chair. The typewriting made the words stand out on the page. He'd counted his money again this morning. He had enough for another four weeks in the studio. Then his rent would fall due again. If he paid it, he wouldn't have anything to buy food with. Not even two weeks' worth.

He swept the papers together. It had looked like it would work. But his luck wasn't going to turn.

Automatically, he began to shuffle the pages into a neat pile. Why make him go to all this bother if they weren't going to even let him call to find out if he had a chance? Six weeks was long enough to starve to death. Didn't they know that? Or didn't it matter?

But they wouldn't believe that anyone in this country in this half of this century could starve to death. He thought of the way his wallet had thinned in the last month. The papers dropped to the table. They might get a chance to have it proved to them.

There was no point in returning the forms. He picked them up. He stared at the top sheet. There wouldn't be anyone at this phone number in six weeks.

Unless he found something else before then. He didn't know that he wouldn't. He hadn't heard from any of the department stores where he'd applied for Christmas temporary work. But if he did, that would start sometime this month.

He stood up. He'd come back to look at the books. There was still time to return the form. If he didn't do it now he never would.

He put his coat on and forced his fingers to pick up the papers. He had reached the point of filling out applications out of habit, not because he thought they would get him a job. This had seemed different.

He went back to the County building, turned in the forms, got his "receipt," and found a bus that would take him back to his apartment. The sky was unseasonably blue. The bus he boarded passed a bit of view to the south. The other passengers' heads turned to look at Mount Rainier. Lawrence didn't notice them looking.

He got off a couple blocks from his building, a half-block from the grocery store.

A few doors from the grocery was a second hand book shop. Usually he passed it without a second look. They sold mostly novels, which he didn't care about, and things like An Herb Lovers Guide to the Pacific Northwest.

Today, in celebration of the sun, the door stood wide open. There were three cardboard boxes filled with books on the sidewalk beneath the window. Above them was a small handwritten sign reading "In Boxes - 15 Cents a Book."

He stopped and nudged the box nearest him with his toe. Old torn-up novels. A Farmers Almanac for 1973. What looked like somebody's old diary. Half a dozen Reader's Digest condensed books. He crouched down.

Here was something with possibilities. The Idea of History. Its cover had once been blue-gray. Now it was just dark. The binding was still intact though. Its paper felt smooth and firm beneath his fingers, not like the cheap rough stuff most of the library's books were printed on.

He opened it to the flyleaf. Printed in 1941. He looked at the sign over the box. Even fifteen cents was more than he could or should afford.

What the hell. It was going to go sooner or later. Faster than he wanted it to, no matter what he did. He might as well enjoy what it went for.

He bought the book, stuck it in the outer pocket of his jacket, and went on to the grocery store. He purchased two loaves of their cheapest bread, a jar of their worst-quality peanut butter and a dozen small eggs.

But buying the book had released the tight rein he'd been keeping on his wallet.

He paused in front of the wine shelves. There was a large sign above the gallon jugs on the bottom one. Three dollars.

The money was going to go before he knew it, anyway. Might as well get some pleasure from it.

When he got back to the apartment he rinsed out his coffee mug, then filled it carefully. "Probably cheaper than coffee," he muttered as he recapped the jug.

He lifted his new book from the table. He took a mouthful of wine as he crossed the floor to the couch. He stopped and looked into the cup. "Whew!" He reached the couch and looked into the cup again. He tried another sip and then swallowed quickly.

"Well, it's not meant for tasting," he muttered. A warm hand slid over his chest as the alcohol went to work. He took another drink and stretched his legs out on the couch. Better than coffee. He reached for his book.

When he woke the next morning the jug had moved from the table to the floor beside the couch and the book was under his head. He couldn't remember what he had read.

He stumbled to the bathroom and carefully patted his face with a towel. A heavy bass beat a rhythm at the top of his skull. The red mark on his cheek would have to fade on its own. Rubbing it gave the bass a staccato force that made his eyes hurt and his jaws ache.

He didn't have to look pretty anyway. He'd filled out an application for every available job in the city. Now all he could do was sit and wait. Six weeks. Well, the book would give him something to do.

Deb was wearing the new gray suit the night she was mugged.

She'd gotten used to the old man at the lamppost below her window. And there was the gray haired woman outside the Arctic Building who really seemed to be living out of the dozen shopping bags she guarded all day. But Deborah hadn't paid any attention to the growing numbers of people in the small park she'd eaten her lunch in the day she was apartment hunting.

She only passed the park on the nights she went by the grocery for food. There were usually a couple odd looking people standing in doorways or coming toward her on the sidewalk. But there were never more than one or two. She'd learned quickly that if she didn't meet their eyes and kept walking they wouldn't give her a second glance.

But that evening the weather was more May-like than October. She swung along cheerfully, glancing at the people she met. She'd found a pair of pearl earrings for her mother's Christmas gift at a bargain price. She was feeling good.

There were so many good buys, if you only looked in the right places. She studied the woman coming toward her. A polyester top that looked like part of an old nurse's uniform. Torn blue jeans. Tennis shoes that were obviously too big. The two men with her weren't much better.

She passed them and turned the corner. There was an alley ahead and then another corner and past the post where "her drunk" would be leaning. Then she'd be home. The groceries were beginning to pull at her arms.

She'd done more than the usual number of errands today. She was beginning to see what Peter and Al meant when they rolled their eyes and said "Ms. Susan."

She didn't hear the feet behind her or smell the mixture of urine and stale wine until they were crowding her into the alley.

She jerked her head. A dark, bloated face was six inches from hers. She pulled back. A hand pressed down on the bag containing her mother's gift.

"Excuse me!" she said. She jerked her arm away from the woman reaching for her packages and brought her heel down sharply on the tennis shoe of the man at her other side.

"Ouch! Goddamsonofa—"

She didn't wait to hear more. She clutched at her slipping packages, dodged around the woman and ran for the corner and light. The other man started to follow, but he stopped when she reached the sidewalk.

She slowed down after she got around the corner. She gripped her groceries tighter, from the bottom. Another two yards and the sack would have slipped to the ground.

"I guess I could have left it for them to deal with," she muttered. She forced herself to breathe more slowly.

There were footsteps behind her. She jerked around. It was Sam, going to his lamppost. He looked at her and she dug into her purse for her keys. She should have had these out anyway. Gouging with keys was supposed to be very effective.

Lucky she'd thought of the heel trick. She opened the iron gate. Actually, she hadn't thought anything. It had all been pure instinct. Including looking the woman over like that.

"Pretty stupid," she muttered as she unlocked her door. She tossed the sack with the earrings in it onto the table and took her groceries to the kitchen counter. She took her time putting the food away. If she kept her hands moving long enough, they'd stop shaking so badly.

This probably wasn't the best place in the city to live, what with the park nearby and the mission just down the street with its free beds for the homeless.

She shivered. Where would she be now if she hadn't gotten away from those three? The woman had looked as willing to kill her as the men had. And as able.

She was being ridiculous. They'd just wanted her money. Or her packages. She should have just handed them the groceries. Or dropped them, that would have been better. But no, she had to be heroic.

Next time she'd think more clearly. The sensible thing to do was to give them what they wanted and then get away quickly. She was lucky they'd been too drunk to pursue her.

At lunchtime the next day, instead of her usual shopping, Deb walked to the grocery store. She was going to retrace the route she'd taken last night. It should be possible to buy groceries during her lunch hour. She should have just enough time to get them home and be back at work by one o'clock.

She looked at her watch as she reached the store. Maybe she was just overreacting. Were these people really a problem? She couldn't tell.

She'd told Al and Peter about it this morning. She wouldn't have been able to keep it to herself if she'd tried. Like telling your nightmares. It helped just to say them out loud.

"Doesn't really surprise me." Al had bounced onto the balls of his feet. "There's been a significant increase in street people recently. It's a classic example of Reaganomics at work."

"There are always some people on the streets," Peter said. "It's the nature of cities. If I were you I'd start carrying one of those cans of mace."

"I thought of that." She twisted her pencil between her fingers. "But besides the fact that they're illegal, it wouldn't have done much good last night anyway, with a sack of groceries in my arms. And I don't know how I could carry it so I'd get at it in time."

"Mace isn't going to give those people a shelter from the environment." Al rocked back on his heels. He braced himself against the sides of the doorway. "What do you want to wager that those three curled up in a corner of that same alley and went to sleep after you disappeared?"

It was easy enough to talk about it. Not easy to decide what to do. Deborah turned away from the store and walked slowly past the park. There did seem to be more people in it now than there'd been that day in September when she'd eaten her lunch here. And it was colder now than it was then.

She looked at the figures huddled on the benches or standing in groups with their backs to the wind. Many carried backpacks. Some had suitcases and sleeping bags at their feet.

What about the ones without even sleeping bags? she wondered. There was the mission, of course. But Al had said that the workers there were reporting more and more applicants for the little they could offer. All they provided was a meal of soup and sandwiches and a thin mattress laid out on the floor.

Her feet quickened as a bony old man wrapped in two sweaters and an oversized coat moved toward her with his hand out. "Say Miss?" he croaked. She hurried by, eyes straight ahead.

- 65 -

7

Lawrence read the book during the next two weeks. Without it the time, with no phone calls or interviews, would have seemed endless. With it, he hardly noticed.

It wasn't the book as much as the ideas it triggered. He read it through and then laid it aside. He paced the floor, putting the concepts into his own words. He ate automatically, slept when he was tired of thinking. For the first time in two months he had found something to focus on and he wasn't letting it slip away from him.

"If I'd seen it a week before—" he said to himself. "If I'd seen it a week before I would have ignored it. The idea of history? Foolishness, I would have thought it. Facts were what I wanted. Dates, times and places."

He wheeled around to walk the length of the floor again. Outside, past the raised blinds, the street lamps shone on the damp pavement. Somewhere a siren howled, lonely and haunting in the sleeping city.

"But ideas, now—"

The ring of the telephone jarred him. He shook his head sharply. He picked up the receiver.

"This three twelve?" The man's voice was raspy with tiredness.

"Pardon? Oh. Yes. Yes, it is."

"Hey, it's like two o'clock in the morning, man, and I'm gettin' phone calls from the lady downstairs from you. She don't like the noise that you're making."

"Noise?"

"Yeah. Feet, she says. Sounds like you're walkin' back and forth, back and forth. I told her you can't be, 'cause it's two in the morning, but she says whatever it is, it's drivin' her crazy 'cause it's been going on it must be a week. So whatever it is, do you mind?"

"What? Oh. All right."

"Just what you been doin' anyway, pal?"

"What? Oh. Thinking. Walking, I suppose."

"You suppose. Oh Christ. Well stop walkin', hey buddy?"

"Yes. All right. Goodbye."

"Thanks pal."

Lawrence put the receiver in its cradle and paced back to the door. He stopped suddenly and looked at his feet. Walking. Two o'clock in the morning. He frowned and looked at his watch. The man on the telephone had been right, whoever he was. His mind worked through the problem slowly. It must have been the manager, since he'd known where he was and what room he was in. And the woman downstairs had known who to call.

Odd, to think that his floor was the ceiling over someone else's head. It made him feel the awful fragility of the building.

The way history was fragile. He paced back to the wall, then realized what he was doing and went to sit on the couch. Sometime in the last few days he had made it out into a bed and left it that way. He didn't remember doing it though.

The thing was, this was a new idea. Maybe a revolutionary one. He rubbed his hand across his face. God, he was tired.

He sat down on the bed and leaned against the couch where it met the mattress. He couldn't walk, but it made him sleepy to lie here and think. But the idea of history. History as an idea—

He woke to gray sunlight trickling through the smudged window panes. The room was cold and he pulled the blankets over his arms and wondered at the emptiness he felt. The way a young child does who, punished, falls crying to sleep and wakes with no tears left in him. He pulled an arm free of the blanket and looked at his watch. Eleven o'clock.

He turned his head slowly. The room had grown shabby with clothes and dishes left where he'd stopped using them. It seemed foreign to him and empty.

His eyes fell on the book. Not everything had to be empty, however. He still had his mind, if he didn't have a job or much else.

He rolled onto his stomach and began fingering the pieces in his mind, putting the puzzle together. The book didn't state it, of course. The authors didn't seem to realize the implication of what they were saying.

Lawrence sat up. It was, in a real sense, his own. Get this in the journals, get it into print, and then see what happened. He could make a good living, propounding his theory. Why, it could change the very way history texts were being written!

Ideas as influence, as actually creating the history that supposedly produced them. They talked about it, of course, in the books. Rousseau and the French Revolution, that kind of thing. But when they came down to why things happened, they ended with measurable actions. With this speech and that war and those treasons.

He rolled off the bed and began pacing the floor. He stopped in mid-step. Damn it. He frowned at the floor and went on. He had more important things to do than worry about the woman downstairs.

It wasn't so much ideas in general that he was after, though. It was ideas about history.

"What my book will explain—" he said aloud. He stopped in the middle of the floor. He grinned. A whole book, it was now. Well, and why not? The energy surged in him along with the plan.

He had plenty of time for writing, that was certain. For the first time since he'd gotten to Seattle he felt as if there was a reason for the things that were happening to him. A purpose behind the hunt for a job and the long wait, for the stretches of inertia that resulted from it.

Over-educated and no experience. Well, maybe his schooling hadn't made him worth a lot when it came to the stupid little jobs the business world wanted you for. But for what he was going to do, it was just what he needed.

It was over a month before Deb had any more problems with street people. She couldn't help but notice that the groups in the park were larger. There were young men now too, and more women than there'd been before.

She kept away from the area as much as she could. It reminded her of the three in the alley. She felt conspicuous, though she told herself she was being ridiculous. Her new winter coat and the small hat with the satin ribbon weren't that luxurious. They weren't nearly as nice as the outfit she had wanted to buy but couldn't afford.

But the next time she was approached she wasn't anywhere near Pioneer Square.

She'd taken the bus to Northgate Mall to look for a Christmas present for Bobby. She hadn't found anything for him, but there was a sale going on in one of the many shops lining the echoing hallways. She'd discovered a pair of leather boots that went perfectly with her new coat. They were a third of the price she'd expected to pay when her budget would allow her to buy them. At the sale price, she'd be silly to wait until January and pay the full amount.

She swallowed hard, wrote the check and pinched the plastic bag greedily as she left the shop. It was a wonderful buy. And there was nothing for Bobby here.

She took her place among the crowd of people at the bus stop outside the mall. It was the usual Saturday afternoon mixture. Golden-age ladies in cloth coats with fur collars. Teenage boys with portable stereos hanging from straps over their shoulders. Fashionably dressed college students. Refugee women with solemn-faced children.

A group of young oriental women stood directly behind Deb. They chattered softly in their native tongue, English mixing in from time to time.

Deb heard the one at her left elbow say "Look!" and then finish her sentence in the other language. Deb turned her head casually to glance at the double glass doors leading into the mall.

A thin, boyish figure with an orange hunting cap on its head had just come through the door. A large backpack was slung over its shoulder. One hand kept the strap in place and the other arm half carried, half dragged a stuffed duffel bag.

There was a delicacy about the face, a certain patient look in the eyes, that said the person was female. Deborah turned her head to face the bus stop.

She heard a soft giggle, then the women behind her began a slightly too loud conversation in their own language. "Excuse me ma'am?"

It was a soft and feminine voice, but insistent. For a split second Deb thought she was the one being addressed. She looked around without thinking. One of the oriental women was the target.

"Could you spare any change?"

The young woman giggled. Her companions stopped talking.

"I am in need of bus fare," the soft voice explained. "It would be most appreciated, if you could spare—"

The voice trailed off. The young woman giggled again and watched her face. One of her friends said something sharply and her eyes slid to the duffel bag.

"Me no English," she said. She laughed again, gave Deborah a half-pleading look, and moved toward her friends as if for protection. They moved aside to let her pass, then followed her to the other end of the crowd.

"Excuse me ma'am?"

Now it was Deborah's turn. But she'd learned a few tricks in the past few weeks and, though her stomach twisted sharply, she looked straight ahead, the tight fingers on her package and purse the only indication she'd heard the soft, pushing voice.

There was a pause, then "Could you spare any change?"

Deb turned her head in the opposite direction, looking to see if the bus was in sight yet.

"Thank you for your kindness." The voice held no reproach, but Deb's head jerked. She looked at the woman and then away again and moved back into the crowd. She looked at her package and purse.

"Excuse me sir?" The woman pulled her bag slowly toward a boy with a stereo.

He twisted a button and pulled his earphones off his head. "Yeah? Oh, you don't got your fare? Well, let me see. Hey, Angeline, you got some money? I don't have much more than what I need to get home."

The girl nearest him was wearing a very tight, sparkling white tee shirt. A carefully torn black sweatshirt was draped over it. She dug a hand into the pocket of her tighter than skin blue jeans. "Yeah, I got a few dimes. How much you need?"

Together they had enough for a fare. Deb tried not to watch the woman's face as the boy poured the coins into her palm.

"I thank you kindly," she said.

"Yeah, yeah." He waved his hand at her and pulled his headphones on. "I know how it goes man, I know how it goes." He twisted a dial on his equipment.

The woman moved a few yards off and eased the pack from her shoulders.

When the bus came she was one of the last on, pouring the coins carefully into the fare box and asking softly for a transfer. She settled onto one of the side seats directly behind the driver's small pen and poked at the cloth which covered the opening at the top of the duffel bag.

The teenagers who'd given her the fare were in the back of the bus. Deb had a seat near the front. Where did the woman come from, that she carried her belongings with her like that? Deb lifted the plastic bag containing her boots onto her lap. She turned her head to look out the window.

~

The day came that the rent for December was due. Lawrence had only enough for food and note paper. None for rent. But he was so absorbed in the development of his idea that he hardly noticed.

The words came slowly to the paper. He waited until he had a sentence, writing and rewriting it in his mind, before putting it down. He couldn't waste the paper or ink on first drafts of revisions. It had to be right the very first time he curved the pen around the words.

He was in the middle of rewriting a sentence when there was a knock on the door. He repeated it twice as he crossed the room and opened the door.

"Do you have your money, man?" Calvin stubbed his cigarette out on the doorjamb.

"Pardon?"

"The money for your rent. You're ten days overdue now."

"Oh. I don't have enough."

"Then you'll have to leave."

"Oh. All right." He stood looking at Calvin's unshaved face.

"Today. You'll have to leave now."

"Oh. All right. Right this moment? I'm in the middle of something."

"How long do you need?"

"An hour. Perhaps two."

"I'll give you an hour and a half. Then you'll have to get out."

"All right." He ran his hand through his hair. "I'll be through with this sentence by then."

Calvin stared at him. He poked his dirty tee-shirt into the top of his jeans and turned away. Lawrence closed the door. He went back to the table and his small pile of paper. Now how was that going to read? "Therefore, I propose that the concept of history is not only mutable, but—"

He wrote it out carefully, reread it, ran his hand over his face, and stood up. He'd known this was going to happen. He didn't have much anyway. Just the suitcase and the sleeping bag and blankets.

He hummed under his breath as he folded his clothes into the suitcase. He'd read about people who'd had to go through all sorts of things. Wasn't it Edgar Allan Poe who'd died in a gutter? And look at him now. And Samuel Johnson, starving in a garret for years, living on potatoes. But in the end he'd been famous. You had to suffer for what you cared about, that was all.

Down on the street, suitcase in one hand, bedroll dangling from the other, he decided to walk downtown. He could think while he walked and there was more likely to be a place there for him to sleep. Capitol Hill's streets were lined with small houses and tired-looking apartment buildings. The few parks had no hidden, enclosed areas.

He trudged off, muttering to himself. When he had the next sentence firmly fixed in his mind, he stopped in the middle of the sidewalk. He knelt beside his suitcase, pulled out his papers and wrote the words out carefully. Then he put the pages into the breast pocket of his coat for easier access.

He was still feeling good when he reached the freeway bridge which marked the boundary between First Hill and downtown. His legs were tired, though. He found a bench in a corner of Freeway Park and pulled out his papers. He reread them slowly.

He had only two pages so far, but they read clearly and concisely. Those were the attributes they'd need if they were going to make themselves heard.

He refolded the papers and looked around. He was starting to feel hungry and a light rain had begun to fall, misting the evergreens. He needed to find a place to sleep.

As he stood up, a half-forgotten ache twisted his stomach. The unsure feeling of looking, of searching for a place to be. It had been there every time he'd asked for an application form. He'd forgotten it in the excitement of working on his idea. But leaving the apartment had guaranteed this grabbing, turning sensation for a long time to come.

He picked up his suitcase. "I'll just have to finish this," he muttered. "Get this done and to the right people and I'll be all right again. It doesn't matter where I sleep, anyway."

He wandered aimlessly for a while, getting thoroughly wet before the rain stopped. He was too tired to find something to eat and when he saw the park he knew he'd found a place to sleep.

It was sheltered on the north side by an old fashioned concrete-brick building. There were bushes planted in half circles along the edge of the building. They curved away from the lawn and pushed their full sides toward the wall.

The bushes protected benches set in the concrete of the areas they partially enclosed. There were dark figures huddled on several of the benches, heads protected from the weather with plastic bags and old paper sacks. Lawrence moved quietly until he found a bench in a section with no one else in it.

He rolled the sleeping bag out on the bench. He laid one blanket underneath, to soften the boards, and another on top to keep him warm. He slid the suitcase under the bench, his shoes on top. He laid his overcoat over them and crawled into his bag.

As he began to relax, he realized he needed to use a restroom. He sat up and looked around. He climbed out of the bag and reached for his shoes. Surely there was one somewhere nearby. He looked down at his suitcase.

He looked around again. The lamps along the sidewalk didn't give much light where he was. None of the black heaps on the benches in the next area moved. He moved toward the bushes behind his bench, then stopped. Off to one side, at least. Hell, dogs did it all the time and they must smell more than humans.

Relieved, he took off his shoes again, dusted off the bottom of his socks and crawled back into the sleeping bag. He'd have to find a place to wash his hands before he ate in the morning. He drifted into the deep, unmuscled oblivion only those who have walked a good deal in one day can experience.

It began raining again, the same gentle mist. Still asleep, Lawrence pulled the bag up over his face. He turned onto his side and pulled his legs up, instinctively finding the street person's protective sleeping position, upper legs giving warmth to lower chest, arms holding upper chest, and face tucked in out of the cold and damp.

It was several hours later and he was still in the same position when the voice spoke into his ear. "Here son, wake up," it said sharply.

He groaned and tried to roll over. The back of the bench got in his way.

"No son. You need to wake up," the voice said. The hand shook his shoulder again, firmly enough to wake him this time. "You can't sleep here, my son. It's going to start raining again."

The hand gave his shoulder yet another firm pull. He struggled to sit up. The voice was talking to a bench beyond his.

Someone must have come searching for a place to sleep after Lawrence had closed his eyes. The dark form that had roused him was bending over a bundle of rags on a bench near the bush where he had relieved himself.

"Here son. Wake up," the voice said.

There were soft mutterings near the bushes on his other side. Lawrence looked around. Several dark shapes stood just beyond the semicircle he was in. They carried bedrolls and pieces of luggage sat at their feet.

On the other bench the rags stirred, then suddenly sat up. "Well, hello Mother Ann! Where you been?" said a muffled voice. There were snickers from the group at the edge of the bushes.

"Well, hell, if it ain't the old codger." The woman in robes laughed. She patted an edge of the rags and the ones at the upper end came off with a flourish. A tiny old man, cheeks gaunt even under his half-grown beard, grinned up at her. He pulled off a few more of the rags and rummaged at her sleeve. She gave him her hand and he kissed it gallantly.

The group at the edge of the bushes laughed again. "It's the old codger all right," someone said.

"Okay you guys, get your shit together," the woman in robes said. "It's fixing to rain like hell and I don't plan on catching pneumonia because you've got no better sense than to sleep in the open."

"Now Ma, don't go getting your pants in an uproar," the old codger said. He sorted his rags into a pile, put part of them back on his arms and head, and stood up. "Here you youngie, you better get movin' or Mother Ann'll be leaving you to freeze in the rain."

"Now, nobody's going to get left," the woman said. "Just get yourselves going and we'll feed some hot soup to your stomachs and put you to bed with a roof over you."

"Ah, that's what we needed." The old man grinned toothlessly. "We've been gettin' bad habits, without you around to cuss us out. It's been your fault, y'know. Desertin' us like that."

"Yeah, where you been, sister?" asked one of the group at the edge. They crowded closer as Lawrence got out of his sleeping bag. He reached for his shoes. They were more interested in the woman in nun's clothing. She couldn't really be a religious person though. He'd heard her swearing himself.

"Hell, you know the people up the hill aren't too sure about me," she said. She counted heads. "Looks like everybody's awake. You all got your stuff? Oh, not him." She looked at Lawrence. "New here, huh? My name's Sister Ann and you might call these reprobate sailors my sheep. God knows, nobody else is going to claim 'em."

"Ah, but you love us, don't ya Ma?" The old man was still sitting on the bench, a small backpack beside him and one knee tucked up under his chin.

"That's as good a reason as any to come traipsin' round after you all, I suppose," she said. She glanced at Lawrence. "Well, now, if you s.o.b.'s are ready to go—" She waved her arms up and down and her sleeves flapped like wings. "Go on! The van's ready and waiting and warm even, by the grace of God."

Lawrence bundled his bag and blankets together hurriedly. He tucked them under one arm and grabbed his suitcase with the other hand. He followed the group of dark figures to a battered, grayish colored van at the edge of the curb.

The rain started falling again, harder now, as they drove off. The wipers on the windshield didn't work properly, so they moved slowly through the wet and black city. The street lights shone feebly.

8

Deb stood in front of the full length mirror which hung on the bathroom door. She was warm with her hat, coat and boots on and the mirror was wavy with age, but she wanted to see the full effect.

She stepped back, her heels hard against the side of the tub, and looked again.

It still didn't feel right. The pieces were good, but the overall picture wasn't as sharp as it should be.

She watched the mirror and moved her elbow, turning sideways to smile at herself. Her hair fanned out over the coat collar and she brushed it away impatiently. She paused. She pulled the hair away from her face, against the brim of her hat.

That was it. She took off the hat, pulled her hair onto the top of her head and carefully put the hat on again. You noticed the eyes more this way. She pulled the hat off and hurried out of the bathroom, pulling off her coat as she went.

Here it was. The hair styling page in the magazine she'd just bought. Short but not too severe. She ran her hand along her scalp and her fingers slowed. Just there Andrew had gentled her head. It was the only gentle touch he had given her. But he had said that he liked her hair. Her fingers tightened. And that's how his hand was later, when he was—

She wondered why it had taken her so long to think about cutting it. Removing every trace of that night and what followed.

She left work at two thirty the next day for her appointment. It was an expensive salon and she wondered if she really should be doing this. It would blow a big hole in her budget.

But it was worth it, she decided on the way home. This was the third time she'd glanced at a shop window, seen a reflection of herself, and turned to see who was behind her.

It made her feel different, too. As if cutting away the hair had removed the last of her childhood. She felt more confident than she had ever before.

There was a gallery opening that night which Peter had given her the office ticket for. She hurried into her apartment and pulled out a dress without the usual worrying about appropriateness and accessories.

The gallery was only two blocks away. She swung up its steps and presented her ticket. As she walked away from the small desk at the front, she noticed a man lounging in a chair in the opposite corner. He was good looking in a blond playboy way. He seemed to be waiting for someone, but she felt his look sweep over her anyway. He made as if to get up, then sat back and re-crossed his legs. She turned her head.

The showing was "new medium." Collages of newsprint on clay boards. Oils and "found objects" combined. Lots of metal and fabric. The pieces were done by different people and Deb made a first tour looking for familiar names. She didn't see any.

Al had a point. Their agency's profile wasn't terribly high. Could that really make a difference though? She began her second round, maneuvering past other viewers. The gallery guests tended to bunch in small groups, talking quietly. The air of intimacy was part of what she liked so much about these events.

This tin and wood sculpture was interesting. You felt the contrast between the tin's fragility and the solidness of the oak. She stood back and put her head to one side, to get a better feel of it as a whole. There was a sudden movement just outside her peripheral vision and she turned her head.

The blond man was standing alone before a hung fabric piece. Interesting that a man would notice it. Most of these pieces were done by women. There seemed to be a tacit agreement that they be appreciated by them too. Maybe he wasn't as arrogant as he had looked.

Not that it mattered. She swung her head and her hair moved gently against her cheek. It felt odd, nothing but air on her neck. She watch him out of the corner of her eye as she drifted away from the sculpture toward the hung clay pieces. They weren't the usual masks, but bas-relief representations of daily scenes, highlighted with garish colors that made the clay look vaguely dirty.

"Do you find that attractive?" asked a voice just above her left ear.

She turned. It was him.

"Actually, I'm not sure I do," she said. She moved her head and felt the hair against her cheek again. "Artistically, I find it interesting. A statement of the way we look at the world, perhaps? Or as the way media changes things, bright colors on a drab world that is actually quite valid in itself."

She looked at the hanging again and felt a surge of power go through her. A woman walking by glanced at them and Deb's back straightened. "Though I wouldn't want to hang it on a wall which I wanted to exude peacefulness," she said.

He chuckled. "That's how I felt the first time I saw it, but it's growing on me. There are so many interpretations, I think it could do well in an atmosphere of meditation. As something to think about, perhaps philosophize on."

She smiled.

"Now what about this next one?" he asked. "I can't decide whether it's just a new-style Mark Toby or has merits of its own. The colors are very appealing."

"They are attractive," she said. "But I get the feeling the artist had one eye on someone else's work on the opposite wall."

"Too aware, perhaps?"

"Yes, I think so." She stood back a little. "Yet, you know, I might be willing to have it on a wall by itself." They were silent, looking at the painting. "No, perhaps not," she said. She put her finger to her chin. "Perhaps not."

They wandered some more. "Now these I find intriguing," he would say, and they would be off on another discussion. They went a third round, he attentive, she alive with perceptiveness. Finally they drifted toward the back of the gallery, where a bar had been set up.

They were serving white wine from a regional winery. Deb swirled hers in her glass. The blond man drifted toward a group of people at one side of the bar and Deb followed him. The talk was artistic and Deb felt a pleasant glow. She stood listening until a woman nearby suddenly looked at her watch and gasped. Deb looked at her own.

It was eleven o'clock. The party was breaking up. The blond man was near her in the group which went down the stairs.

"I'm hungry," he said as they broke into the street.

"Look, the sky's cleared," Deb said.

He stood beside her, looking up.

The people who had come down with them were halfway down the block. "Are you coming with us, Bob?" a woman's voice called.

"Wouldn't miss it!" he answered. He grinned down at Deborah, lifted a hand in farewell, then moved after his friends.

The steaming van emptied itself into an echoing wooden warehouse near the waterfront. Inside, make-shift partitions marked off sleeping areas on each side of a central gathering space. In the large middle space which they defined stood a wooden picnic table badly in need of another coat of brown paint.

On the table were a ten-gallon bucket filled with homemade soup, stacks of chipped hotel ware bowls, and several rows of cheap aluminum spoons. There were two bathroom/shower areas beyond the table. One had a cardboard sign reading "Men" tacked on the door. But Lawrence was more interested now in the smell of the soup.

The group shuffled into a crude line. Most of them were still carrying their packs and sleeping rolls. With whatever hand they could work free, they held out their bowls.

First came a piece of bread, then steaming soup and finally a spoon stuck in at one side. They moved slowly to the edges of the empty space, soaking in the drafty warmth of the hall. The woman—they called her "sister," "mother" or "ma" alternately— handed out sheets of paper toweling to use as napkins.

Lawrence squatted next to his suitcase and sleeping bag. The man they called "old codger" crouched beside him.

The old man finished his first bowl of soup and bread and had gone for a second before he took any notice of Lawrence. He wiped his greasy mouth with his paper towel and looked him over. "Hey sonny, what's your name?"

Lawrence looked up. "Pardon? Oh, I'm Lawrence. Lawrence Anderson."

The old man took another spoonful of soup, his bowl level with his chin. His eyes watched Lawrence. "You look more Italian than scandhoovian," he said.

"My father was part Italian," Lawrence said. He drank the soup slowly, getting the most from its warmth.

There were a few minutes of silence. The slurping of soup and clink of spoons were loud in the drafty air.

"You been on the street long?" the old man asked suddenly.

Lawrence turned his head. "No."

He nodded. "Didn't think so, by the looks of ya. Y'know, it's not good to keep your stuff underneath the bench the way you had 'em. They gets ripped that way."

"Ripped?"

"Yeah. Stole. Like ripped off. First rule of the streets is, keep what ya have to a bare minimum and never let it out of your sight." He chuckled. "Or your hands."

Lawrence reached for his suitcase and blankets with his free hand.

"Ya don't gotta worry in here though." The old man tilted his head suddenly. He drained the last bit of moisture from his bowl with a drawn out sucking noise and wiped at his face with the paper towel. "Mother Ann'll skin you alive if you're caught stealin' in here and she's got a memory like an eliphant's, Sister does. You'd never get back in if she caught ya rippin' stuff off, and everyone knows it."

Lawrence looked around. The walls had once been painted a greenish yellow. Now they looked like faded wood. "What is this place anyway?" he asked.

The old codger looked at the table. The bucket had been taken away empty and there was no more bread. He put his bowl on the floor, hitched up his ragged substitutes for pants and edged closer to Lawrence. He smelled of stale sweat and old urine.

"Well see, it's like this. This here's an old warehouse and Sister's got the bizness that owns it to let her use it for a consideration. Meaning she gots to keep it clean and the windows not broken or nothing like that."

"Is she really a Sister? A nun, I mean?"

There was a short bark of laughter behind them. Lawrence turned his head. The square black-robed figure stood on the other side of his suitcase and bedroll.

"Not exactly what you'd expect, son?" She nudged his bedding with a solid black shoe. "You can take this into the men's partition anytime. The showers are ready. You gotta get one quick if you like it warm." She nodded at the old man. "Don't let this old codger fill you too full of bull. This one is full of adventures."

She turned and was gone, informing an especially filthy old man in the opposite corner that he was washing himself before he laid down on "my mattresses."

Lawrence looked at the old codger.

"There's a nunn'ry up the hill name of Sisters of Providence. She stays with 'em," he explained. "But whenever she can she's 'round and hauls us in here. Her people don't like what she's doin', of course. Not safe for a woman or some shit like that. Like anybody'd do anything to old Ma." He got to his feet unsteadily and hauled at his pack with a gnarled and dirt-stained hand.

Lawrence stood up too. He picked up his things. "So you come here quite often?"

"Whenever she's here." He motioned for Lawrence to follow and dragged his pack behind the nearest partition. He heaved it onto a mattress.

Lawrence sat down on the pallet beside it. Even its thin lumpiness was a relief after the hard damp of the bench in the park. He was suddenly dizzy with tiredness. He forced himself to roll out the sleeping bag, get out of his clothes and into the pajamas from his suitcase. Then he stood the suitcase at the head of the mattress and fell into sleep.

Next morning there was coffee in the ten gallon bucket and bread and hard boiled eggs beside it, two apiece. But nothing was eaten before showers in the room beyond. Even if you'd showered the night before. That was the rule and no one dared break it. Sister Ann guarded the food.

Lawrence was still clouded with sleep. He followed the others into the locker room, out of his pajamas and under the faucets jutting high from the wall. The ice of the spray hit his skin like a million small knives.

He jumped back, looking wildly around, hurrying for soap and to be out of the water. He stood just out of range, shivering nakedly, and shook the water from his eyes. There was no soap, except for the slivers a few of the men guarded zealously. Obviously their own. Lawrence had some in his suitcase.

He turned his head, his teeth chattering, to look at the room. No towels. He edged back into the cold stream, getting hair and body as wet as he could as quickly as possible, muscles tense, willing himself not to feel.

The water rolled off his thick curls and he scrubbed at his scalp with his fingernails until he couldn't feel his hands anymore. Then he hurried from the spray's range again and shook himself off as best he could before shivering his way into his clothes.

He sat on the bench with his arms crossed, trying to get warm again. No soap and no towels and no one noticing or offering to share. They'd seemed friendly enough before. He brushed the drops of water from his hair away from his eyes. The others were shivering into their own clothes and running fingers over their dripping heads.

He turned and looked at the shower. The men there were following the same procedure he had as if it were a matter of course. The only difference was that they were yowling with pleasure at the feel of the water. As if, even cold, it was luxury.

An old man came shivering from the spray, his belly a hard ball below his bare ribs. His left hand was only a claw and he pulled awkwardly at a tee-shirt two times his size. This was followed by a pair of jeans which were more than skin tight and a large hand-knit sweater with the sleeves torn off haphazardly. He didn't pull on any socks before he stuck his feet into a pair of battered but still stiff hiking boots.

Lawrence looked around and into the measuring eyes of a young man with wild red hair which fell over a faded and stained blue sweatshirt. Lawrence looked at the floor as he buttoned his shirt.

He pulled on his socks and shoes and hurried out, water still dripping from his hair. He got into line for his coffee, bread and two eggs, then crouched on his heels and watched those around him.

Most of them were wolfing their food voraciously. He realized with a start that he was eating with both hands too, stuffing first bread, then egg, into his mouth. He slowed down to chew.

He had a reason for being here, he reminded himself. To give more time to the reading and writing, less to the worry of looking for work and money to live on a fancier scale.

He forced his eyes away from the old man he'd watched dressing and thought of his suitcase with its pan, silver, kitchen knife and towels. It wasn't like he was reduced to only the clothes on his back. Yes, he couldn't find work now, but it left more time for his writing. He wondered if he'd be able to come back here often.

He asked the old codger as they tied up their sleeping bags but the only answer he got was a curious look and "You never can tell, you never can tell."

The old man yanked the string at the top of his knapsack and tied it into a knot. "Come with me today lad, and I'll show you a few sights and clue you in on the town."

Lawrence looked at his suitcase. He had writing to do, and how could he think with this talkative guy in his ear? But he needed to learn to fend for himself. He'd already overheard enough to know that there were things you did and didn't do, as a street person. Places to go or not go.

There seemed to be certain places the street people were looked on with fear and even suspicion. His mind groped at his history idea. Was there a way this time on the streets could relate to his work?

"You ready?" the old man asked, a little too cheerfully. Lawrence looked up and a smile twitched his lips. His spirits rose. If there were things here which would add strength to his book, this was the man to learn them from.

Deb still couldn't believe that her parents hadn't fussed about Thanksgiving. "Not enough money" she'd told them, only half truthfully. She had enough for the bus fare, but she wasn't quite through with her makeover. She wanted to look like a stranger to them. A person with a life and will of her own.

Why it was so important, she couldn't have said. But the humiliation of last summer—Andrew Simpson's elopement with the Kennedy girl, the sharp pity on her mother's face and the disappointment in her father's eyes—they were things still to be fought against.

She'd made a mistake in thinking he cared. When she thought about it now, she didn't know why or how she had thought he would ask her to marry him. She knew better now, too, than to ever again confide in her parents. Too much of a dream, given away, became guaranteed. If it faded, as she knew now that dreams could, she had failed.

Well, coming to Seattle had been a dream too, but it had worked. Now for the rest of it. It was difficult, but in reach, with the help of her magazines and her own careful shopping and makeup.

She had bent her back to the burden of improving herself, decided Thanksgiving wasn't enough time to show to best advantage, and written, "Sorry, can't make it."

They were coming to her for Christmas though, and Christmas was only three weeks away. She was in a mad orgy of shopping and clothes and getting the apartment just right. Clothes for herself. New paper to line the kitchen cabinets and dresser drawers. A sachet for the closet and new hangers, puffy with satin, to show her wardrobe to best advantage.

And there were still gifts to buy. At work, she ignored Peter and Al, who were huddled over Peter's desk muttering about layoffs and funding and strikes. Under the forms she was working on lay an extra sheet of paper for ideas. She filled it with careful lists of possible presents for Bobby along with approximate prices and places they could be purchased.

She had already budgeted down to the last penny, taken another look at what she needed to buy, added up the money she'd have and marched herself firmly into the department stores. She was going against everything her parents had ever taught her about money. Credit? For clothes? But she stiffened her fingers and filled out the forms. There was more than one way to break away from one's parents.

She'd been startled at how quickly the cards were approved. She'd have to repay the money she used, she reminded herself. It wasn't as if she could just spend and spend without having to pay.

But it was a nice feeling to know she had a card for the Bon. Nordstrom's too. These were things she'd need anyway. Shoes and a dress and a belt. Costume jewelry for that final touch. When she took her purchases to the counter the register totaled to half the limit on the new card and her stomach tightened. She handed over the small plastic rectangle and the cashier slipped it into the machine's slot. "There you go!" she said. "Have a good day!"

Deb smiled back at her, piled the bags into her arms and hurried back to the office through a light rain. There'd be a paycheck next week and she'd get Bobby's present then, she decided. If she could ever figure out what it should be.

It was two minutes after one when she got back, but Peter wasn't at his desk. Deborah piled her packages carefully into the large bottom desk drawer beside her purse and set to work. There were more forms than usual today. The rush before Christmas and January 1 deadlines, Peter had said as he handed them to her.

"The rush before no money's left," Al had said as he put a similar pile on Peter's desk.

At ten after one, Peter still hadn't come back. The telephone rang beyond the partition and Deb lifted the receiver on the third ring.

"Deb? Al there?"

"I guess not Susan. He must have stepped out."

"Peter?"

"He's not here either. He should be back any minute."

"Tell Al, call me immediately." Her voice was even sharper than usual and the receiver almost crashed into its cradle.

Al sauntered in at twenty after, Peter behind him.

"Susan called," Deborah told him. "She said to tell you to call right away."

He nodded and disappeared around the corner. His voice was low as he spoke into the phone.

Peter sank into his chair. He kicked his shoes off and they hit the underside of his desk with a bang.

"Have a good lunch?" Deborah asked.

"Wonderful. Lovely as the last meal before execution."

"They say those are usually pretty good," Deborah said. "It always seemed pathetic to me. The only thing you're allowed to do is eat, but how much good is all that food going to do?"

He shrugged. "How much good does anything do?"

"Lord, you're in a good mood. What happened to all the Christmas cheer I was hearing this morning?"

"I was told there probably wouldn't be any."

She put down her pencil. "What?"

"Haven't you heard? Susan told Al right before lunch."

"I left early to go shopping, remember?"

"You may want to go get your money back."

"What are you talking about?"

"It seems that the federal bureau which handles our finances has finally decided that we are unnecessary."

"What?"

Al appeared in the doorway. He bounced forward on the balls of his feet. "I see Peter's been sharing our good news with you."

"Is this some kind of joke?"

Peter chuckled. "Don't I wish."

"But we're part of a County agency."

"We're operated by the County but seventy-five percent of the grant section's budget comes from the Feds. And we weren't important enough to be continued."

"Did you really think you were so disposable?" Peter asked him

"Well, I had a suspicion I might be." Al leaned back on his heels. "That's what I've been telling you, isn't it?"

"Yeah, yeah." Peter flipped a hand at him. He kicked his feet up and out, then looked at them in surprise. He bent down and looked under the desk at his shoes. He looked up. "So I guess we'll be getting the sack," he said to Deborah.

"But what about the other twenty-five percent?"

"Not enough to operate anything," Al said. "Besides, they figure they can get along easily enough without artists. That's the Republicans for you."

"It's a bureau decision," Peter said. "Not a political one."

"It's a bureau decision resulting from a political mandate to cut all non-military expenditures." He grinned. "Perhaps we can obtain positions as coordinators for artists wanting to paint camouflage on the outer shells of space stations."

"I still don't see why the County doesn't try to keep something going," Deborah said. "Besides, they can't move that fast. It'll take them a couple months to close us down completely, won't it?"

"Couple of weeks is more like it," Peter said.

"But that's Christmas! They can't—"

"Like hell they can't."

"But that's inhuman! How am I—" She'd been going to ask how she was going to buy Christmas presents. The look on Peter's face made her mouth numb. His wife was pregnant.

"Well, the County won't leave us totally helpless," Al said. "My understanding is that we are each to receive a hundred dollar severance check."

"Big deal. Groceries for a week, maybe two," Peter said. "Nothing for the doctor bill."

"Oh, I'm sure welfare will be happy to oblige you. What the top dogs forget is that people out of work still require food. They'll just go to welfare or the food stamp bureaucracy."

Peter dived under the desk suddenly and came up with his shoes. "Haven't you got anything better to do?" His accent was more clipped than ever. "Or do you enjoy saying 'I told you so'?"

"Now, I wasn't—"

He stubbed his feet into the shoes and got up. He started for the door, turned and grabbed some papers off his desk and waved them at Deb. "I'll be in Susan's office," he said.

"This is all just rumor, isn't it?" she asked Al.

"Verifiable rumor, I'm afraid. The Feds have cut off the money supply. The agency will fold. That's already been decided." He crossed his arms and rocked back on his heels. "I don't have the timing, if that's what you're after. However, they've called a meeting for tomorrow morning. We should be getting the notice in the afternoon mail."

"I suppose the meeting's to tell us the news officially."

"Yeah, but you can't reasonably expect to keep such a development secret for long. Especially since the papers last week were discussing the effect of government cuts at local and state level and predicting this very thing."

"So it's a matter of time."

"That's one way of saying it." He bounced forward on the balls of his feet. "At any rate, I'd start looking for another position, if I were you. Myself, I've been putting out feelers for the past month, developing contacts, and the outlook isn't too healthy. There isn't much happening this close to the holidays and this conservative mood is putting the squeeze on all the programs having to do with the arts."

She stared at him without hearing. The holidays. What was she going to do about Christmas?

9

It was a beautiful day. One of those rare Northwest winter days when you expect flowers to bloom in December. Sometimes they do.

As they walked along, the old codger gave Lawrence a short history of his life. His name was Jonny Hansen, he said. Johnny without an "h." That was why he'd taken to Lawrence, with a name like Anderson. He came from "these parts." He'd been one of the original pioneers of the area, to hear him tell it. His parents had practically founded the city of Bremerton. He'd never taken to their hard way of living though. He preferred to take life as it came.

And so he was on the streets. Had been, more or less, since the Great Depression. He'd worked as a dock laborer for a while, but gotten restless and moved on "to more excitin' things."

He regaled Lawrence with stories of life on the streets. Adventures he'd had and fights he'd gotten into when he was younger. "There warn't nobody would come looking for trouble 'round me," he declared. He poked a bony finger at his thin chest. "I ain't what I used to be m'lad. No I ain't. Ain't nobody used to mess 'round with me."

Lawrence looked at him. "Do you have problems now?"

The old man looked at him out of the corner of his eye. "Naw. They know better than to bother me. I don't got anything anybody'd want. Ya keeps things simple and nobody wants to take nothing from ya. You don't have anything to make 'em hungry-like."

A black limousine drove slowly by. "Now these people with their fancy cars and their stereos and their furs, they gotta worry all the time. Worry worry, that's all they got time for, beings as they're afraid someone'll rip off their things."

Lawrence tightened his grip on the suitcase and sleeping bag. "This is all I've got."

The old codger looked at the suitcase. "Well, it ain't bad. It ain't bad. If'n you want, I can lighten it for you. Tell you what's important and what ain't. Makes it easier to carry that way."

They were walking in the Denny Regrade area. The buildings were bleached gray by the weather. A sign on the corner of one announced that it housed the New Life and Gospel Mission.

"Now the first thing you gotta learn about bein' independent is how to find food," the old codger said. "Ya gots the mission here, for example. They always wants you to pray and get saved 'fore they'll feed ya. And they don't like ya to come back. Mother Ann now, she's different." He shook his head. "Wish we had more like her, that's fer sure."

Lawrence nodded numbly. They'd been walking for two hours and his feet kept time with each other wearily. His mind refused to ask how much they hurt.

The old codger pointed up the street. "Now here's a good oppitunity." They turned into a dirty alley of brick and concrete walls. Several large metal-boxed garbage containers had been wheeled to one side. Their heavy metal lids were level with Lawrence's chest and the old codger's shoulder blades.

Jonny put his pack down and pushed at one of them. "Ye'll have t'help, m'lad," he gasped.

Lawrence pushed up on the rounded edge and the lid lifted.

"Now the other side," the old codger said. While Lawrence did this, he dragged an old cement block to the edge of the bin.

He stood on the block and peered inside. "Ahhh," he said. He lifted his head. There was a neat blue door set in the grimy brick of the nearest building. Above it a small sign read, "Northern Delights Bakery. Delivery Only."

The old man winked at Lawrence. "That there's a bakery," he hissed. "These're their castoffs."

Lawrence looked into the bin. A bakery box containing perhaps a dozen cookies lay on its side. There was half a cake in another box. The red and green frosting had begun to separate and the colors leaked grotesquely onto the white cardboard.

"Come on! Dig it out!" the old codger hissed. He turned to look at the door. "We ain't got all day!"

Lawrence reached for the cookies.

"The cake too!"

The old man held the boxes against his chest and turned sideways on the cement block to peer inside the bin.

"There isn't anything else," Lawrence told him.

"Shhh!" Jonny said.

Lawrence looked into the bin again. A five gallon shortening can, empty. Several boxes which had once held cookies. The tattered edges of the paper lace used to line wedding cake platters and bakery shelves.

The bin had the tart stink of food coloring. He reached for the lid.

"Careful now!" the old man hissed at him. Lawrence lowered the lid carefully, trying not to let it clang.

The old codger took the cake and Lawrence carried the cookies. The suitcase handle pressed the sleeping bag strings into the palm of his other hand. The arrangement felt almost comfortable.

The old man peered around the edge of the wall at the end of the alley, then darted into the sunlight.

"Oh what a haul!" he exulted. "Lawrence m'boy, we did good!"

Lawrence looked at the cake.

They had the cookies and cake for lunch. The old codger ate most of the frosting.

That afternoon they walked to the park the nun had found them in the night before. This was one of the best places in the city to sleep, the old codger explained. The police didn't bother them here and sometimes Sister Ann came and took them to her warehouse. There was also a certain amount of seclusion created by the way the bushes were planted.

But there wasn't a restroom nearby. Lawrence was glad he hadn't gone looking the night before. The method he had used was the most common. Anything else had to wait until the downtown department stores opened. Their restrooms weren't watched as closely as the ones in the cafes near the park. They weren't accessible unless you could afford a cup of coffee.

That was another thing he learned quickly. Money was only for the few essentials: Cigarettes, wine and maybe soap. Then came food. This was mainly the stale doughnuts, cookies and overripe bananas sold in a grocery store near Pioneer Square.

Food could be gotten other ways. There were soup kitchens scattered throughout the city, as the old codger had said. None of them were open every day of the week, but with judicial timing and some walking, you could get a meal almost every day.

This was only the evening meal and usually made up of soup and bread, with an occasional sandwich. But it helped fill your stomach.

Their wandering led them back downtown to the brick and concrete bulk of the Federal Office Building. They sat down on the steps and looked at the stone arch in the building's plaza. It looked lonesome, the old codger said. Lawrence said he thought it looked mysterious and strong. They argued good-naturedly about it until the old codger ran out of things to compare it with.

It began to grow dark. Lawrence stirred uneasily, but the old codger didn't move. Workers from nearby offices were beginning their daily trek home. The old man eased from his spot on the steps.

"Now you jest stay here," he said. "You watch me and see if'n you can't learn a thing or two."

He began at the bus stop at the edge of the curb. "Got change for a cigarette?" he asked a man in a suit. The man turned his head and looked right through him. The old codger shrugged and moved on.

He asked a woman in blue jeans this time. She looked him up and down, then dug a few coins from her jacket pocket.

He grinned at her. "Thanks miss," he said. He drifted away, waited until she'd caught the next bus, and started again.

After a while, the crowd began to thin out and he came back to Lawrence.

He sat down. "Not bad, not bad atall," he said as he counted the money. He poured the coins into an inner pocket of his rags and fingered one of the two cigarettes he'd received. "This is a Camel," he said. "I saw the pack."

They sat for a while longer, watching the lamps overhead cast shadows on the cars passing by.

At last the old man stubbed his cigarette out. "Ah, what a life," he said. He stood up. "Time to find us some food and a bed, m'lad. There's no missions gonna be open tonight, that I know. Woulda been crowded anyways and you ain't learned to pertect your stuff yet." He looked up at the sky and fingered his money again. "I s'pose we'd best try to buy us a bed," he muttered. "It's gonna be cold tonight. Clear and cold. That's always the worst time to be out."

By now Lawrence was too tired and hungry to do anything but numbly follow him through the streets. After several tries, the old codger negotiated a room in a hotel on Third Avenue whose only access was a narrow and very dirty stairway.

The old iron cots were dirty too. The linen was yellow and worn almost transparent in places. Lawrence didn't remember the sheets in his suitcase. Lack of food had made his head fuzzy.

He lay down on the bed in his clothes and looked at the rotting linoleum beneath the sink without seeing it. There were no rugs.

~~~

It hadn't been the ill-founded rumor she'd hoped against hope that it was. Deborah picked up her pencil that Tuesday afternoon and stared at the doorway opposite her desk. The meeting last week really had been to tell them they were losing their jobs. Had it only been a little over a week? It seemed so much longer. Though she was still feeling stunned.

Today really was their last day. Her paycheck, with its extra hundred dollars, lay in her purse. It seemed very small.

She reshuffled the forms Peter had handed her so silently. He was still hunched over the open drawers of his desk, sorting their contents. She went back to work, grateful for something to fill the time with. She was typing the last page when Al came in.

"Well, gentlepersons, have you made your final salutations to the old work place?" he asked.

"Don't you have anything to do?" Peter's accent was more clipped than ever. "Clean out your bloody desk or something?"

Al winked at Deb. "This gentleman is certainly in an outrageous humor. You'd think he'd just gotten laid off."

Deb turned her lips up in imitation of a smile. Her fingers tapped the next word out carefully.

Al was talking to Peter again, though Peter's back was still hunched over the desk drawers.

"I thought you were all for layoffs and cutbacks and all such amenities. Cut out the fat. I distinctly remember you saying it." He bounced forward onto the balls of his feet.

Peter grunted and the top drawer of the desk closed with a hollow bang. He bent to look for his shoes.

"We're not the bloody fat," he said from under the desk.

Al grinned at him. "Oh really?"

Peter sat down again. He pulled on a shoe and yanked at the laces. "Bloody fools."
~~~

Al looked at Deb. "Now what did I do to deserve that?"

"Oh damn!" The lace broke. Peter threw the portion in his hand at the wall. It hit and fell onto the desk. He swiveled around. "You know very well I didn't mean you."

He reached for his shoes again, realized the lace was gone, and glanced at Deb. "'Scuse the language," he muttered.

She smiled thinly. "I'm not arguing."

"But I thought you appreciated all these wonderful reforms," Al said. "They here and Thatcher in Britain were going to make the world all bright and shiny again." He leaned back onto the heels of his shoes. "Why the sudden change of heart?"

Peter adjusted the lace so he'd be able to tie it. "I didn't know they were planning to do it at my expense."

Al bounced forward onto the balls of his feet. "Somebody has to take it, doesn't he? Look at those poor bums stretched out in the park every night. Do you suppose they relish their lifestyle?"

Peter straightened up. His chair swiveled back toward his desk. He picked up the other piece of shoelace. "I always figured they were there because they wanted to be." He ran the lace between his fingers. "I don't know anymore. We have one month's salary saved. By the time it runs out I have to have another bloody job. And Sandra's due any day now."

"You'll still have the insurance," Deb said. "They said at the meeting it'll cover preexisting conditions. That's pregnancy too, isn't it?"

"Yeah, at a hundred deductible and them paying eighty percent." He scrunched the lace into a ball. "The question is, where do I get the twenty we have to pay? The unemployment figures are the same every damn week." He tossed the lace onto the desk. "If we had the money, I'd go back to England just to be near my folks. God knows Sandra's can't help us. He was working for a sawmill three years ago and doesn't even have unemployment anymore."

He turned around suddenly, the chair creaking. "Sorry folks. Just getting a bit morbid, that's all. British humor, you know."

He stood up and slapped Al on the shoulder. "When are you leaving, old chap? Shall we stop for a beer and celebrate our deliverance from Ms. Susan?" They went out.

Deborah picked up her pencil again. She chewed on the metal band circling the eraser and looked down at the typed form. At least he had a month's salary. She had only enough for a little over two weeks.

There was Christmas to get through, only a week or so away, and her parents' visit. She pushed the form to one side, reached into the bottom desk drawer, and pulled a piece of paper from her purse. She brought the telephone from Peter's desk to hers and smoothed out the paper. It had the numbers for three temporary agencies on it.

She hoped to God they needed people, because between now and the first of next month was a very short time.

She had two appointments set up when she got off the phone, but she was careful not to mention them when Peter and Al came back. They both seemed a little more cheerful though. Slightly giddy, in fact.

Not that there was much to celebrate. Susan was a pain sometimes, but then, Deborah had a feeling that supervising Peter and Al wouldn't be easy. They both said they believed in equality, but the fact that Susan was female probably didn't help their attitudes.

But they had to have some reason to feel good about leaving, to make it easier to plunge into the market. It wasn't going to be much easier for Al than for Peter.

She took the last pile of forms to Susan's office and was grateful that she was on the phone. Deb caught her eye, nodded and hurried away.

She was glad when Al and Peter left abruptly a few minutes before five. "Keep in touch!" Peter called as they disappeared around the edge of the door. She was left empty-handed on the almost deserted floor. Closing desk drawers echoed from other sections.

She got ready to leave. The last time. At least she had those appointments.

It was raining when she reached the street. Even Elliott Bay was gray, water and mist forming a solid wall that hid the Olympics, though they were only a ferry ride across the Sound. A fog horn bellowed, mysterious and lonely, and she shivered. She put her head down and hurried across the wet intersection. At least she had those appointments.

She was especially glad of them the next morning. But once the forms were filled out and the talking was over, she had to go home and wait for a telephone call. She busied herself through the next two days, dusting and sweeping and always listening for the phone. If she didn't get something soon— She couldn't tell her parents. They'd want her to come home.

She waited until after office hours to go to the grocery store, though she dreaded the blocks near the park. But she couldn't risk missing a call.

On the third morning she woke at six thirty, thinking she'd heard the phone ring. A fire siren sounded several blocks away and she drifted into an irritable doze.

It came that afternoon. The second agency she'd gone to had an assignment, to begin the following day. It was only three days, but still a paycheck. She scribbled down the information, her fingers shaking so hard she could barely write.

Lawrence learned a lot in the next week or so. The old codger had a routine he followed more or less every day. In it there was much of the street's wisdom.

Where the night had been spent dictated where one would make the morning's ablutions, but wherever they were, these must be short. The old hotels didn't have a bath in each room and other people would pound on the door if you took too much time. And when you used a public restroom, you were even quicker, for fear of being caught and thrown out.

Then the search for a meal. This was usually a breakfast and lunch combination, but seldom resembled either of them. The bakery was the old man's first choice, though Lawrence's stomach still churned at rich pastry first thing in the day. The working mission was the one place in the city which gave out breakfast. It also asked that eaters make themselves available for daily work. That limited the old codger's freedom. He told Lawrence it was too far and not a safe area.

Instead they inspected more garbage cans. The old codger had several routes, peering into bins behind the few grocery stores and many restaurants downtown. Most contained only rotten vegetables.

There was a food bank as well, but it was no use. You had to have identification showing you lived in the area the bank served. Neither of them had an address to give.

There was no systematic program for feeding the poor in the city. It had never even been thought of officially, though Sister Ann muttered about it often enough to her superiors. The street people had to fend for themselves as best they could.

If you weren't fussy and were willing to walk, food was more or less taken care of. Keeping clean was the biggest problem. One could wash face and hands in any restroom with soap, but hair, body and clothes were impossible. Even tooth brushing had to be done on the sly. A man in a suit brushing his teeth in a department store restroom would be considered health conscious. A man in grimy jeans and two days growth of beard was going to be asked to leave. Especially if he carried a sleeping bag.

There were barber shops one could go to for a shave. Lawrence and the old man used them as often as they could afford to. And Sister Ann was an angel of mercy primarily because she'd harassed a church member plumber until he had installed showers—labor and parts free of charge—in the old warehouse.

But they didn't see Sister Ann very often. Sometimes she would disappear for several weeks. Or they would happen not to be in the park the night she made a roundup.

For Lawrence, going without washing was almost worse than the meager amount of food. The unwashed feeling of his body and clothes wasn't something he could get used to. It made him edgy and lonely, even in the old codger's group of friends.

But then, he knew none of them well. It was a constantly changing group and the old codger was prone to attacks of restlessness. He could sit on the same bench for days, begging from where he sat or telling Lawrence tall tales. Then one afternoon he would blink his small eyes rapidly, purse his mouth and look up and down the street. "We ain't got no fortune to make here, Lawrence m'lad," he would say. "How much money you got?"

Lawrence would count out any loose change he'd picked up. The old codger would look it over gravely, empty his own pockets and announce that there was enough for a bus ride at least.

In this way, guarding their transfers carefully, the old man harassing the drivers for directions, Lawrence saw the Ballard Locks and heard the roar of the lions from the zoo.

Several weeks after this adventure, the old codger got bored again. They headed toward Lake Washington this time.

It was an overcast and windy day and the water whipped gray on the lake while the trees, houses tucked into them snugly, looked stolid and menacing. Lawrence shivered.

"'Tis a bit cold at that," the old man acknowledged. He was wearing his usual layer of rags.

They had taken the bus to Montlake. The old codger decided that since they were so close to the University District, they might as well try their luck there.

They started to get on a bus but the driver said their transfers were too old.

The old codger spat after the bus's exhaust and hobbled off purposefully. Lawrence hurried to catch up with him.

"Where're we going?" he asked. His hair had begun to grow out and it hung in his eyes. He pushed it back.

"The U District, like I told you." They could see the water of the Montlake Cut ahead. A narrow bridge crossed it.

"Can pedestrians go on that?" Lawrence asked.

"We will," the old codger said.

The hike over the bridge and past a big hospital complex took twenty minutes. Lawrence looked at the wooded bank on the other side of the road as they walked. It had been so long since he'd seen trees that looked like they belonged where they were growing. He hadn't realized how tired he was of the skimpy attempts the downtown merchants had made to brighten the streets.

They were soon past the trees, though. There was only over-cultivated lawn now. Lawrence stared at the buildings beyond. "What are those?" he asked.

"That's the U," the old codger said. He looked at Lawrence. "We got one, ya know. Most cities do."

Lawrence nodded. It seemed so long ago that he'd been part of a campus. He brushed his hair back and looked down at himself. He didn't look much like a student now.

It was just as well. There was no money for school. And the time would have been taken from the book, he reminded himself. Not that he'd been spending much time on it. He followed the old man up the street.

The District was different from downtown. There were only a couple of buildings that were more than two stories tall. And they weren't all shaped the same way. Some looked more like old houses than storefronts. It gave the area a village-like look which was appealing after the gray uniformity of downtown.

The people were different too. Fewer standard business uniforms and a lot of cotton and sweaters and beards. Lawrence could almost have fit in as one of the crowd. But he knew that he wasn't. He kept close to the old codger.

The old man perched on top of the concrete block wall surrounding the post office. Lawrence looked over it. The ground had been excavated from the area in front of the building's basement. Steps had been built and doors and windows put in. The basement was now the ground floor. There was a wheelchair ramp at one side, parallel to the sidewalk above. A narrow ledge ran along it.

The old codger had his hand out and was doing well. Students were more free with their cash than business people, he explained during a short lull. They wouldn't keep giving if you came every day, though. That's why he didn't show himself here too often. Lawrence nodded and eyed the ledge by the ramp.

He waited until the old man was approaching another student, then gestured to him that he was going below. The old codger nodded impatiently and went on talking to the young man with a bushy red beard and very thick glasses.

Lawrence took his suitcase with him. He sat on the ledge, opened the case and carefully pulled his papers out.

He began at the beginning and read it over again. It was only two and a half pages. How long had it been since he'd added the last sentence? He opened his case again and took out his pen. He shook it carefully, looking at the words on the paper. It was a good idea. He could feel that it was.

He looked up at the wall. The old codger was leaning forward. "Hey, could you lend me a quarter? Say, could you spare a smoke?"

Well, that's what he was good at, Lawrence supposed. It was certainly what he liked doing. Lawrence pulled a smooth surfaced book from his suitcase and bit the end of his pen. The writing was his thing to do. He looked up again. The old man was still begging. He looked like he'd be there a while.

10

It was a mild winter for the Pacific Northwest, though the rain fell steadily cold. The street people who gathered around the park benches near the County Courthouse comforted themselves with stories about colder years, when the drunks sleeping too near the waterfront had frozen to death.

"Alcohol may not be good antifreeze but it sure beats water for keeping ya warm while yer awake." The old codger yanked at the rags that he used for trousers.

"Me, I'll take cigarettes," said the fat woman at the end of the bench. She shifted a heavily bandaged leg under her thin skirt. "'Course, with my extra padding, don't need me no blankets!"

"I'll take food over either," the dark eyed boy behind her said. He pushed his matted hair away from his face. "Or the money for it."

"Won't do you no good to go asking for money for food or for booze," the old man told him.

"Yeah, the old codger should know," said a man wearing orange suspenders.

Somebody snickered. "He's been at it longer'n any of us, that's for sure."

"It's the only danged life," the old man said. "Naw, Lawrence m'boy, you know what you gotta ask for is cigarettes."

"I don't smoke."

"Ya ask for the money for 'em," he said. "Or for bus fare, if there's a stop anywheres close." He turned and looked down the street. "There's one right there."

"I'd rather stay here."

"Well then ya asks for cigs or the money. If they give you a light, than ya gives it to Cheryl. She might even give you somethin' for it."

The man in suspenders snickered and Cheryl tried to turn. "Don't get smart with your mouth, kid, or I'll blast ya!" she said. "I'm not that kind of girl and the old codger knows it." She settled into her place again and winked at Lawrence. "But I do have a few pennies set aside just for cigs, if they're reasonable priced."

The old man looked down the street again. "Must be about quittin' time," he said. "There's a passel of folks coming this way. See that man in the suit? He's lightin' up. You could ask him."

Lawrence shook his head.

"There's another one. And that one there too. See that fur collar? She's rollin' in dough." He looked at Lawrence. "Ah, you're chicken, that's what!" He spit on the sidewalk in front of the bench.

He looked up the street again. "Wanta start small now, there's that young lady there. The one in the hat, she looks kinda sweet. And she's goin' slow, like she ain't sure where she is. I bet she could be talked outa some cash."

"He's too chicken," said someone at the back of the group.

The fat woman smiled at Lawrence. "He's shy, that's what he is." She patted his arm and he felt his jaws clench. It wasn't just Cheryl's pawing. Anyone touching him grated his nerves. Just the brush of someone else's clothing against his felt like fingernails scraping on chalkboard. He shifted away from her. This need for control made him even more sensitive, in the end. He had to pull back on every reaction, measure his feelings for the reasonable thing.

He looked down the street. The old Indian at the back of the group muttered "chicken" again. Lawrence glared at him, then looked down the street again.

"Come on boy," the old codger said. "They can't hurt ya. All they can do is say no."

"There's one there. That old lady," the fat woman said.

He watched her pass.

"You're lettin' all the good ones go by," said the old man. "Won't be anyone left on the streets 'for you make up your mind."

Lawrence wet his lips. "Just ask for money for cigarettes."

"Yeah, that's the way."

"And say please," Cheryl said. "Polite always gets more than rude."

He stepped out onto the sidewalk.

The girl saw him coming and veered to her right. Her eyes flickered over him, carefully indifferent but watching to make sure she was out of his reach. There was a whole crowd of them around the bench at the edge of the park and she didn't want to get caught between him and them. Her hand went to her purse and she moved toward the curb without looking at him.

"Excuse me miss?"

The voice was oddly familiar. She looked up without thinking. What a mess his hair was, matted and dirty like that. She caught herself and looked away, suddenly alert to the light at the corner ahead. She quickened her steps to reach the crosswalk before it turned red.

"Could you spare a cigarette?"

"I don't smoke." Both "don't walk" signs were blinking. She tucked her purse more firmly under her arm as she waited.

"Some change so I could buy a pack?"

The light at the other angle turned green. She looked at him again, this time with irritation, and stepped onto the street without checking for turning cars.

She hurried, half running, across the street and down the next block. She slowed down a little only after she'd turned the corner. These street people were getting worse. Deb's hand tightened on her purse again. She forced herself to walk slowly. The drunk lounging under her window looked positively friendly compared to the man who'd just approached her.

Odd how familiar he'd looked. She must have seen him this morning when she'd passed the park on her way to the new temporary assignment. They wanted her tomorrow too. She'd have to take a different route to get there and back.

Lawrence turned back to the group around the bench. He sat on the ground beside Cheryl's fat knees.

"Now don't give up," the old codger yelped. "Ya gotta keep tryin'. You younguns have no perseverance. No push. Here, let me show ya." He scrambled onto the sidewalk and, by persistence and luck, got a cigarette for Cheryl and a handful of change for himself in the next fifteen minutes. The rest of them watched.

The sidewalks began to empty. The old codger poked at Lawrence's shoulder. "No use tryin' no more," he said. "Let's go see if we can dig up some eats at the Mission. Mother Ann's not been around for a while. Maybe she'll show up tonight."

Lawrence nodded. He ran a hand over his face. "I hope so," he said. "I could do with a shower."

"And wash off all that warm dirt?" The old codger chuckled as he picked up his pack.

Lawrence smiled sourly and reached for his bedroll. He picked up his battered suitcase and followed the old man up the block. Some Christmas he was going to have. Out in the street and only two pages added to his manuscript since he'd gotten there. He hadn't even learned to beg properly.

11

Deb's first temporary secretarial assignment hadn't been bad, as far as work went. But the money could have been better.

At the end of the last day of the assignment, she multiplied the numbers, then figured it out again. After taxes, approximately eighty dollars. Not even half her rent. She stared at the paper, unwilling images of the people in the park floating in front of her eyes. If she didn't find a job soon—

There was always her parents. They were coming tomorrow. She looked at her carefully decorated room. Each piece had been chosen and arranged so particularly. She couldn't go back now to the room in the attic with its bumpy bed, battered dresser and ugly wallpaper that her father wouldn't change because it was "still in good shape."

But it wasn't the bedroom so much as the feelings. Tightness and hurt and Bobby's eyes mocking. Her mother with her "I wish it was different but I knew it would be this way" look.

"Oh God, I can't," Deb said aloud. "Oh God, don't make me. I'll do anything, but don't make me go back." She stopped. It was childish, bargaining this way. She clenched her fists. Tomorrow was Christmas Eve. They'd be arriving sometime in the afternoon.

Her hand tightened even more and then relaxed completely as she decided. She wasn't going to tell them. She'd been afraid she wouldn't be able to keep it in, but now she knew that she could. She would have to.

She could feel her muscles against the back of the chair, tense and strong with sudden vigor. She wasn't through fighting yet.

She left the apartment early the next morning to return the application she'd filled out for the law firm next to her assignment. The clerk who left her holiday party to take the form raised her eyebrows, but Deb didn't care.

When she got back, Deb did a bit of last minute dusting, gathered the ingredients for her dinner soufflé into one place and looked at the clock. She changed out of her gray suit into something less obviously job-hunting and looked at the clock again.

She looked through her magazines for something to read, paced the floor for a few minutes, then put the Cosmopolitan and its suggestive cover at the bottom of the stack. She looked at the clock. She changed the towels in the bathroom and scrubbed out the sink. The door-bell buzzed as she was drying her hands. She raced for the button.

Her mother looked like she was trying not to look anxious as she came through the door. Her father's face was a blank. His eyes darted around the room once and then came back to Deb.

"I was half expecting a young man to be sitting on the couch," her mother said. "Your letters have been so short lately, I thought you might have met someone at one of your art thingies."

"At the gallery openings, you mean? Well, I have met a few people, but nobody special." She hoped she didn't sound nervous. Of course the letters had been short. There'd been nothing to say but "I've lost my job."

"I've been busy getting ready for Christmas and everything," she said.

Her father went to the window. He looked at the bench her plants rested on, then turned to the couch. He sat down. "This is sure low," he said. He poked at the material.

"It's my bed," she told him. "It folds out and I put on sheets and my quilt. It's really comfortable. You get to sleep on it tonight, as a matter of fact."

He looked down at it. Silence fell.

"Where's Bobby?" she asked.

"He's looking for a place to park," her mother said. "There are 'No Parking' signs all over the place. We went around the block three times and finally he let us off and said he'd find something. He's bringing the presents with him."

Deborah nodded toward the pile of gifts on the dresser. "We can put them with those," she said. She looked around. "I couldn't figure out what to do with a tree in here. The space is just a little too small. So I didn't bother. It would have been hard to get it home without a car anyway."

Her mother looked startled at the word "home" and Deborah sat back in her chair. Then she got up. "But you must be freezing! The weather's supposed to drop again tonight, too."

She went into the kitchen and her mother followed her.

"There are rumors floating around that it'll snow but I don't think anyone believes them." Deb filled the teakettle and put it on the stove. "So far, what I've heard is that it never snows for Christmas in Seattle. If we get it before, it'll melt on Christmas Day. Usually what happens is that it rains and then it snows on New Year's Eve, in time to make the roads icy."

The buzzer sounded again. "Oh, that's Bobby, I bet!" She went to the speaker, waited for his response to her "Yes?," then pressed the button that released the door catch.

"See Dad! I'm perfectly safe!" she said. "As a matter of fact, I turned down an apartment because it didn't have security locks." She opened the door at Bobby's knock. He stumbled in, arms awkward with packages.

"Just put them there." The kettle started to whistle and she darted into the kitchen. "I've got coffee and tea and hot chocolate. What do you want?"

The others sat down with their cups and Deb poked at the presents as she piled them onto the top of the dresser. "Hmmm, this looks interesting." She shook a knobby package. She grinned at her father and began arranging them in a more artistic pile. "I'm still poking at everything I see, aren't I Dad?"

The dinner soufflé was as much a success as it could be with people who were more used to hamburger and noodles than "anything fancy." Her mother protested that she'd taken too much trouble and Deb said it was super easy. She brought out the mincemeat pie and then hurried them to get ready for Seattle's traditional Christmas Eve service at St. Mark's Cathedral.

This too was an awkward success. The next morning fell into the same category. Her mother protested again that she'd gone to too much trouble, with bacon and English muffins for breakfast, orange marmalade on top. Her father thought the eggs in their small cups were a "nuisance," but when they got to their presents Bobby seemed suitably cowed by the wool sweater she'd finally decided upon.

All in all, it had been a successful visit, she decided as she closed the door at three o'clock Christmas day. They'd only arranged to have the animals taken care of for one night, so they had to catch the ferry before milking time.

Deb moved slowly through the apartment, massaging her temples. Her head was suddenly throbbing. It had been hard work to be so upbeat when the weekend and Monday were facing her.

She began piling dishes into the sink and went to the closet for a towel. She'd have to do laundry this weekend. They'd gone through all of her linen, with her parents on the bed and she and Bobby in sleeping bags on the floor. She reached for her purse. She'd probably have to go to the store for quarters for the machines.

She counted out her change, then reached into the bill section to see how much money was left. At the back, her fingers touched paper which was larger than the bills. She pulled it out.

A check. For one hundred dollars. Signed by her father, made out to her, and "with love" scribbled in the corner in her mother's handwriting. She closed her eyes against the sudden tears.

Though there was little sense of community among the street people, there was a vital grapevine. One person in one loose group knew another in another group, and so on. Survival could depend on the information they got this way and they all knew it. There was little reluctance to share information, though parting with food or clothing was almost incomprehensible.

When it came to the business of Christmas, the grapevine was buzzing. The city's poor might be invisible the rest of the year, but the weather was too cold and the season too bright for most people to have a free conscience without at least some effort to aid the poor.

Several large suppers were being given and one of them would be superintended by Sister Ann. Because she took care of them throughout the year, her "regulars" were torn between her comforting warmth and the certainty of better food at one of the other "shindigs" as the old codger called them.

He talked about it a lot to Lawrence. He didn't get much of a response outside of an occasional "umph" and a pushing back of matted black hair. Lawrence knew he was being rude but he couldn't bring himself to care.

"They say the people at the Pesbeterian Church are gonna have turkey," the old man would begin. "Stuffin' too. The kind they make inside the bird."

"Real food would be nice," Lawrence would say and then fall silent while the old man began at great length to compare past dinners he had attended.

Lawrence didn't believe the old codger's stories. So many weren't true. Like the ones about living off the fat of the land after the war. If it'd been anything like now, it couldn't have been fun.

They certainly weren't eating well with only the soup kitchens and cheap cookies purchased with whatever the old codger could beg. The bakery whose garbage they'd stolen had gone out of business.

After the one time, Lawrence wouldn't try to beg for money or cigarettes again, although Cheryl almost always had money to buy them. She had a sister whose address she used to collect her Social Security payments and proof of residence at the food banks.

He satisfied himself with watching the street corners and areas near bus stops. It often happened that just as someone had given up on the bus coming soon and decided to smoke while they waited, the bus would roll up. They couldn't smoke on board, so they'd toss the cigarettes on the sidewalk to die out in the damp.

If you were quick enough, you could grab what they'd dropped before another pedestrian squashed it. Cheryl only paid him a nickel, but it was something. Often, she paid him in pennies, so his pocket felt pleasantly heavy. He didn't let himself think about how little it actually held.

There were still a few bills in his wallet but not even the old codger knew about them. They were for paper and pens and not to be touched, no matter how cold or hungry he felt.

And he was hungry and cold. Bored and frustrated too. What with looking for cigarettes and checking the coin return slots of the pay phones and waiting while the old codger begged, there wasn't too much time for consecutive thinking, and no time at all to put the thoughts into ink.

It was too wet most of the time anyway. There was no protection from the December rain. It had an added, icy edge to it the day he waited for the old codger to finish gossiping with the elderly Indian man he had just met. The two of them sat on a bench in a small park overlooking the freeway. Lawrence had refused the old codger's invitation to join them. He stood at the edge of the park and watched the cars on the freeway below.

Finally, the old codger broke away, patting the old man on the shoulder.

Lawrence trailed behind him as he started down the hill, onto the freeway overpass.

"Good man, the chief," the old codger said, shaking his head. "Lives with his daughter and it's a good thing. He'd never make it outside at night. Don't see why he comes out durin' the day even. But she's got two little uns and does embroidery with beads, the way the old injuns did and the place gets kinda crowded. I ast him to come with us tomorrow but he don't know if he will."

"Tomorrow?"

"Tomorrow's Christmas, m'lad! Don't you remember? I been telling and telling you! There's a big turkey feed at the Pesbeterian Church. The one that's right next to Freeway Park. I got it all figured. We can go there for supper and then to Mother Ann for a bed."

"I thought she was giving a dinner."

"Ah, we don't want none of her food. Not if'n we can get better. The Church people now, they know how to put on a shindig. Had cranberries last year. 'Course, if we're not too full we can always have seconds at Ma's."

Lawrence pushed his hair away from his face. Sister Ann was doing all she could to make life at least bearable. It seemed mean to go someplace else, using her only as a filler.

But he was too tired to argue. After they'd searched for two hours for a grate, then huddled over it until morning, keeping warm with what little extra steam the city's buildings weren't using, he would follow numbly wherever the old man might lead. If he could by some miracle provide a warm meal and a real bed under a dry roof, so much the better.

It hurt Lawrence's head just to think and his suitcase was heavy with books. What good were they doing him?

The warmth of the big room in the church basement the next day and the sight of the food-heavy tables revived him a little. But there were people all over the place and that made him tense. Teenagers in jeans and sweaters dashed back and forth. Older women carried trays of food from the small kitchen near one end of the long room.

A man in a suit said a long prayer before they were allowed to find a seat and begin passing the food. As the first edge of his hunger went, Lawrence slowed down. He looked around. He had spent Thanksgiving in Sister Ann's care and this was the first time he had seen this many street people together.

Did they all search for warm grates at night, when they hadn't the inner heat or the covers to sleep on park benches? The man across the table from him was slipping pieces of food off his plate and hiding them in his coat pockets. They all knew better than to eat too much at one time. Stomachs used to being fed soup and day-old bread couldn't handle a lot of turkey and cranberry sauce.

They left the table reluctantly and were herded into a ring of chairs set up at one end of the room. Now it was present time. The gifts had been donated and wrapped by church members. There was a package for everyone. A middle-aged woman slowly began to hand them around Lawrence's side of the circle. She had a gracious smile for everyone.

It was a sickening smile, Lawrence thought as she made her way toward him. She was approaching a frail woman in her early fifties who, Lawrence knew through the grapevine, had been released from the mental hospital a few months before because she was "capable of self-sufficiency."

The street had done its work and her body was already that of an old woman's. A stroke had left her almost speechless and the clothes on her back were all that she owned. She had sold the rest for a few dollars because they were too heavy for her to carry and she could last a day or two on the food she bought with the money. None of the hardier street people expected her to live through the winter.

The lady with the presents was turning her smile on the hunched over woman. "Really my dear, you'll catch your death, wearing those clothes in this weather," she said reproachfully. "You should bundle up more."

Samantha looked up at her and her face twisted as if to smile. A glob of spittle clung to her lower lip and the woman reached into her pocket, then dabbed at the spot with a lacy handkerchief.

"Now here is your present," she said. "Do be sure to wear it along with your other winter clothes. It'll help you stay warm."

Why was she so sure Samantha had other warm clothes, Lawrence asked himself. Did she think these people with blankets for coats and boots with flapping soles liked it that way? That they wore bits of dirty yarn for hats because it made them feel good? He felt his hands become fists as she came toward him.

"And here's something for you," she said to the old codger. He nodded and thanked her, ducking his head, and Lawrence saw, as she looked down, the disgust in her eyes. She was still smiling. She went to the pile of gifts to get another arm load. Lawrence ran his hand over his face. Maybe he was just overreacting. God knew, his nerves were a mess.

As she came back, his hands began to tremble. He had a sudden picture of himself throwing the present she offered him into her face. She held out his gift. He looked at her. Her smile was carefully in place but her facial muscles were tight with the effort.

He rose suddenly. His chair scraped loudly on the tile floor. She motioned at him with the gift. He pushed it away.

"No," he said. He backed away from her and his chair fell. He turned and almost ran to the other end of the room.

The old codger turned, his face full of reproach. He didn't get up.

"Now Lawrence, don't be a fool," he called. "Come back and take a look at yer present."

"No," Lawrence said. He must have gotten some of his feelings into his voice. The old codger's face changed and he turned to the woman.

"I'll take it for him if ye like," he said ingratiatingly. "We're friends, y'see. It bein' Christmas, he ain't his most natural self."

She nodded, one eye on Lawrence. He watched her from the other end of the hall. She handed the old codger the gift. She turned to give the next present to the man who'd been sitting on Lawrence's other side.

Her smile was more subdued as she continued around the circle and she kept glancing toward Lawrence. He edged toward the plate glass door leading onto the street. His hands clutched at the curtains to keep them from trembling. He stared out at the overcast sky without seeing it.

~~~

The telephone rang while Deborah was in the shower that Monday morning. She was still dripping onto the rug as she scribbled the information down. Another temporary assignment.

This one was at a development company, whatever that was. They wanted her this morning. That was what was important.

She grabbed the nearest dress, ate a piece of toast while she combed her hair, and dashed on her makeup. As she hurried down the stairs, she went over in her mind what she'd been told about the assignment. She'd be answering phones and acting as receptionist. It was only today but could continue through the rest of the week. A lot of rushing around and getting ready in a hurry to sit and look at the phone all day for four twenty-five an hour. It wasn't much, but if she could work every day at that pay, she could manage.
~~~

It was the "if" that was so difficult about temporary work. There was her parents' check though. She wondered how long it would have to last.

She hurried into the building, waited impatiently for the elevator and clenched her fingers around her purse strap as she looked for the room number.

The other bad thing about temporary jobs was the first day of work jitters you had to go through every time. Psyching yourself up to understand all you were told, trying not to look dumb and hoping they liked you enough to ask for you the next time they called the agency.

They sat her at a desk in the lobby area, showed her the telephone system, and gave her a list of things to do when people called with questions. The woman who normally acted as receptionist was home with a sick child. They didn't know if she'd be in tomorrow or not.

After an hour of no phone calls, Deb began to wonder if the woman she was replacing wasn't really out looking for another job. She grinned. Working with Peter and Al had made her cynical. They were always extremely understanding when the other called saying he'd be out for the day.

She'd been sitting at the desk for an hour and a half before she got her first call. It was a wrong number. This seemed to spark a flurry of activity. She got four more calls within a few minutes of one another.

Then the phone went dead again. She re-sharpened all the pencils in the electric sharpener on the desk, rearranged them in their holder, and straightened the pads of message paper. She carefully rewrote the one message she'd taken and stood it neatly in the note holder at the corner of the desk. She folded her hands and looked at the clock.

She was grateful when twelve o'clock came and the woman who'd shown her the desk at nine reappeared. She would take over until one o'clock. She looked at the three messages on the desk. "If you want to pick up a magazine or paper to read this afternoon, go ahead," she said. "It's pretty slow around here today. Really odd for a Monday."

Deborah moved as quickly as she could through the slushy sidewalks and breathed in deeply, trying to get some energy into her system. If this was what being a receptionist was like, she'd been crazy to take that application to the law firm. That's what they were looking for.

But it was better than nothing, even though it was only a job. If she'd wanted only a job she could have stayed on the farm.

She shuddered. There was more to her moving here than the art. The urge to get away had piled on her so quickly with the Andrew situation. Even now she didn't like to think about it. Then there was Bobby. And Mom's knowing looks. And her father's long silences. If she was going to be an old maid, at least she could do it without them making comments or looking so upset about it.

Not that she was going to be an old maid. She remembered the man at the gallery and smiled.

And not that it mattered. She could be herself. That was enough. She didn't need a man to be happy.

But she did need her art. Something to make her feel somewhat intelligent. She stopped to buy a newspaper as a cheap alternative to a magazine. Above the name of the paper was a box containing headlines of articles inside. "Hard Times for the Art Industry" one of these said. "See Section E."

She knew without looking what it would say. At least being a receptionist paid the rent and bought groceries, she told herself. She tried to picture filling a succession of days with what she had done this morning. She felt tired. Before, she had at least been doing something that was part of something she was interested in. Something to care about.

Of course, not all receptionist jobs were so boring. Maybe if she could get one that was busy, with things going on all the time, the days would go faster. Besides, the position she'd applied for paid more than she'd been making before. That would help.

12

There had been mattresses laid out in the hall where they'd been fed dinner. Once the shakiness of Lawrence's anger subsided he had no energy left. He'd followed the old man's instructions like a sick and lonely child and they hadn't gone to Sister Ann's after all.

But New Year's was another story. Whether the old codger was afraid of another outburst or if he thought Lawrence would simply desert him for Sister Ann and the warehouse, Lawrence didn't know. He didn't care. He was as sick of the old man as he was of everything else.

He knew he couldn't have survived without the old codger's street-wariness, including his gift for wheedling money and cigarettes. But the excitement and adventure had worn off. Lawrence's only feeling now was cold weariness overlying a fierce anger. The dirt and the cold and the hunger had numbed his mind and grated his nerves until he hardly knew what he was doing.

One thing he did know. He wasn't going back to that church for New Year's Eve dinner. He was going to Sister Ann and the warehouse, even if she wasn't there.

It had been several weeks since they'd seen her. He had a deep urge to look at her square face and hear her rough voice. As if she were the last link with serenity.

So they trudged down the hill to the waterfront late New Year's Eve day. Neither had ever walked to the warehouse before. They went slowly, slipping on the icy pavement beside the railroad tracks along Elliott Way, peering up at the building signs.

They finally saw it. They knocked on the door but nobody came.

"I'm not leaving," Lawrence said before the old man could start talking.

They waited five minutes, then ten. The old codger began to pace up and down in front of the old building. Lawrence wondered if they'd have to spend the night lying against the closed door. It would be cold this close to the water. It was down here that people froze to death in their sleep.

And the air had suddenly become sharper. There was almost a spiciness to it. He wondered if it would snow.

Thirty minutes. The old codger stopped pacing. He stood in front of Lawrence and peered into his face. "Listen m'lad, if we step to it lively it might be we'd get to the church in time for leftovers."

"You go," Lawrence said.

The old man waved a hand at the building. "She's not coming," he said. "If she was, the lights'd be on, wouldn't they?"

"The lights wouldn't go on until she got here." Now that he had made a decision, he wasn't changing it. His head felt less tired than it had in weeks. He watched the stream of headlights pushing steadily along Elliott Way. "She could come any minute," he said.

The old man edged closer and peered into his face. Lawrence could smell the stale wine on his breath. His fingers curled toward his palm. He looked at the headlights.

"I think you've gone crazy, that's what," the old man muttered. He started pacing again.

They'd been waiting forty-five minutes. Suddenly a pair of headlights swung away from the street, blinding them. The lights jerked awkwardly as they crossed the railroad tracks. It was Sister Ann's van.

"Well, whatya know," the old codger said. He came to stand beside Lawrence. "Ye knew all along, didn't ya?"

Lawrence picked up his suitcase and bedroll. He waited beside the door. The passengers in the van spilled out of it. Sister Ann came toward the door, swinging her keys.

"Well now, if it ain't the old codger! And Lawrence too! Wondered where the hell you were. I didn't see you at Christmas. Still putting up with his bull, are you Lawrence?"

She unlocked the door and switched on the lights. "Soup'll be on in ten minutes!" she called to the group behind her.

"Can I help?" Lawrence asked, at her elbow. She turned. "Put your things in the sleeping area and come along then," she said.

She waved the others into the large space between the partitions and ordered them into the shower rooms to wash.

"Celebrate New Year's with a clean face!" Her long sleeves flapped against her gown as she said it. Lawrence followed her into the room between the two restrooms.

It had once been an office. Now two portable stoves stood on top of a battered steel desk. There were five-gallon aluminum buckets on three of the four burners. A huge blue-speckled coffee pot sat on the other. She turned the knobs on the stoves and stirred each pot, looking at the steam intently. Finally she seemed satisfied. She turned one of the knobs off and gave the soup on that burner a final, vigorous stir.

She waved a hand at the filing cabinet in one corner and began searching in the boxes stacked under the desk. "Dishes are in there," she said. "You can carry those out. Silver's in the desk here and so're the napkins." She straightened and grinned at him. "We've got real napkins tonight. The man that owns this place had some left from his office party and asked if I could use 'em."

He slowly began to take the bowls from the drawer. She stirred another pot of soup and looked at him. Her square face settled into less busy lines. "All right son, what is it?" She waved at a small stool beside the filing cabinet. "Sit down. I'm not a damn priest though, remember. If it's something to do with the law, they can get it in court."

"Oh, it's nothing like that." Lawrence twisted on the stool. "It's just— I want to get out, is all."

"Out? You mean off the streets?"

He nodded.

"Well, that's not easy but it is fairly possible," she said. She looked at him. "You say you ain't been in any trouble?"

"I'm just sick of it. I'm not getting anything done."

"What do you want to do?"

He told her about the book. He knew he wasn't being very clear but he managed to say enough that she knew he had an idea of what he wanted from life. "Not like these others," he said at the end.

"Now, I wouldn't judge 'em too harshly." She looked at the door to the other room. "We all are where we are by the choices we make and the luck we run into. Sometimes it's not easy to tell them apart. It's not for us to judge any but ourselves." She grinned at him. "That's hard enough."

She opened a desk drawer and pulled out a handful of spoons. "I'll see what I can do, but for now let's carry this stuff out. Those buggers have been sitting in the cold long enough."

He stood waiting.

She lifted the bucket of soup from its burner and motioned at the coffee pot. "You help me with this and I'll see if I can't help you. That a deal?"

He picked up one of the small edge-worn towels she used as pot holders and lifted the pot carefully. He followed her into the other room.

Maybe it was just the new year starting that made her so restless, Deb decided the next evening. Or realizing that she was probably the only person in the city who wouldn't be doing anything on New Year's Eve. Parties all around her and she too broke and friendless to go anywhere. If she'd still been at the

County there would have been a gallery event or something. Maybe the blond man would have been there. But now, nothing.

She put the teakettle on to boil. Hot chocolate might make her feel better.

The things she'd told her mother were pure fabrications and her mother probably knew it. They'd obviously known she didn't have as much money as she pretended. Remembering that didn't help much.

Probably the real reason she felt so lousy was that the development company had decided they wouldn't need her after that one day. The woman who'd sat in for her at lunch time had said she'd bring her work out to the desk. There was no point in boring Deborah for another eight hours straight.

"It would have been eight hours of pay, though," Deb muttered. She went to look at her plants. There was a draft from the window and two of them were drooping. She moved the pots carefully, trying to get them out of the stream of air without making the rest of the bench look too crowded. She peered out the window. Gray drizzle. Too cold even for the old man at the lamp post. He was nowhere in sight.

She suddenly wondered what would happen if she got sick. There was no one nearby to know she wasn't well. The occasional calls from the temporary agency were all the outside contact she had.

It was too depressing to think about. She made her bed out and fixed her hot chocolate. She flipped through an art magazine while she sipped it.

At last she put the cup on the saucer and closed the book. She fell asleep thinking about the connections between El Greco's coloring and that of Miro.

The telephone didn't ring the next morning. She waited, hating herself for her anxiety. She hated the sight of her checkbook even more, when she rummaged through her purse for her hairbrush.

When it rang that afternoon she sprang for it.

"Hello?"

"Miss Brownell?"

"Yes? I mean, this is she."

"I'm calling from the firm of Yardley and Hines," a male voice said. "You were interested in a position with us."

"Yes."

They were anxious to get it filled right away and they saw she was available immediately. Could she come in for an interview?

She tried to sound calm. "Yes, I guess so. When would be best?"

"I know it's the day after New Year's Eve, but would it be possible for you to come in today?"

"What— What time?"

"It's one thirty now. Would three thirty be too much to ask?"

"Excuse me?"

"Could you make it at three thirty today? You are available immediately, aren't you?"

"I didn't have anything planned."

"Available to start working, if we should offer you the position."

"Oh! Oh. Yes." She laughed. "I wasn't expecting a call so quickly."

"We're in a hurry to fill it," he said. "Can I put you down for three thirty, then?"

"Yes. Yes, that would be fine."

She took a deep breath and arranged where she was to go and who to ask for at three thirty. When the phone clicked into the receiver she walked to the couch and sat down hard.

"Oh God, please," she said. She closed her eyes tightly, then opened them. She looked at the window and the gray day beyond it without seeing them. She took a deep breath. "I don't care if it's not art. I don't care if it's boring. Just let it be something."

She was ready, dressed and businesslike at two forty-five. It was a ten minute walk. She paced the length of her single room. If she got there too early, she'd look overeager and they'd wonder if there was something wrong with her.

She fidgeted her fingers and looked at the clock for the third time in five minutes. Maybe if she was early, she'd make a good impression. They did want someone right away and she hadn't sounded terribly eager on the phone.

But it wasn't good to seem too anxious. She looked at the clock again. On the other hand, she was making herself more nervous, waiting for the clock to move. She went into the bathroom and checked her lipstick. She closed the door and looked at herself in the mirror.

Gray suit, to look businesslike, but a pale green blouse instead of a white one. She was asking to be a receptionist, not a partner. Black pumps. She went to the closet, put on her coat, and went back in the bathroom. She stood another five minutes, debating about looking too fashionable if she wore her hat, then decided it was too cold out not to.

For all of her excitement about it, she never remembered afterward what had been said at the interview. The man she talked to had seemed to decide the minute he saw her.

It seemed a rather abrupt way to give her a position with higher pay and less work than she'd been doing before. Her only real responsibility would be answering phones and sorting mail. She'd start January 2. This firm didn't believe in wasting its time!

She was in the lobby at eight o'clock sharp that morning. Robin, the woman who'd been acting as interim receptionist, would train her. The person before her had left without warning two weeks before Christmas.

"But I'm a legal assistant, not a phone answerer," Robin said crossly. She yanked the chair back from the desk and glanced up. "Not that there's anything wrong with phone answerers."

Deb smiled. Robin showed her what buttons to push and gave her a list of people in the firm and some cursory mail-sorting instructions. They'd go over it at nine when the mail was delivered, she said.

The hardest part would be recognizing faces. Deb hadn't really believed Robin when she said it, but she realized it was true just after eight thirty. The elevators across the lobby suddenly began disgorging passengers with frightening regularity.

The firm had an "in and out" board. Each person was supposed to move their name tag to the correct space when they came in or left. That way she'd know who was there and who wasn't. They didn't always use it though. And sometimes they would ask her to do it for them, Robin said. She'd have to know their names, either way.

She could feel her head starting to buzz. There were several father and child combinations and three people with the same first name but different lasts. There was also a senior and junior.

As the flood became a trickle, she looked at the board by the phone. "This may take a while," she said.

Robin laughed. "It'll be all you have to do," she said. She pointed out her own name and extension number and said, rather unwillingly, to call if Deb needed help. She also made sure Deb knew the name and number of the secretary who was to relieve her on breaks and at lunch time.

Then she disappeared. Deborah knew she'd be back only when asked to. And then not happily.

But it was a job. She began looking through her new desk drawers. She eyed a youngish lawyer as he walked up. He pushed a tag on the in and out board and went to the elevator.

There were plenty of nice looking men around. Not that they'd pay attention to a receptionist. She reached for a pad of paper and began filling in message forms with the date and her initials. With this many people, the phone would ring fairly often. She hoped so anyway.

～

There was no point in his going to Welfare, Sister Ann said the next morning. They'd see that he was healthy and male and ask why he wasn't working. She scowled at the dish she was drying.

And he hadn't been in the military, so he couldn't go to the County for veteran's aid. Really the only place she could send him was the Salvation Army. Her lips twitched as if she'd thought of a good joke but couldn't say it.

She gave him directions, a piece of paper with her address on it in case he had problems, and best of all, a warm clasp of the hand that didn't grate on his nerves. His feet were full of energy as he headed for the Army headquarters on Fourth Avenue. There was a dirty slush of melted snow on the sidewalks which had been muddied still more by passing feet. He had to walk carefully to keep the hole in his right sole from letting in too much dampness. But that was habit. His emotions didn't notice.

He didn't feel so wonderful as he talked to the Salvation Army woman with her clumsy blue suit and brown hair in a bun at the back of her neck. She wasn't nasty or pitying, but there was simply no room.

"I'm sorry," she said again. "We don't have space for a single bed more and the rehab center is at more than peak capacity now."

He looked at her.

"The only thing I can do—" She pulled open a drawer of her desk. Its runners squealed. "I can send you to the city housing authority. They have temporary housing for people out of work that they'll let you stay in for a limited time." She searched through the drawer. "Didn't you say you also needed money for food?"

He nodded. She looked at the raincoat he was still wearing. "How are your clothes? Have enough to keep you warm and sufficiently dry?"

He looked at his feet. "I've got a hole in one of my shoes."

She nodded and pulled out some forms. She filled them in, asked for the correct spelling of his name, wrote some more, then handed the papers across the desk.

"This is for the Army store here in this building. It's good for one pair of shoes, any price. I hope we have something to fit you. This is a coupon to give the clerk when you get your shoes. She'll give you ten dollars for food. I know it's not much but I'm afraid it's all we can afford."

Her bun had slipped to one side of her neck. She pushed it back into place. "Everybody in the city seems to be hungry this winter. Or cold. Sometimes both."

She shook her head and her bun slipped again. "Anyway, that envelope contains a note to the housing people. There should be someone there this afternoon, if they've gotten over their New Year's hangovers yet. They'll tell you if there's anything available and where to go and who to talk to when you get there."

She stood up when he stood and shook his hand. The clerk in the store smiled at him too and wished him luck as he hooked the laces of the new shoes over his fingers. He picked up his suitcase and smiled back at her. Maybe he really would have some luck this time around.

It looked like it when he was at the housing authority. He was surprised by how quickly they came up with an address for him to go to. They also had a phone number to call if he couldn't locate it.

Even the twenty-block hike to the place, lugging suitcase and bedroll along slippery sidewalks, didn't wear his spirits. He was still cheerful, though his lungs ached with the cold, when he knocked on the door of the small, shingled house. The early winter dusk had already fallen, but there were no lights at the windows.

"Yes?" A short wrinkled man with bronzed skin and dark hair had opened the door. He spoke with a heavy accent.

"I'm looking— I'd like to speak to the manager."

"That me."

Lawrence held out the note and the man's eyes narrowed. There was a dim bulb burning in the hall. He stepped backwards and his lips began to move silently. Lawrence stood on the steps. A television set blared in the dark house. Children's voices rose, squabbling. A woman called from a room farther back and the noise fell.

The man refolded the note. He gave it back to Lawrence. "You lucky you get here when you did," he said. He turned. "You, Sung. Tell Mama I be back in minute."

He stepped over the sill, shut the door, and went past Lawrence down the steps. "It next door," he said over his shoulder.

There was a large old wooden house beside the small one. They went up its cracked walk and creaking steps. It needed a paint job, but there were lights behind the stained shades.

Immediately inside the door were the stairs. He followed the man up two flights and down a hall. They walked slowly and Lawrence glanced into a half-open door as they went past. A tousle-headed middle aged woman sat on an unmade bed. The old man stopped in front of a door at the end of the hall.

"This all we got," he said. He flung the door to the alcove back. "Not much but door locks."

Lawrence walked in. If this was a step up from the streets, it was a very small one. Where the dirty green wallpaper still hung, it was splotched with damp. Brownish growths spotted the middle of the worst areas. Two window panes had been broken. The glass had been replaced with pieces of cardboard. Several other panes were badly cracked. The floor was so heavily stained he couldn't tell if it was clean or not. An army cot stood in one corner. Its mattress was bare.

The only other furniture was a wobbly straw chair with a badly frayed seat and two nails driven into the wall. They were for his clothes.

He felt even worse by the time the old man had finished his short but memorized speech about "house rules" and left. There was a common toilet on each floor. The one on this floor was at the other end of the hall. There was a washer and dryer in the basement. They each cost fifty cents a load. He had only a few coins. It would have been so good to be really clean again.

And then there was the final thing. He wasn't allowed to stay more than four weeks. He was expected to have work and be ready to leave at the end of that time. The city needed the space he was sleeping in for other people.

"So the man said," he muttered. Being told polite lies and half-truths while he looked for work had soured him. Being around the old codger had finished it off.

The only thing the old man was romantic about was street life itself. The only way to make a living, he called it. But then, he said that because he regarded people who worked in offices all day, the ones striving and scheming and butt-kissing, as fools. Why bother, when you could sit and gas in the park with your friends and the others would feed you if you only asked the right way?

The asking was just as striving, scheming and butt-kissing, to Lawrence. And you never got enough to stay warm and fed. He wondered if the old man would carry on much because he'd disappeared the way he had.

He hadn't said goodbye. Just muttered a lame excuse about "talking to Sister" and said he'd meet him at the park later. Though the old codger must have realized something was up when Lawrence insisted that he not wait. He'd gone too docilely, with far less of the usual grumbling when things didn't go his way.

Not that it mattered. Lawrence unrolled his sleeping bag. He began pulling clothes out of the suitcase. Nothing mattered now but the writing. The obsession of it, which by any logic should have been cooled by his time in the street, had only risen stronger for being denied. Four weeks. Didn't they understand that what he was doing would take longer than a single month?

But he did have some time. And a little money. With the ten dollars and the cash in his wallet, he could buy food for a couple weeks. And he'd have a roof over his head. With that and without the old codger's badgering, he could finally get something done.

He began to pace the floor. The usual panic of writers with clean paper in front of them had never bothered him and it didn't now. He felt as if he was more in control of the words than he had ever been, though he was almost dizzy with hunger.

But the luxury of thought and knowing where he was sleeping that night made food unimportant. He walked some more, then sat cross-legged on the bed, his smoothest book propped on his knees. He wrote until long after midnight, deliberately ignoring thoughts of food or employment. He had four weeks. He'd do what he could.

13

Deb settled into her new job quickly. And just as quickly, realized the routine was going to be even more deadly than she had feared. It was one of those jobs which is given interest only by the occasional strange phone call. Even then, there was no one to share her amusement with.

A few of the youngest lawyers did say hello when they went by. Once in a while they'd stop to chat about the weather or make rude comments at their mail as a prelude to a semi-conversation of silly remarks. There was no real friendliness.

That was the thing that was hardest. She seemed to be an embarrassing fixture. Like a spittoon or a toilet or something. Even the secretaries acknowledged her only in the briefest possible way.

Deb had never been introduced to any of them. She seemed to be expected to know their names automatically though she only saw them at coffee breaks and the lunch hours she stayed in the building. The gossiping made her shy anyway.

The loneliness made the days longer than they really were. She kept reminding herself that she'd prayed for this job and was grateful for it. She really was very lucky to find something so quickly and at better pay.

Maybe it was just the grayness of a Northwest January. Or the fact that she wasn't doing what she really wanted to do. The problem was that she didn't really know what she wanted to do. She knew she couldn't have gone on filling out forms about art forever. She would have started to feel about that the way she did about routing telephone calls.

She took her frustrations out in buying new clothes—and in daydreaming. One of the younger lawyers, Randy McDonald, did occasionally talk to her. He actually seemed to be looking at her when he stopped for his messages.

It was hard not to think about him. She had to remind herself that he used those brown eyes on everyone else too. And his conversation was always about what to say when so-and-so called or where he would be and when he'd be back. It wasn't exactly flirtatious.

He seemed so nice though. She had noticed that some of his calls were to and from art organizations in the area. Her daydreams, more often than not, consisted of getting up the courage to ask about them. What would he say, with surprise and delight in his voice, when he discovered that she was interested in art, too?

He wasn't married. She knew that much from the lunch and coffee gossip. The secretaries and assistants were unanimous about him. Not very many people got labeled "a nice guy." And they'd give anybody who'd listen a rundown on almost everybody in the firm.

"Arnie is a lech," was another unanimous opinion. This was one reinforced by experience.

"Arnie" was short for Arthur Arnache, pronounced "shee." It was fitting that he had a boyish name, one of the secretaries had commented. He had pinched her quite openly at the Christmas party and a month later she was still angry.

Robin was the only assistant Deb had become a little friendly with and she was one of the most adamant about Arnie.

She hadn't said much about him to Deb until the day the secretary who normally relieved Deb for lunch was sick and Robin took her place. She found Arnie perched on the corner of Deb's desk.

"Hi Robin," he said. He waved the papers in his hand in Deb's direction. "About time they found us a decent receptionist, huh?" He winked at Deborah. "The last one we had was a dud."

The phone rang. Deb picked it up.

Robin busied herself at the racks of sorted out mail. Arnie suddenly put his papers down. "I almost forgot. I need pencils."

Deb was still on the phone. She already knew what number the woman needed but she had to listen to the woman's explanation before she could give it to her. She gestured at Arnie to wait.

He grinned at her, flapped his own hand playfully and came around to the back of the desk. He squeezed between Deb and Robin, facing the desk. He put his hands on Deb's shoulders as he moved past.

Robin had half-turned to give him room. He got the pencils from a drawer and she moved out of his way. Deb told the woman the number and pushed another button. She answered the next call. Arnie squeezed past again, though Robin had given him plenty of space. He put his hands on Deb's shoulders again.

He picked up his papers, waved goodbye as Deb transferred the call, and disappeared down the hall.

Robin moved to the end of the desk and looked back toward the office area. When she was sure he was gone, she turned to Deb.

"I would be careful with him, if I were you," she said.

The phone buzzed and Deb reached for it. "Why?" There was no one there. She put the receiver down. "I mean, I've heard a few things, but that could just be gossip." She stood up.

"Gossip or not, you don't want him hanging around." She spread her mail out on the desk. "Part of the reason Marilyn left—the girl here before you, I mean—was that there were rumors they were sleeping together."

Deb leaned against the side of the desk. Robin frowned at her. "He made her life miserable with his innuendos. The bosses, being stuffy on principle, were very displeased and that's putting it mildly. She got called in and asked to please keep her private life private, poor kid. I don't think he'd so much as asked her out. If he did he probably slept with her. Not because she meant anything to him but because he's a creep."

She lowered her voice. "So just be careful, okay? I'm not kidding when I say he's trouble. I know he's kind of hard to avoid. I suppose all you can do is be polite but not too friendly. Especially if there's a boss anywhere nearby."

She jerked a finger at the drawer where the pencils and pens were kept. "He's not supposed to be behind the desk anyway, except to get mail if you're too busy to get it for him. I guess you can't be too busy for him, no matter what."

"Well thanks for warning me," Deb said. She headed for the break room. She was more worried about Randy than Arnie. If the head people were so strict, she didn't have a chance. Not that she did anyway, she told herself firmly. Her daydreams were nothing but dreams, and she knew it.

—

Two weeks of writing went by in a blur. Lawrence came out of his room only to use the bathroom or to go to the small grocery store on the corner for bread, coffee and apples. He was so intent he didn't notice the spots on the walls or the puzzled look of the manager when they met.

"How it go?" the old man would ask. His hand jingled the keys in his pocket and he would squint at Lawrence's face.

"Pardon? Oh! Fine. Thanks."

"I don' see you. Got job, huh?"

"It's not easy."

"What you do?" He'd walk beside Lawrence down the hallway.

"Pardon? Oh, I'm writing. I'm working on a book about history."

"So you don't found work. If need help, tell me. We get call sometime, ask small thing. Sometime they want fulltime."

"Pardon? Oh, all right. I'll let you know." And Lawrence would hurry up the stairs or out to the grocery. He had work to do.

Slowly the pages filled. He read the sentences over and over, forcing himself not to notice the haziness in his head, gulping glasses of water down in one swallow to keep the hunger from growing too imperative.

The writing was good. It seemed clear to him, and concise. Almost obvious, yet he'd never seen the idea printed before. Surely here was something one could get hold of.

He found he liked the writing process itself. The power of pen over paper, of mind over pen. The fighting to find just the right words to express the thought in your mind. And the feeling of victory when he felt that he'd said it.

But then his money gave out completely. He was down to his last half-loaf of bread. He didn't even have money for paper and pens. He could try fasting. He remembered reading somewhere that it cleared the mind. It might give him more insight into his work.

He felt that he needed more. He'd said all that was in him, explained as thoroughly as possible, given clear and comprehensive examples. The book was basically done. But it was only fifty-three and a half pages, hand written. A long paper, a very very short book. What he had to say was important, in spite of its length, and he knew it with all of his heart.

He paced the room an entire day, trying to decide what to do, rubbing his hand over his face, talking to the four walls.

"It needs to be longer to get attention. I need to supplement it. And I have to think clearly in order to do that. I've eaten so little food lately, if I try to go without completely, my brain will stop functioning. I need food in order to think. And food takes money."

He wheeled around, taking the cramped space in two strides. "It isn't right, the way everyone's supposed to go out and earn in order to live. What about people who think? The ones who have ways to express what's inside of them by doing something besides selling?"

He wondered how many creative efforts had been killed, how many books and paintings and how much music destroyed, because those able to make them were rendered incompetent by the need to eat.

He stopped in the middle of the floor and rubbed his face with his hand. He could feel the anger growing inside. It felt good.

"If they want me to write, why don't they let me do it?" he said aloud. "I'm using my education, aren't I? Doing what I've been trained for—to teach others? Well, this is my way of teaching." But it was going against the usual definition. That was the problem.

He paced around the small room again. "It just seems silly to waste time on a job picking up garbage or something. Not that they'd hire me. I'm overqualified. Too much education." He kicked the frame of the bed. It lurched against the wall.

"What I should be doing is what I was trained to do in the first place in the way I'm best able to do it. If there's no place for me to do what I should be doing without worrying about food and a bed— If they don't have some kind of place where I can just think in peace— Then they shouldn't ask me to work my tail off just to survive. Who wants to survive, if you only have to do what you hate?" He sat down on the edge of the bed.

"All I want is a roof over my head and some food in my stomach." He looked at the splotched and molding wallpaper. "If they could just give me that for a while, I'd give plenty in return."

He rubbed his face with his hands. "It takes time and thought and concentration and that's what they won't give me. I have to be out by the end of next week and I have nothing to live on. No job, no food, no money and this—" He flicked the pages with his finger. "This still has a long way to go. A week without food won't help it."

He propped his elbows on his knees and put his hands over his face. He stayed like that for a long while, then got up slowly and began to put the pages away. It was a waste of time, but he'd have to find something. At least try. If he said he'd tried, how could they kick him out? Maybe he could work on the manuscript in the evenings.

But he knew that he couldn't. This was something he had to do full time to make any headway. The discouragement huddled in a dark mass around his shoulders as he went down the stairs. He'd have to talk to the manager.

"I used to write in my language," the old man said as he began pulling out listings. He handed Lawrence some slips of paper. "These people call in past week. You use this phone, if you need." The sound of squabbling children rose from the back of the house, but Lawrence had no quarters for phone calls. He nodded.

He looked at the papers. Help in the yard. Shoveling snow. Someone to move boxes out of a basement. They were all odd jobs, probably taken already and almost certainly too far to walk.

"We got bus passes if it far," the man said. Lawrence began writing the numbers on a separate piece of paper.

"Yeah, I write poems," the old man continued. "Pretty good. Pretty good. Teacher proud. Win national contest in my country. But no money. Can't live on words. Childrens need clothes."

He gestured toward the back of the house. "Writing no pay. You think so. People gonna buy books. My daughter, she read more than help mot'er. But I tell her it no life. Specially for girl. No money. No monies at all."

Lawrence looked down at his list. So it didn't pay. Did that make it any less worthwhile? Was pay all that mattered?

Yet he knew that it did. If it didn't, he'd be in his room right now, not calling someone up to ask for the privilege of shoveling their snow or moving boxes. It didn't pay, so you couldn't do it. Because, above all else, you had to live.

Lawrence looked at the manager. He hadn't been able to do it. He'd had to give in. Therefore, no one should be allowed to find freedom. Jealousy, that's all it was.

Lawrence fought down the sudden sourness in his throat. He asked for the phone. He made a few calls and got the answers he knew would be there. They'd already found someone or else decided it didn't need doing.

Yes, you were to work. The very people he'd just spoken to would have said so. But would they give you employment? Of course not. He turned to the manager with real satisfaction. Now he could go back to his work.

But no. The old man had rummaged out another piece of what he said was good news. There was a place called the Millionaire's Club near the waterfront. It was for people like him, especially men, who needed work. He should try there.

~~~

And so Deborah's days went by slowly, long and predictable except for Arnie. She snubbed him once or twice and he seemed to get the idea, but he was still there, like an animal at the edge of a group of prey: The group is tense, aware of the predator's presence, but still they don't move and still he waits for an opening.

He evidently thought he saw one the day she wore the new dress. She'd been shopping again, pawing through racks of on-sale resort wear, looking for spring and summer clothes. The dress was a long sleeved, straight tube of sky-blue material topped by a large square white collar. She purchased it impulsively, because the warm blue of it made her feel good.

Arnie must have thought it looked good. When he came in that Monday morning Deb and Randy were conferring about a telephone message she'd taken Friday afternoon. The people who'd called had been confused about what they wanted and she was trying to explain what they'd said.

She answered an incoming call, then put the receiver down. "I'm sorry I didn't give you everything you need," she said.
~~~

Randy smiled at her. "It's not your fault." He flicked the paper with a finger. "These people are always like that. This is a very clear message considering what you had to deal with. Especially with two of them on the phone at the same time."

She grinned. "That was a little confusing."

Arnie peered over the desk. Deborah avoided his eyes but he looked her up and down anyway.

"You know, I've never liked that style of dress until now," he said. He came around Randy, putting his hand on his arm. Randy drew back.

Arnie picked up his mail and waved it at her. "Really, it looks good on you. Normally I hate all that material, but it drapes you nicely."

Her cheeks flushed. She looked at Randy. "Thanks," she said. She nodded at the messages in Randy's hand. "Who are you supposed to call, anyway? Or should I ask? I mean, I was curious, by the time the whole weird conversation was over, about who was who and what they wanted you for."

Arnie looked from Randy to Deb and, for once, left without any more comments. Randy watched him go as he began to unravel relationships, explaining names and people as well as he could. "I'm not sure, to tell you the truth," he said finally.

She laughed and got up to push some mail back into the slot it had slipped out of.

He was so silent she thought he'd gone. He was still standing there when she turned back to the desk.

"That dress really is nice," he said abruptly.

Her cheeks pinkened again. "Thank you," she said. She met his eyes and blurted, "Why do his compliments always make me feel embarrassed? Nobody else here does that."

Nobody else gave her compliments and Randy should know it. How could she compare the two of them? She looked at him again, willing him to understand. He looked at the carpet.

"I wouldn't worry about it." He looked up. "He's just one of those people who always say the wrong thing."

The phone rang and she pushed a button and lifted the receiver at the same time. He fingered his messages and watched her. She spoke into the phone and he lifted his hand at her and walked away.

The previous feelings of loneliness had been nothing to this. "Nobody else here does." What a dumb thing to say. "You don't embarrass me," would have been worse, she supposed. Only slightly, though.

The telephone buzzed and she answered the call. She transferred it and stared at the elevator doors across the room. He probably didn't care what she said, anyway.

She reached for her scratch pad. Her pencil moved carefully, grateful for something to do. She'd been finding herself doing this a lot lately. Sketching the silk flowers on the stand near the chairs. The elevator doors, half open or closed, with people in pieces behind them or stepping on or off. She'd even drawn the in and out board and the small shadows cast by the magnetic clips clinging to it.

She hadn't drawn since she'd graduated last year. Her art teacher had said "Some talent but no genius." If that was all, then why bother?

So she'd gotten a job filling out grants for those who did have some genius and filled her spare time with art gallery openings. With that outlet closed, she'd started drawing again, simply for solace.

And her drawing had changed. There was a certain instinct in her pencil that hadn't been there before. She felt more relaxed about what she was doing and her drawing was more sure because of it. It still wasn't genius, but she wasn't sure she cared about that anymore, anyway.

"It makes me feel good and that's good enough." She dropped her pencil and looked around. There was no one to hear what she'd said. She picked up the pencil again.

It was an especially quiet day. She had filled an entire scratch pad by four o'clock. She was adding light touches of shadow to a ghostly drawing of one of the foyer chairs when the elevator doors began closing behind the departing lawyers and their assistants and secretaries.

The floor had pretty much emptied when Randy came out. He stopped at the side of her desk to pull on his coat. They exchanged the usual good nights.

But still he seemed to be hesitating. She looked up at him.

"What are you doing?" he asked.

She covered the paper with her hand before she looked down. "Just doodling," she said.

"May I see?"

She handed it to him and began organizing the pencils in their container.

"This is good!"

There was surprise in his voice. She laughed. "Thanks," she said dryly.

His face got red and he smiled at her. "Sorry. I didn't mean it like that. It really is." He took another long look and handed it back. "I didn't know you drew."

It was five o'clock. She locked the desk and switched the phone system off. She slipped the pad into her purse and began gathering her coat, hat and gloves. He watched her.

"Have you been drawing long?" he asked. They walked to the elevator.

"Several years." She looked up at the elevator light. This was her chance and she felt so stiff and almost panicked.

She fought it down and tried to speak more naturally. Pretend it was a phone message she was talking about. That was the trick. She glanced at him.

The brown eyes met hers solidly and then looked away. He was as nervous as she was! The tension ebbed out of her legs.

The elevator doors opened and he waited for her to get on. "Why are you answering telephones if you can draw like that?" He asked it quickly, like he was afraid his time would run out.

She made a face. "You can't make a living with mid-talent drawings."

He looked at her. "Mid-talent. That's an interesting phrase. I don't think it applies."

The elevator was already on the ground floor. They stepped off. They stood in the echoing lobby, looking at one another.

"Look, I'd really like—" He stopped. She waited without daring to hope. "Would you mind having dinner with me?" he said in a rush. He grinned. "I want to convince you that you really can draw."

She felt real laughter ringing inside her for the first time in weeks. "One batch of doodling has proved that to you?"

"Not if you'll let me see more." He frowned. "Will you have dinner with me?"

"Why I— I'd like that," she said. The words and the tone were right, almost comfortable. It was a kind of magic that she should feel this good. His face relaxed and she felt a strange warmth rush through her.

They stood looking at each other as more people came out of the elevators and walked around them. Impulsively, she laid her hand on his arm. He slipped it into place without looking at her.

They went through the revolving doors in one compartment.

14

It was the first time he'd been outside for any length of time since he'd moved into the old house. The cold and damp were a shock. One thing about that building, the steam radiators kept it warm, even with the drafts from the windows. It was actually stuffy most of the time. He'd taken to removing the cardboard from the windows while he worked. It helped him stay awake.

It was surprising what minor things had become luxuries. Rest. A roof. Heat. "Better than the streets," he muttered. He could feel the panic rising inside. He only had about a week left.

He knew the chances of finding any kind of work in that length of time. The even slimmer chances of finding something that would give him enough to live on. It was so impossible that he didn't even want to start looking.

But it was even more impossible that he should be back on the street. His coat was ragged now with dirt and wear. It felt thinner. He shivered. It was cold on the street at night. Colder than now, and the ice of the wind was driving into his bones.

He walked to the Millionaire's Club but they were no help. There was nothing on their bulletin board. The man in charge was nice without being pitying, but it was clear that he was tired and overworked.

"Come back tomorrow," he repeated three times. "If we have anything tomorrow morning, you can try then."

Lawrence would have taken a sales position now but he knew his clothes were too shabby to even apply. Even the security guard places wouldn't talk to him. On the way to the Millionaire's Club, he'd walked into the office of a firm with a "Help Wanted" sign in the window. They'd looked at his coat and the shaggy black curls in his eyes and said, "Sorry, not hiring."

He wasn't unqualified now. He was undesirable. He didn't even exist.

He didn't want to go back to the old house yet. He'd have to pass the manager's place. What if the door opened as he went past? What if they met in the hall? There was no work. But that wouldn't be good enough. It would be Lawrence's fault, for wanting to write.

He stood on a grate outside one of the large department stores to warm his feet and tried to think. It was mid-afternoon. He hadn't eaten since breakfast. But it wasn't late enough in the day for him to go back. He moved his feet on the grate and held his coat out to let the warm air draft onto his upper legs and trunk. The old codger had showed him how to do it.

He watched the shoppers going in and out of the glass doors lining the street. He wished he could just write and tell them all to go to hell, including his stomach. His body warmed bit by bit but his hands were cold from clutching his coat. It was crazy to keep looking for work he knew wasn't there.

He crouched down and spread his hands out in the steam. He looked at the people going by. He was lost in his thoughts and the warmth seeping slowly into his body made him drowsy. He watched the passersby like a child, looking at them more openly than they at him.

The backs of his hands were still cold. He put the right one out, palm up to soak in the warmth. The other went into his pocket, hugging his coat to his body to keep in the moist warmth.

The people passing directly in front of him tended to circle out and away, toward the walk's outer edge. He wasn't too tired to understand what they were doing. His lips twisted.

He watched a middle-aged lady in a full length mink coat move carefully away from him without once looking at him. As his eyes followed her fur-covered back down the sidewalk, he felt a hand against his, a cold piece of paper between.

He jerked around and pulled back his hand at the same time. The paper fluttered away and he grabbed it.

The man whose hand had touched his was already moving away. His wool overcoat and felt hat disappeared through the door of Frederick and Nelson. Lawrence looked down. Twenty dollars.

He looked again. A real twenty dollar bill. His fingers closed around it. He put his hand into his right pants pocket. It was the only one he had left without a hole in it. He pulled the bill out again. He looked at it carefully. He put it back in his pocket.

He shifted his feet on the grill. Maybe the old codger had known what he was talking about, living off the fat of the land. Why hadn't he ever come up here by the big stores when he needed money?

Perhaps he'd been afraid of the lights. And more than one person would be too conspicuous. But Lawrence was alone. He could stand or sit here, whichever he preferred, and no one would pay much attention.

He looked at his hands. Maybe if he said something? The shyness of a month ago was behind him, lost in hunger. His lips moved soundlessly, experimenting. "Ma'am, could you spare a few dollars? A dime or a quarter?" He knew their giving was triggered by guilt. He wondered what sin the man in the hat had committed, for twenty dollars to expiate it. But why should he care? It was money, and that's what he needed.

He shifted his weight onto his haunches. He kept his hand up. A young woman dropped a quarter into it. He looked at his palm. If he could get enough money this way, maybe he could still find a way to write. This wasn't like swinging a snow shovel for eight hours or lifting boxes around. It wasn't as tiring and there wasn't any commute to pay for either. It wasn't regular, of course, but neither were odd jobs from the Millionaire's Club. It might be enough to feed him, at least.

He thought of the twenty lying in his pocket and all the food it could pay for. Suddenly, knowing he actually had money for food, he was hungrier than he'd been in weeks, knowing he didn't have any.

And with food in his stomach, what he couldn't do! Suddenly even the short time he had left in city housing gleamed with potential.

He stayed in the same position for three hours. His muscles ached unbearably, but there were twenty-five dollars in his pocket when he stood up. If he could gather this much every day, he could save enough to live on when his time at the housing was up.

He couldn't expect to have twenties pressed into his palm every day, of course. But if he saved up what he did get— He walked slowly back up the hill, thinking about the food he would buy.

During the next week he carefully avoided talking to or even seeing the manager. He stayed in his room until noon, thinking and writing, pouring the words carefully onto the paper. He knew that the noon meal was a major one for the manager's family. Lawrence slipped out of the building then and around the block in the other direction. He walked rapidly down the hill toward the main shopping areas downtown.

In the following days he didn't make anything close to the money he had that first afternoon. Yet there was usually enough pressed into his palm to buy food and put a few quarters away in his one holeless pocket.

He dressed carefully for these excursions. He needed warmth, at least a semblance of cleanliness, and ease of movement. First he would pull on a turtleneck sweater, then his one heavy vest. A sweater went over this. It was too large for him and so most comfortable as a third layer. The overcoat went over it, as clean as he could make it with a damp washcloth and scrubbing with his worn-out lint brush.

After he'd stood or crouched over the grate for a few hours the crowd would thin out for home or dinner. If he waited long enough they could be seen leaving nearby restaurants with small white sacks in their hands. The women in their snug coats and high heels usually carried them. His nose immediately recognized the bags for what they were. Leftover food from overloaded plates.

He eyed the bags jealously. These women, artificially slim even under thick wool and fur coats, didn't need or even want the food they carried so carefully.

Should he just ask? He watched them and argued with himself. What was the difference between waiting quietly, hand out, and simply asking? Through history, the ones who received—who achieved—were those who asked. Or they didn't ask, they just took what they needed or wanted. And he needed that food far more than these slim women beside their paunchy men.

—

They found a restaurant three blocks up and four over. Deb thought fleetingly that this must be how it felt to do drugs. As if you had no part in the things surrounding you, yet were aware of them with crystal-sharp senses.

Like the way the air felt after rain, only more so. She didn't tell Randy that, but they talked about other things and the words tumbled out of her in a way she'd never talked to a guy before. Or a girl, for that matter.

And Randy talked too. They were so absorbed in each other they were hardly aware the waiter had brought their food. There were no false starts, after that first one.

From her drawing, they went to his interest in art and the theater. And that led to music and drama and then to the city and the life it contained. She found herself saying things she'd hardly been aware that she thought.

She didn't realize it until Randy was trying to explain the odd excitement which shopping at the downtown outdoor market could give him.

"It's the colors," she said suddenly. He looked at her. "It's something I still haven't gotten used to," she said. She toyed with her water glass. "I hadn't thought about it in relation to shopping, but it does add to the fun of it. Just to look and to soak everything in. Color for me has always been connected to art."

She was suddenly pensive. "Though this is the first drawing I've done in ages." She looked at him. "Do you really think I have talent? I mean, I know I'll never be rich and famous, but I'm beginning to wonder if being a receptionist is good for my sanity. And the drawing keeps pulling me back. But I know I'm not good enough to do portraits or anything like that. Not 'great art' as my teacher in high school would say—"

She stopped. Her hand went out to her tea cup. She looked at her food, then up at his face. "I don't usually talk this much. Really." She smiled at him. "It's just good for my vanity to have someone tell me I can draw."

"But you can. I really mean it. I think you're good."

She sipped her tea. She waved her hand at her face and put the cup down. "It's making me warm," she said.

He smiled at her. She grinned. "Thank you."

He reached for her hand. "No," he said. "Thank you."

She looked down at their fingers, linked so lightly on the smooth wood of the table. She smiled at him and tried to keep her voice steady. "And what have I done that you should be thanking me?"

"For being you." His face was flushed.

Deborah looked at him. For a man to feel and to show it—

Her fingers tightened in his, then she caught herself. She pulled away and fingered the napkin in her lap.

"This is a very good steak," she observed to her plate. She smiled at him and then looked around the room. "I like the way this is arranged. The plants and booths back to back give it more privacy than open tables ever could."

He nodded. "I've heard that it was private, that's why I thought—"

She looked at him.

"I just wanted to talk to you," he said lamely.

"But you hardly know me." She smiled at him, knowing they could never go back.

He looked at his watch. "An hour and a half ago I hardly knew you," he said. "It's already changed to past tense."

"Yes." She picked up her fork.

"Do you believe in God?"

She blinked. "I— I don't know," she said. "My mother does, but I've never been sure enough myself to decide."

"I never have either. But this makes me wonder."

"I know." Only after she'd said it did she realize that she really did know what he meant.

"It's like a miracle or something." He caught her hand in his. "This suddenness and the right feeling— You have it too, don't you?"

She nodded. They looked at each other. She glanced at her place. "I'm really not hungry for this. It's delicious, but—"

"We can get the waiter to give you a doggy bag if you like. But let's have a glass of wine first." He grinned at her. "I feel like celebrating."

Though Lawrence was convinced what he was doing was necessary, he knew that it wasn't usual. He would pace the sidewalk outside a restaurant for an hour, eyeing the bags going by. His nose twitched visibly at the smells that drifted out when the restaurant doors opened. There was food there and he needed it with a need that had no place for what the old codger would have called foolishness.

Though the old man wouldn't have understood that it was the writing that drove him. He thought about that a lot as he watched outside the warm doors. It made him feel colder.

But no matter how long it had been since he'd last eaten, no matter what delicacies he might hope to find in those bags, the hour of walking must be fulfilled. It was a penance he paid to the politenesses he'd learned so early in life. The ones that had failed him in the end.

Tonight the penance was as long as usual, though he hadn't eaten since the evening before. For some reason, all he'd been getting the past week was cold garlic bread. He wondered if the waiters knew he was out there and were doing it on purpose.

He had stopped coming to this restaurant for a while. He'd been afraid they'd call the police because one of the women he'd approached had screamed when he'd touched her arm. She'd turned and run hysterically back into the building. Lawrence had quickly disappeared by a roundabout way, just in case someone was watching him.

That had been two weeks ago. He'd stayed away a week and then come once or twice last week. He'd gotten garlic bread here as well as the other places he'd been. He paced back and forth under the arches decorating the bank building next door.

He no longer had his watch. Even a battered old pocket watch will bring a few dollars at a pawn shop, and he'd needed another ink pen.

He didn't need a watch anyway. On the street there was little need to know anything beyond the sun's rise and fall. His stomach told him all he needed. As for the pacing, he knew when his hour was up. Time is something you find in your bones when the trappings of it are discarded. An elemental thing that needs no hand circling a face to tell when things need doing.

And now it was time. The restlessness had worked itself out. He waited at the edge of the rain.

He cursed the damp softly. The cold of it got into his skin, no matter how many layers he wore. He couldn't keep it out.

When he had first begun panhandling here, the food in the bags had been warm. His tongue stroked his dry lips. Pork chops and chicken. Warm fish in a buttery sauce. Even vegetables. Slim green tubes with a bland taste and warm corn on the cob. But then that woman had screamed.

The door of the restaurant opened and he stepped out onto the sidewalk. They were going the other direction.

He watched them. He hunched his shoulders and bent his head to keep his face dry and his chest semi-warm.

Two men and their girls passed him and went into the restaurant. Maybe they'd come out later with food. They usually did, the women with men. Even if the man carried the food, you knew it was the woman's leftovers. Too dainty, too much on a diet, yet willing to be taken to dinner.

It made him angry until he remembered that it was their leftovers he was most likely to get. Two old ladies walked up to the door from the opposite direction. Those two would have bags for sure, as skinny as they were. Especially two dressed up like that. And if he asked them, they'd hand their food right over. They'd be afraid of someone who looked like he did.

He had become aware of his appearance in a new way. The looks of distaste from passersby brought a sardonic grin to his face. If they didn't like it they could bribe him to keep away, if they didn't feel sorry enough for him to give him a handout. He had two things working for him now, guilt and disgust. Both were equally strong.

Not that he liked it. He didn't recognize himself when he happened to glance into a department store window. But anyone's hair would look wild if it was cut with a kitchen knife. It was one of the few things he hadn't sold and he used it sparingly, to keep the blade sharp.

And it wasn't his fault his hair was matted. Curls like his couldn't be washed properly in a bathtub or sink. There had been no showers in the old house the city used for people like him. Not that he had had much time there.

And not that it mattered, he supposed. He had what little money he'd saved and the work he'd done on the book. He comforted himself with the writing, shutting his mind to the knowledge that he couldn't finish it if he stayed on the streets. Knowing without putting it into words that he wouldn't know what to do with himself when it was done.

There was someone coming out of the restaurant. He pulled back into the shadows. Only a man with a briefcase. Lawrence's stomach growled and the man glanced toward his corner.

He shrank farther back. He forced his mind blank, refusing to feel the pain in his bowels. The pavement was slowly getting wet from the mist. The wait would be worth it if there was meat at the end. Even bread would do, at the moment.

But he couldn't think about it. He settled himself to waiting again. It was the penance he paid, though he dared not think about that. It made the anger rise in him too sharply.

He watched the sidewalk growing damper under the street lamp. The restaurant door would open after a while. Then time would begin again.

15

The door swung open suddenly and a rush of light and the smell of food spilled onto the damp sidewalk. Dishes rattled. It was drizzling now.

A man in a dark raincoat stood in the doorway of the nearest building. He blended into the shadows so well that only the most observant entering patron would have noticed him. He was almost completely hidden by the dark arches to the left of the door with "Blondie's" emblazoned on it.

The man's shoulders were hunched against the cold and he only moved when the door of the restaurant opened. The noise would spill into the street again and he would move forward and peer at the people going in and out.

This time it was a man and a girl leaving. The man carried a briefcase in one hand and an umbrella in the other. He held it over the girl. She was wearing a dark hat and coat and a white paper sack gleamed from her right hand.

She tucked her left hand into the crook of her companion's arm and they turned in the direction of the building the man was sheltering under.

As they turned, he cleared his throat and moved from the doorway. He fell into step beside them. They were looking at each other.

"Excuse me, ma'am," he said. His voice was loud in the dark street. She jerked around and shrank against her companion at the same time. "Could you spare that bag of food?" the man said in a rush. "I'm very hungry."

She thrust her arm at him, almost throwing the bag. She pressed more closely against her escort.

He had transferred the umbrella to the other hand. It was awkward, with the briefcase. His arm went around her waist protectively and he opened his mouth.

But the man in the overcoat was already gone. He'd hurried back to his shadows and was ripping the bag open.

Randy and Deborah hurried down the sidewalk and around the corner. His briefcase bumped at her waist as he tried to keep the umbrella over her. He was still carrying them both in one hand.

"It's okay," she said breathlessly. "I'm all right." She put her right hand on the arm he had at her waist.

He dropped his hand, switched the umbrella back to it, and looked down at her. "He startled me," he said.

"Me too. Otherwise I wouldn't have given it to him." She laughed. "That was good steak!"

"I'm glad you did. I wouldn't have wanted him following you."

"Oh, I'd have been all right. I've been reading up on taking care of myself. I'd know what to do. Besides, you were with me." She took his arm again and they turned a corner. They were going down one of the city's steepest hills.

"I'm glad I was." He looked at her anxiously. "Does this kind of thing happen often? Is that why you've been reading up on it?"

"Well, once." She told him the bare details of the attack in the alley. He moved his arm, pressing her hand closer to his side.

"You're being more careful now, aren't you?"

They were almost to her apartment. She saw him looking at the old drunk by the lamppost and smiled contentedly.

He put down his briefcase and touched her cheek. "Do be careful," he said. "Coming to work tomorrow and everything, I mean." His hand fell away. He looked at her. "I wouldn't want anything to happen now."

She moved to his lips. By the time they had said their last good nights, the steak was completely forgotten.

Lawrence was happy, too. He sat munching contentedly beneath the dark arches beside the restaurant.

16

In three weeks, Deborah's life went through a metamorphosis. Being in love literally changed everything.

Randy had contacts in the art world and the businesses connected with it. One of these was a graphics and magazine design shop. The owners were looking for a new person. There was a quickly filled out application and an interview on her lunch hour, then several days of waiting before they called. They were willing to give her a try.

Deb reveled in the change. This was far more involving than the office work she'd been doing. She found herself trying layout designs and making sketches for illustrations wherever she went— including dinner with Randy.

And this was often. She worried about the expense, but he wouldn't discuss it. He only said cheerfully that it was money well spent, and refused to go near the place where they'd been approached by the man in the overcoat.

They didn't see each other as much as they would have if she'd stayed at the law firm. He had meetings and dinner appointments and she sometimes worked late to meet a deadline. But if they didn't meet, he called to say that he'd missed her. Then they'd talk until midnight.

They would have talked until then whether they were on the phone or together. She had never found anyone she could say so much to. And he listened. She was so grateful for this that she learned to care about his law cases. And to remember the basic outlines of arguments he was working on.

But then, it was easy to care about what he said. More often than not, the cases he spoke most passionately about involved art organizations and tax credits for businesses helping them. She was fascinated with the complications of keeping the local ballet corps solvent and the problems downtown theaters were having in holding their leases.

She could stay curled up on the couch for hours, listening to him, asking questions and playing devil's advocate until he demanded to know just whose side she was on anyway, and she could slip laughing into his arms.

For here was the other side of their talking. The warmth of their bodies and her own sweet desire expanding inside her. She'd never felt such stirrings before. The intensity was frightening but she welcomed the sign that this was no normal friendship.

This wasn't the way she had felt when Andrew had kissed her. She clung to Randy as he held her, afraid to give way, and he, smiling a little grimly, would take himself home and then call her at six the next morning just to say that he loved her.

And then there was her work. Drawing illustrations was a shop specialty. It wasn't simple. One had to evoke an entire world in a newspaper ad, with its smeared ink. Lines not too heavily blackened. Mood and atmosphere but no fine detail that the ink couldn't catch. And a grace of line that could come out fresh and alive no matter how much the picture was enlarged or reduced according to the customer's need and the space and design of the ad.

Deborah found herself looking at everything differently. The sides of buildings, the way lampposts leaned into themselves. Children's arms clinging to parental hands.

It wasn't color she wanted now, but lines as clean as possible. She bought new sketch pads and pencils and spent every odd minute drawing whatever happened to be available. It wasn't boredom that drove her now. This was something she loved and she could also make money at it.

Her new supervisor was a large square woman named Evelyn. Ev didn't seem to care about anything except drawing and the plants at the small window beside her desk which looked onto the alley. Even Deb's frequent calls from Randy didn't faze her.

The phone had its own stand between the two drafting tables. Ev usually answered it. It was always for her unless it was Randy.

"Your friend," she would say, handing the receiver over. She'd hunt through the in and out boxes, pull out some papers, and stand up. Through the buzz of her own feelings and the warmth of Randy's voice, Deb would hear her chatting with the layout people next door, asking about this project and that, checking on deadlines she knew by heart, running errands to the back rooms and the cameras.

This was enough to endear her to Deb, but Ev also cared about her drawing. She fussed at her lines, helped with perspective and corrected without ever reproaching. But she never spoke of her own family or friends or ambitions.

It took a while before Deb got up the nerve to question her. "Why are you working here anyway, Ev? You've got a real talent for showing people how to do things." She leaned back from the paper pinned to her board and looked at it critically. "To me, anyway. How come you're not teaching?"

Ev erased a line carefully and reached for her brush. "Couldn't afford it," she said. She looked out the window, past the well-tended plants. Then she looked at Deb. "Are you and your boyfriend serious?"

"We love each other, if that's what you mean."

"Are you planning to get married?"

It was a question Deb had been trying not to ask herself. "I don't know," she said.

"You have talent, you know."

Deborah made a small, self-conscious face. "You and Randy. I wish I could believe it as much as you do."

"Just don't let him convince you your talent should only be used at home."

"What do you mean?"

She shifted her bulk on the chair. "Men. They may encourage you, but it's a game. Keep the lady happy. Then they marry you and chain you to the house. There's no getting out then. Art classes are only for playing with. The real business is doing dishes and buying new lamps to match the living room curtains."

"Oh, but Randy would never—"

Ev nodded. "I thought that once, too. Better ask him. Or tell him. That's better." She looked at Deb sharply. "Better find out for yourself what you want, though, before he does pop the question. It may be best to let him know beforehand, so he can decide without being embarrassed. It's harder getting out of marriage than into it."

"I don't think Randy's like that at all."

Ev shrugged. "Forewarned is forearmed. Isn't that how they say it?" She turned back to her drawing.

Deb waited, watching her, but her shoulders were steady over her paper and pins and she didn't look up.

The money Lawrence had scrounged so carefully lasted exactly two weeks from the day he left city housing. Even sleeping in the dirtiest, cheapest rooms he could find wouldn't stretch it any further.

And there were no cheaper rooms to be had. The torn naugahyde on the chairs in the dark lobbies, the old-fashioned and filthy cuspidors, and the urine smells told him that. This was the bottom.

For about ten dollars a night he got a narrow room with a bed and cold running water. The commonly-used, dirty restrooms were at the end of the hall. He still had his single electric burner and he used it, though discovery would have meant he'd be in the street for the night, less the money he'd paid for the room. He heated water on it. The hot liquid in the mug kept his fingers warm as he tried to write, squinting in the uneven light of the single uncovered 60-watt bulb.

But now he had no money for even those beds. It had been small comfort, but still something to look forward to. More importantly, it had been a place to write. Now survival again took precedence over the only reason he had to survive.

He tried panhandling for more cash, but there was never enough for food and lodging too. And it was hard to panhandle and search the restaurant garbage cans at the same time.

He decided he was getting too familiar to the people who frequented the stores and restaurants he shadowed. The pickings seemed slimmer. He didn't know that they were the same—that his body's needs were becoming greater with each day's drain on his system.

He wasn't eating properly even when he did eat. The closest he came to a vegetable were the occasional pieces of limp lettuce clinging to a hamburger bun. There was seldom any meat on the buns. And the little milk he found to drink was sickening with sourness.

The pull on his physical resources weakened him emotionally too. It was tiring to be always hungry.

He was also dirtier now than he'd been and that bothered him more than he knew. His hair hung in mats around his eyes and his coat was streaked with the grime of the dirty steam gratings. Just keeping his face and hands clean was a battle. There was seldom any soap in the few public restrooms he dared to use. And of course, there were no showers.

He didn't notice the smell anymore, but he did notice the way he looked. He could be startled by his own face in the mirror, the blue eyes staring out of the pale dirty face. His diet kept him pale in spite of the constant exposure to weather and wind.

His looks did help him pick up a few quarters from frightened old ladies at bus stops. Once or twice shopkeepers had called the police and reported him for harassing pedestrians. But the old codger had taught him how to disappear when a police car was anywhere near. He knew all the alleyways now.

He learned again to sleep in them at night, curled out of the wind into a niche in the wall, huddled close to the brick or concrete. This was to avoid being seen as well as for the little wind protection the wall offered. He steered clear of the park he had slept in while he was with the old codger. When he did glimpse the old man on the street, he hurried into an alley or around a corner. He avoided all of the other street people.

He had failed. He hadn't climbed out of the streets, and the thought of the old man welcoming him back made him almost beside himself.

"Oh God," he would mutter, rubbing his face with his hands. "Oh God, it didn't work. They wouldn't let me. The book is still there and they wouldn't let me do it." He'd look around wildly, expecting the old man to appear suddenly from behind a garbage bin. "But he's not here. He doesn't know. Bad as them. Yes, he is. Wouldn't let me write. Always pestering."

He would rub his hands over his face again, then suddenly punch at his stomach. "Always pestering! Stop it!"

But it was never enough. He would have to turn and turn again, hitting out at the nearest wall until his knuckles dripped sour blood. "Don't talk to me! Leave me alone. Leave me alone! Just let me write!" His hands rubbed up over his face, the blood streaking his skin, sticking to his matted hair. "Just let me think," he would moan. "Let me write!"

But the hunger always got in the way. He went back to the garbage cans, forgetting the need for money and bed. The cans near the fast food places and the bus stops were most profitable. Remnants of hamburger, last drops of milk shake still in the cup, bits of chocolate on candy bar wrappers.

But the hunger was always there. Even when he did steal a few minutes from the long days of scrounging to sit on an old board in an alley and think, the pangs rose louder than his thoughts, confusing themselves with the writing.

"Now a prime example of this process is the elimination of the Russian peasant from the bread-—from the land," he would mutter. "Oh God, let me think."

He would grab his abdomen, pressing roughly through the layers of sweater. "Shut up," he would mutter. He would pick up the pen stiffly, forcing the words from his chilled fingers onto the smudged, much-folded papers on his knees.

The ink would spell out, "Now a prime—" and he'd pause, trying to remember. "A prime example of this process is the elimination—" His bowels would grumble again, sharply.

He would fold the paper hastily, tucking it with the pen deep into his only whole pocket, and hurry to the nearest restroom he could use. The scraps of food, never clean, eaten at strange hours and hurriedly with filthy hands, were never enough to fill his hunger and they ran through him like water. He ached with the cramps, not knowing precisely where they came from, and hated "them" and God.

He understood through his haze that the pain was what soldiers spoke of as the plague of battle and war. But the knowledge was no comfort as he bent almost double, hurrying to find a restroom.

So many were closed to him. Few of even the fast food places would let him in, and the ones that did never had paper towels and didn't always have toilet paper. When it was there, he was as capable as anyone else of taking it. His nose seemed to run constantly and sometimes he was forced to use the dark corners of alleys for his diarrhea.

And so it went. Nights in the alleys, curled tight to the buildings for futile warmth, hiding hopelessly from the wind and the lights of night watchmen.

They had their orders about vagrants. Not to obey would be to lose the jobs that were often their only protection from the street. They were efficient at kicking sleepers awake. The watchman would be gone before the job was fully done, but the sleeper would know without doubt that he'd been there. He didn't want the timing of his round to be interrupted. And moving quickly meant less danger of being attacked.

Lawrence considered himself lucky when he slept the night through in one place. The watchmen, the retching, the hunger— They were all part of a whole. A constant craving for filling and warmth.

It was only now that he began to feel a sexual craving along with the others. The warmth of a body to replace the sleeping bag he shivered into each night. The sense of release from the all-invading tensions. But he knew the fantasies were hopeless. Even the most desperate prostitute moved aside when she saw someone like him approaching. He rubbed himself nightly to sleep but it didn't really help.

One place he did find some warmth was in the foyer of the post office in the early mornings. He often stood in the echoing lobby, watching through the street-grimed windows as early office workers tumbled off the buses or made their transfers. He learned quickly that it wasn't a good time to beg money. People were too sleepy to hear him or too grumpy and tired to feel guilt, much less pity.

So he stayed inside, moving sullenly out of the way of the janitor and his wheeled bucket. The smell of his disinfectant thickened the air, but Lawrence only edged as near as he could to the heaters.

There were always other street people there, but he never saw the old codger. Lawrence stayed near the door, just in case. No one else tried to approach him. They were warned off by the wild hair and staring eyes. They had enough trouble.

Later, when the streets grew crowded with lunch hour shoppers, he would try his luck outside a department store. He'd get a few quarters if he did well, then begin to look through the garbage cans, hunting for food.

But there was never enough. The money would buy a doughnut or cheap loaf of bread and then he would go back to panhandling, lurking outside restaurant doors or digging through their trash cans.

It was an endless orgy of dirt and shame and though he had no choice that he could see, each day was a self-flagellation by begging. "Ma'am, could you spare a quarter?" It ate into what was left of his soul.

His clothes grew even dirtier and his hair was more matted than seemed possible. Yet he was hardly aware of the mere bodily needs, except for the demands of his stomach. They only served as annoyances. Deeper than food or the sexual desire was the craving for the idea and the writing. It haunted his dreams and tormented his thoughts and in a fierce anger he would snatch moments away from his body's demands.

He had to do this more than anything else. He would crouch muttering into a corner of an empty alley, trying to think but not feel, pushing the pen with cold and shaking fingers. He seemed barely human at these moments, his concentration was so centered. Yet this was all that was left to make him feel like a person.

~~~

And she'd thought she'd been so careful.
~~~

Deborah groaned and reread the letter. When she'd told her parents she was seeing someone, she'd tried to make it clear it was only friendship. Now her mother was inviting Randy to visit at Easter.

The letter had come in the Saturday morning mail. Randy would be here in a few minutes. They were going to see a new display at the University gallery, then eat a late lunch. She bit her lip. Would he realize that this was the summons for approval she knew it was?

But if he was aware of the implications, he didn't say anything. He just handed the letter back to her and said he would love to meet her parents. Really, it was time that he did and wasn't Easter next weekend? When did she want to leave? Friday at noon? He pulled his pocket calendar out, scribbled it in, and gave her a kiss as they went out the door.

She wrote the next day, saying they'd come, then waited nervously through the following week. Her stomach could cramp into knots at the very thought of Bobby and his big mouth. She doubted it had changed much. And her mother with her bright, knowing eyes.

Would she guess how much Deb loved him and that he said he loved her but hadn't yet spoken of marriage? Would she see that the control which kept them from sleeping together was growing more fragile with each touch? That Deb almost didn't care if it broke down completely? Deb knew what her mother would think of that.

A day didn't pass but she wondered if she should have even told Randy about the invitation. Yet how could she have hidden it?

And she wasn't sorry he'd come, she admitted to herself as they paced the ferry deck the Friday afternoon before Easter. It was a typical day in late March, windy and cloudy, then windy and sunny, then windy and rainy, in rapid succession. They braced themselves against the white metal rail of the boat and watched the clouds sweeping toward them down the Sound.

Then they were snug in the car again, pulling across the brown-green of the Kitsap Peninsula and on across Hood Canal Bridge to the mountains. She slipped across the seat to sit closer. He took his hand from the steering wheel and touched her face. "I love you," he said. "Could you—" There was a catch in his voice.

"What, sweetheart?"

"Could you hand me a Kleenex?"

She opened the glove compartment and pulled one out of the small box inside. He coughed into it, wiped his mouth, and put it into the garbage bag at her knees. His hand strayed to her leg. "You know, I don't have any family," he said.

"Yes. You told me the first night we met, remember? Losing your mom and then your father so quickly must have been really hard."

"We didn't really meet before that night, did we?"

She laid her cheek against the soft cotton of his shirt sleeve. She could feel his arm muscles move as he guided the car.

"I just want you to know that I might be a little awkward around your folks because it's been so long since I've had any family— To be around, I mean," he said. "I suppose I'm nervous." He grinned.

She smiled into his sleeve. "I love you. Don't worry. There are only three of them and Bobby's the only real pain. Besides, we'll be going back Sunday. It's not like it will last forever."

His hand stroked her leg, then went back to the wheel. "You're going to have to start giving me directions pretty soon," he said. "This is about as far as I've ever been."

There were only a few to give and those simple enough. He took his foot off the gas as they approached the farm driveway. He squeezed her hand. She kissed his shoulder, then moved away. She was sitting sedately beside the passenger window when they pulled up to the house.

She knew she'd have to work to keep the same distance between them all weekend. She only realized how hard it would be when they were inside the house. It wasn't easy to meet her mother's eyes without showing the way she felt about the man beside her. Especially difficult not to look at him when she talked, instead of at her mother.

And Bobby only made matters worse. Deb and Randy were sitting at the kitchen table when he came in. They were drinking tea and talking to her mother as she bustled about.

"Hiya," Bobby said. He dropped into the chair across the table. He stretched his legs out to their full length, looked down at the mud on his boots, then back at Randy and Deb.

"Randy, this is my brother Robert," Deborah said.

"Bobby," he said. He reached across the table and they shook hands.

"I'm pleased to meet you," Randy said.

Bobby nodded. "Any friend of Debs' a friend of mine." He turned his head. "When's dinner, Mom?"

"Another twenty minutes or so. Dad's working late, but he should be here soon."

His chair scraped back and he stood up. He went out without another look around, his boots clumping on the worn linoleum.

Deb jumped up and began to help set the table. Her mother filled the silence with questions about her new job, comments on the slacks she was wearing and awkward questions to Randy about his work.

The same subjects were commented on again at dinner, her mother pulling out topics of conversation and her father laconically acknowledging he heard the information she presented. Bobby was almost silent.

It all made Deb even more tense. She wished her mother would stop trying so hard to fill in the spaces. She realized her father was being ostentatiously normal and it irritated her. But Bobby's silence worried her most.

Either he'd changed drastically in the six months she'd been gone or he'd been warned not to say anything to "frighten Deb's young man away." And probably in those very words. Which meant he was capable of saying or doing almost anything.

Deb knew her mother was just trying to help. But waiting for the inevitable comment only made it worse. Her nerves were really on edge before it finally came, the next afternoon.

Randy had been asking questions about Bobby's old Ford pickup. He was only being polite, but only Deborah knew of his total ineptitude with mechanical things. She loved him for his questions, because she knew he was trying to get along with her brother. But Bobby was not likely to think a man who didn't understand mechanics was worth much.

Sure enough, Randy was invited to look at the engine. They came back into the house in a remarkably short time. Bobby helped himself to another piece of pie. Randy sat down beside Deb at the kitchen table. She'd been looking through a pile of old art magazines she'd bought during high school.

"For a lawyer, he sure don't know much," Bobby said to Deb. He scraped a chair back and sat down. He reached a hand for her magazine. "Whatya readin'?"

"For someone who's supposedly an adult, you certainly don't have any manners!" she snapped. She pulled the magazine away from him.

Bobby lifted the cover. "Art junk," he said. He looked at Randy. "You let her read that stuff, she'll be getting more ideas about how she's superior than she already has."

"I wouldn't control what she read even if I didn't like it," Randy said.

Bobby lifted his eyebrows and bit into his forkful of pie. "And here I thought you'd gone and gotten engaged," he said.

Deb closed the magazine. "You big— Can't you ever mind your own business?"

Randy's hand covered hers. "Even if we were, I wouldn't ask Deborah or anyone else to allow me to censor their reading, their thoughts or their actions," he said. "I don't know much about engines but I know about people. Telling or asking them not to do something when they see no benefit to themselves is an excellent way to get them to do it, not to deflect them from their intentions."

Bobby stared at him, then went back to his plate. He finished eating and put his plate and fork in the sink. He said goodbye politely enough as he left the room, but the door banged solidly behind him.

"I'm sorry," Deb said. She looked at the magazine.

"For what? I knew he was something of a nuisance. You've warned me enough times. I shouldn't have been so sharp with him though. He is your brother."

She raised her head. "Well, we only have tomorrow to get through." She smiled at him and shook her head. "Now you know what I was talking about."

17

Lately Lawrence had been wandering and begging in the Belltown area, just north of downtown. Here the glass and concrete office complexes were interspersed with old apartment buildings tattered by the grime of the streets. There were also several restaurants whose patrons didn't recognize him as a street regular. They were more apt to give him their doggy bags. And there was a soup kitchen that dispensed meals a few times a week.

Best of all, there was little danger of running into the old codger or his friends. Their territory was at the other end of downtown.

The soup kitchen was run by a large and somewhat shabby church. The people there were called "holy rollers" and "tongue jabberers" by more orthodox congregations. Lawrence knew about the labels. They used the names themselves sometimes. But he didn't understand what they meant and he didn't care.

This was the church he was in on Easter morning. He was only vaguely aware that it was Easter, but he knew there was a big feed planned for the street people.

He had come early, hoping to be able to sit a while in the big room that the food was usually served in. Maybe he could find a corner to himself. Maybe he could just sit and think and even write a little bit.

He knew he was hoping against hope, but it was still worth trying. He'd spent a miserably damp night in a dirty doorway and just the warmth would be a blessing. A real chair for a change, instead of hunching over his ankles to keep the warmth in. His small luxuries were worth fighting for.

But instead of quietness, he found a church service.

He'd slipped halfway through the door before he realized the room was three-quarters full of people. The service upstairs had overflown into the hall below. The preacher's voice was coming into the room through speakers attached to the ceiling in two corners.

The rows of chairs faced the speakers, away from the door. Nobody saw Lawrence and by the time he realized how many people were there, the room's warmth had done its work and he was inside.

They were all standing up, singing a hymn. The song was full of hand clapping and words that meant nothing to Lawrence, but it was happy and strong. The room was alive with it, reinforced with the echoes from the loudspeakers of the congregation upstairs.

He sat down on the chair nearest the door in the last row. He put his suitcase and bedroll on the floor. There were tables in the back of the hall with baskets of cold rolls and plates of lunch meat laid out on them. He could smell baking ham and roast turkey from the kitchen behind the tables.

His stomach growled. He wondered if he could steal a roll without anyone noticing, but the song had ended and the people were settling into their chairs.

Then a voice started talking over the static-filled speakers. Everyone in the room was listening, but they were talking too. All around the room were soft cries of "Yes, yes!", "Oh, please listen!" and "True! True!" Some of them had their heads bowed and most of them had closed their eyes. The voice must be praying, Lawrence decided. He bowed his head too.

One thing he'd never had much to do with was church. His parents had gone when he was very small, but only because they'd lived near his grandparents and were being nagged about it. When they'd moved to the West Coast all that had stopped.

He'd been five when they'd moved, so he didn't remember much. He knew it hadn't been at all like this. Cold and stiff were the words his mother had used. But then, that's how she felt about her in-laws, too.

They'd gone to the church that was most like them, he supposed. Fashioned their religious beliefs to their personalities, the way one's decisions were fashioned by one's own sense of history and one's sense of history molded by the personality you brought to it.

It was an interesting sidelight to the main thesis of his work. Under the rumble of the speakers in the corners and the encouraging calls of the audience in the room, Lawrence's own mutterings went unheeded. He formed his sentence carefully, then worked the paper and pen out of his pocket. He wrote it out laboriously, using his knee for support. It was an interesting concept, if only he could get some time and quiet to develop it further.

But time and quiet, warmth and food were the things he never seemed to have enough of. Even when he'd been in school or while he was at the camp teaching there wasn't enough. There was always something pestering, waiting to be finished, someone to be talked to.

And trying to find work was just as bad. It took every ounce of energy and every minute, searching through newspapers, walking from place to place, filling out applications, and being turned down. All the emotional strength you had was poured into facing rejections.

On the street it was even worse. Every minute was taken up by survival. Food and sleep were paramount. If you were lucky, you got a little water and soap to wash with thrown in.

He reread his sentence, retraced a few words, and carefully put the paper back in his pocket. There were scraping noises around him and he rose too, thinking the service was over. Now they could eat. But the congregation was getting ready to sing another song.

This was a slower one. When it was finished and he sat down again, he began to feel the warmth of the room. There was more singing from the speakers, but now the people in the room only listened. It was a slow, soothing song. He crossed his arms on his chest and his head nodded.

It jerked up again as a voice boomed into the microphone upstairs, then nodded down as it became more melodious. The voice was saying something about beauty and truth and Lawrence's eyes closed.

It was a good twenty minutes before they opened again. He felt better now, though his stomach was beginning to cramp from the hunger. He hadn't eaten anything since he'd found that half loaf of bread in the trash yesterday.

The voice was still going on. "And you will remember that my text this morning is not the ordinary Easter text," it said. "It is not 'He is risen,' though He is risen indeed. It is not 'The stone is rolled back,' though indeed the stone is rolled back. No, it is not even from one of the four well-loved Gospels in which we read the story of our Christ and His working while He walked among us. It is from the Old Testament that I take my text, for in the Old Testament we find the pure and powerful, the wise and wonderful prophecies of the coming and death and the resurrection of our Lord Jesus Christ!"

The voice fell. Lawrence's head nodded, then his eyes opened. "Now I want you all to turn with me to that book which is such a comfort to the soul when all other lights have failed, that book which contains so many wonderful prophecies of our Lord Jesus' coming. I want you to turn with me to the book of Psalms, to the twenty fourth Psalm and I want you to read with me the first verse."

Paper rustled as Bibles were opened and Lawrence's eyes drifted closed. They opened again as the preacher boomed into the microphone. Small voices in the upper and lower rooms read along ahead of and behind his reading.

"'The earth is the Lord's and the fullness thereof; the world, and they that dwell therein.' Now let's turn to another verse that uses this same word, this 'fullness.' This verse is in the New Testament, in the epistle of Paul to the church at Ephesus. It is in the book of the Ephesians, in chapter 3, verse 19. Just the last part now, just the last part of the verse. And it says, 'that ye might be filled with all the FULLNESS of God'! Now do you see what Paul is praying for the Ephesians, beloved? The fullness of God is the very fullness of the earth itself, of springtime and harvest, of sun, moon and stars! God owns everything. He is the keeper of all and He will give us His FULLNESS!"

His voice rumbled lower again and Lawrence's eyelids faltered in spite of himself. It was too warm and he was too tired and hungry to follow the argument properly. Yet what he had heard wouldn't let him sleep. The voice went on and Lawrence listened through the fog of his weariness.

Finally the service was over. The congregation provided an excellent dinner for themselves and the people who crowded in at the alley door. Lawrence gorged his fill, but his heart wasn't totally in it. He didn't stay for the third round of food. Instead he wandered out into the faltering spring sunlight.

He paced the familiar stained concrete with a new refrain in his head. He was hardly aware of where he had found it, but it was a magical promise and he clung to the words. An incantation to give him hope.

"The earth is the Lord's and the fullness thereof. The earth is the Lord's and the fullness thereof. Aren't we all the Lord's creatures? So the fullness is mine too. The earth is the Lord's and the fullness thereof. It's mine, too, the earth's fullness. I should get part of it, too. I'm a person too, though even I can hardly believe it anymore.

But by God I am. The earth is the Lord's and the fullness thereof. If it's His and I'm His then I deserve part of the fullness."

He switched his suitcase and bedroll to ease the pressure on his hands. "The earth is the Lord's and the fullness thereof. The earth is the Lord's and the fullness thereof."

He repeated the phrase again and again as he tramped down the street. His graying and ragged raincoat flapped around his thin legs. His blue eyes stared from under his matted hair. He didn't see the anxious looks of the people who passed him or the way the boys on the corner poked each other as he went by.

He kept repeating the words to himself. "The earth is the Lord's and the fullness thereof." They filled him with such hope that he didn't even pause to consider why he hadn't found them before.

Deborah and Randy made it safely through breakfast and Easter service. She was on edge, wondering what Bobby would do next. Randy hadn't said anything more about it. What had he thought of her outburst? Or what Bobby had said?

Bobby seemed to know he'd overstepped the bounds. He was on remarkably good behavior, though he did drag Andrew Simpson into the Easter dinner conversation at one point. Deb felt her mother's eyes on her as he mentioned Andy's latest tractor mishap and she answered with a steady look. Her only feeling was irritation with Bobby and her mother's inquisitiveness.

She was a little surprised herself at her lack of emotion. It wasn't even curiosity. Only a mild interest in the doings of someone she'd once known long ago.

She and Randy had agreed that they'd only stay an hour or two after dinner before heading back. The ferry traffic would be heavy the last day of the holiday weekend and they didn't want to get back at two in the morning.

Deb began helping her mother clear the table. Randy accepted an invitation from her father to take a tour of the farm and wood lot. He'd always wanted a small place of his own, he said. He'd like to see how they managed it.

"His idea of a small place of his own is a garden and a chicken house," Deb told her mother when they were gone. "He'd have a problem leaving a late meeting or court case to go milk his cows!"

"You could always do it," her mother said. Her head was bent over the roasting pan as she scraped it clean.

"Mother, just because I bring a friend who happens to be male home to meet you doesn't mean I'm going to marry him!"

She looked up. "He hasn't asked yet?"

Deborah put the plates in the cupboard and shut the door firmly.

"It's so obvious that he likes you," her mother said.

"Like is not love. And love is not marriage. Not necessarily. And not immediately, even then." She picked up the dish towel. "You're jumping to conclusions." She put the serving bowl firmly onto its shelf and rattled the pans into the cupboard. "Doesn't the cake pan go on this shelf anymore?"

She was still jerky and tight lipped when the men came back from their tour. She was the first to suggest it was time she and Randy were leaving.

The goodbyes and collections of luggage took another half hour. Deb was using the trip to collect the drawing materials she'd left in a corner of her room in September and had to find a box to put them in.

They were finally down the driveway and gone. Randy reached across the seat to her knee. "We're out of sight now," he said. He grinned at her.

She gave him a small smile and slid across the seat. He took her hand.

"I like your family," he said.

She laid her cheek against his upper arm. "You don't have to be polite," she said. "I know Bobby was a pain. And Dad probably bored you to death, wandering around the farm."

"Your father and I had a very good talk." She pulled back to look at his face. "Actually, Bobby seemed to be on his best behavior, from what you've told me."

She looked out the window. "He could have tried a little harder."

"Male dominance seems very important to him. It must be difficult to establish his superiority when he has an older sister who's so talented and pretty."

"You think I'm talented. I'm sure the thought never entered his head."

"Hmmmm." They drove on a while in silence. He took his hand from her leg to negotiate the curves and she looked at the greenery.

"I hadn't realized how hungry I was for the woods," she said softly. "They used to seem so menacing and dark. Like they'd closed out all the life I had in me. Now they're almost reassuring."

"Still a country girl at heart?"

"I've never really thought about it. Maybe. Though I like the color and noise of the city."

He nodded. "I was only half serious when I told your father I wanted a small farm of my own, but the idea does appeal to me. Just a place to get out in the woods, if only on weekends."

"I wondered how you were going to coordinate late meetings with milking the cows."

"Why? Surely you know how to milk."

"That's a man's job. Besides, my hands are too small." Her cheek was against his upper arm again.

"Chauvinist," he said. His hand moved toward her lap, then back to the wheel. He looked straight ahead. "Would you want that?"

"What?"

"A small farm."

She tried to answer him casually. "I don't know. Maybe on weekends. It would give me a chance to draw from nature."

"You know that I love you, don't you?" He kept his hands on the steering wheel.

"Yes." She put her hand on his thigh.

"Deb— Maybe I'm ridiculously old fashioned, but I wanted to meet your parents and talk to your father before I really proposed." He was still looking straight ahead. "It's ridiculous, but even though I know you love me, I'm still afraid to ask it."

She turned sideways on the seat, looking at him. She touched his cheek. "Can you really doubt the way I feel about you?"

There was a long pause. He turned his head.

"Yes," she said softly.

The car swerved violently. The car horn squawked behind them and Randy pulled to the side of the road. Two cars and a truck drove past. The people in them looked at Randy curiously.

He reached for her. "Get you to marry me and then try to kill you," he muttered into her hair.

They sat there a long time. He explained again that the trip around the farm had been for the purpose of asking her father's "permission." She took a long look at him, breathed in and then explained the reason for Bobby's remark about Andrew.

The story took less time than she'd thought it would. Almost as if it had happened to somebody else. She tried to explain that too, and he shook his head.

"You don't care?"

"It's not that I don't care. I wish it hadn't happened. After all, you were hurt." His face went into her hair again. "The guy was a jerk. And you were too innocent to realize what he was up to." He pushed away to smile at her. "But I love you. That doesn't change. I could wish it hadn't happened, but things like that do, all the time. It's not the end of the world and it's not the worst of all possible sins. You did a dumb thing. I've done dumb things myself."

She waited for him to go on.

He grinned. "Not that kind of dumb thing, as it happens. I know, men are supposed to." He hesitated. "I guess I'm pretty strait-laced. It's not God or morality, though maybe it actually is. I've had urges but I've never loved anyone enough to follow through on them."

"You mean you've never—"

His expression was somewhere between guilt and laughter. "No."

Her lips twitched. "Just shows you how liberated we are. We've switched the old roles completely. Man forgiving woman for wild oats, not woman man!"

His mouth tightened. "There is no forgiveness needed. Only understanding."

"I love you."

His arms tightened round her again.

18

"The earth is the Lord's and the fullness thereof," Lawrence muttered the next morning as he knocked on the door of the cottage beside the old house he'd lived in before. A small girl opened the door. She stared at him.

"—fullness thereof," he muttered. May I speak to your father?" he asked the girl. She shook her head.

"Is the manager here?" he asked. She nodded. "Will you please get him?" She disappeared into the back. "The earth is the Lord's and the fullness thereof." He looked at the worn wooden porch.

A short stout Asian woman shuffled into the hall. She wore a pair of men's slippers on her feet and a large apron over her polyester dress. "What I do for you?" she asked harshly.

"I'm looking for a room," he said.

"You have speak husband. He over there." She waved a hand next door. She peered at Lawrence. "You can't stay always," she said.

"And the fullness thereof," he said to himself.

"What you say?"

"Where is he over there?"

"He fix light two one two," she said. She watched him go down the steps.

He found the manager in the downstairs hallway, and told him the work he'd gotten hadn't panned out. He needed housing again.

The old man looked at him. "Don't have." He walked down the hall.

Lawrence followed him. "You must have something." The earth is the Lord's and the fullness thereof. It was in the pulsing of the blood in his head. The earth is the Lord's and the fullness thereof. "You must have something," he said again.

The manager stopped. He looked at him. "Come back to house," he said.

See, the voice in Lawrence's brain whispered. The earth is the Lord's and the fullness thereof. There is something and it is yours.

Lawrence followed the old man, trying not to show his excitement. You just had to ask and to take, because it's yours if you ask and you take, the voice murmured. And you should ask because you're the Lord's; the minister said so and the earth is the Lord's and the fullness thereof. You deserve some of the fullness. The earth is the Lord's and the fullness thereof—

They were at the manager's house. The woman came out of a back room as they came in. She pursed her lips when she saw Lawrence. The manager said something to her in another language and when she answered she flashed her small black eyes at Lawrence and then back at the man. She moved her hand jerkily. The gesture was obscurely threatening.

Lawrence watched her. "The earth is the Lord's and the fullness thereof," he told himself softly. The woman looked at him again, then at the man. She spat out a single syllable and shuffled back down the hall. There was the sound of furniture grating on wooden floors. A drawer shut with a dull thud.

The old man went to a desk. He pulled out a large piece of paper. It was a rough sketch of the floor plan next door. Into each room was penciled a name or group of names. He studied it, pulled a pencil from another drawer and motioned to Lawrence. He jabbed the pencil at a small space.

"This four floor. What you call attic. Small room. Somebody already there. Young man with big voice. He gone most of day to look work. You have quiet." He looked at Lawrence. "Other all full."

Lawrence looked at the drawing.

"It all I have," the man said.

"All right."

It was the only door at the very top of the stairs. He would be using the same bathroom on the third floor that he'd used before. There was no point in the manager showing the way and Lawrence went up the wooden stairs by himself.

There was no one in the room, but it was definitely occupied. One of the beds was cluttered with neckties, slightly frayed shirts and shoe-polishing equipment. The other was pushed back under the eaves on the opposite side. It held nothing but a bare mattress. There was a rickety wooden shelf made of an old fruit box hanging near its head.

Lawrence unrolled his sleeping bag, took his overcoat off, and pulled out his paper and pen. He'd go out begging after the other fellow came back.

The silence closed in around him and he began writing. He hadn't bothered to look out the dust-smeared window at the sidewalk and street below. There were only small houses, with more small houses beyond. The dismalness wouldn't have mattered if he had looked. His mind was on the papers he had spread out on the book on his knee.

But the heat of the room and the dusty light filtering through the window weren't good conditions for concentrated thought. In the middle of a sentence, hunched in the center of the cot trying to get the words right, his body got the best of him.

He was startled awake by a loud pounding on the unpainted door.

"Hello, hello, hello!" a male voice called. The door opened. A square blond head looked in at him. A thirtyish, stocky man in a brown suit came in.

Lawrence rubbed his hand over his face. He sat up and began folding his papers. "Hello," he said.

"Manager warned me I had a roommate. Thought I'd let you know I was coming before I got here, in a manner of speaking." He scooped up the ties on the other cot. "My name's Jack. I'm just sort of passing through while I scout out some labor to put these here fingers of mine to." He cracked his knuckles expansively. "Mail room, delivery, lugging lumber, pushing buttons, anything somewhat manual, that's me. Jack of all trades, in a manner of speaking." He laughed.

Lawrence looked at him. Jack began moving around the room, putting the ties in one place and then another. "Won't be here long. Got a couple of tracers out there that are looking real positive. Lots of other people looking out there, so it takes time, it takes time. But the right attitude keeps you going when all else fails, in a manner of speaking. Been here a week and I've got some contacts made and some prospects already. Just have to keep pushing, in a manner of speaking. What do you do?"

He really had stopped. "I— I write," Lawrence said. No, that made him sound like a journalist or something. "About history and ideas," he said.

But Jack wasn't listening. "Writing! Now that's something you can really make pay, if you do it right, if you know what I mean. Gotta get the right angle and then go for it, in a manner of speaking! Now here's a book I've been reading. I'm not much of a one for a book, but this one is different. No hoity-toity ideas, pie in the sky kind of stuff, but really practical things. It's idea stuff all the same, if you know what I mean, but more logical, more to the point."

He dropped the ties onto the bed again and pulled a paperback from the bottom of his pile of shoe-cleaning paraphernalia. He waved it at Lawrence. "Now this is a book to give you a new way of looking at things without it being all sugar and spice and everything nice, if you know what I mean. This guy says all you got to do is think positive. You repeat things to yourself and you write them, but I'm not much of a one for writing things down so I say them. Saying comes more natural to me, in a manner of speaking.

Like you say, 'I, Jack Bracket am ready for a new and exciting position.' Position means job, in a manner of speaking. And you say it and you say it and pretty soon you get so excited 'cause you start to believe it and you go out and get busy and then it comes true!"

Lawrence stretched out on top of his sleeping bag. The earth is the Lord's and the fullness thereof, he said to himself silently. The manager was right. This was a guy with a big voice. It was a good thing he'd be out looking for work every day.

As Lawrence closed his eyes, Jack was still waving the book. He was telling him how its author had made his first million. Lawrence nodded to show he was listening and drifted into sleep once again.

~~~

Deb felt so alive with her secret when she got to work the next morning that she was sure everyone would see it. But no one looked at her twice.

Finally, just before lunch, she mentioned casually that she and Randy had gone to her parents for Easter.

"Hmmmm." Ev picked at a piece of tape stuck to the edge of her board. "Have a good time?"

"Well, my brother being what he is, not especially. Though the drive back was wonderful."

"Hmmmm."

Deb looked at Ev's placid face. "Randy liked my parents."

"Parents liking the boyfriend is usually the bigger question," Ev said. She examined the tip of her pencil. "They can make more noise about likes and dislikes than the man himself will."

"Well, they must have. My mother kept asking if he'd proposed yet."

Ev reached for another pencil and frowned at the line she'd just drawn. Deb watched while she carefully drew it again. She shaded
~~~

a corner and leaned back. She looked at Deb. "And that's all?" she asked.

"I didn't think you were interested."

"Figured you'd want to tell it your own way."

"You rat! I think you knew when I walked in here that he'd proposed!"

"I figured something was up, the way you've been dancing around all morning." She waved a hand at Deb's empty work board. "Now that you've told me, you can get something done."

Deb grinned and pulled the next project out of the basket. She pinned the rough sketch to her board and got out clean paper. "Did you know?" she asked.

"Now how would I? But I've been around long enough to recognize the difference between secrets that don't want to be told and secrets that do. This was obviously one you wanted to tell."

"And you weren't going to give me the satisfaction of being asked what it was!"

"It was more fun watching you figure out how to tell it without being too obvious about what you were doing."

Deb made a face at her and looked at the sketch. She reached for her pencil. "I may be late getting back from lunch."

"Okay."

"We're going looking for rings. He didn't want to choose one I might not like and I'll have to get his anyway. I'd rather not make the decision myself. He'll be wearing it for a long time. I want it to be something he likes."

"Ummm."

Ev was working again. Deb watched her. Ev turned her head. Her hand went to her blouse, then her hair. "What's the matter?" she asked.

"Oh nothing."

Now it was Ev's turn to watch. Deb shaded in the shadows she'd just outlined. "Is this going to make a difference in your job?" Ev asked.

"What? Our engagement? No, of course not. Why should it?"

"Well, being a lawyer, his wife won't exactly have to work. Won't you want to just decorate your house and make fancy dinners and things?"

"You make it sound boring."

"It would be, for me. It may be for you."

Deb shook her head. "I hadn't thought about it. I mean, we haven't talked about it." She looked at the ad on her board. "Much as I like it— I wonder just how much we'd have." She looked up at Ev. "What I'd really like to do, if I could do anything at all, would be to go back to school."

"Art school?"

"Not exactly. Commercial art or graphics. Illustration, I guess."

She nodded. "I think you'd be pretty good at it. And it's not like the heavy arts. You can make a living at it. But will he let you?"

"He likes my drawing. I mean, he's forever encouraging it. I don't see why he'd be against it. But it'd be pretty rotten, getting married and then not paying my way."

"You could work part time."

"I wouldn't exactly be paying my half. And I'd get so busy we'd never see one another."

Ev didn't answer. She sat like an old Buddha, slouched on her stool, staring at nothing. At last she stirred. She leaned forward and looked out the small window with the green plants in their neat row. "I'd find out before you got anything settled, rings and dates and all that," she said without turning her head. She went back to work.

At lunch time, Deb was still thinking about what she'd said.

She and Randy were sitting in his car eating hamburgers he'd picked up on his way to meet her. They were parked at the side of the street. The rain drizzled on the windows. The tires of the cars moving past them made swishing noises on the wet blacktop.

She picked at the lettuce at the edge of her burger. "Randy, I have a question that's going to sound really greedy."

"You haven't got a greedy bone in your body."

She grinned at him. "You hope."

"What is your question?"

"How much money do you make? I mean, is it going to be necessary for me to work after we're married?"

"I don't see why you should if you don't want to. I'm bringing in twenty-five thousand a year now. That's not a whole lot, but I'm due for a raise to thirty and if we're careful it shouldn't be a problem." He frowned at her. "But I thought you liked what you're doing? I'm not going to ask you to quit, if that's what you're asking. I want you to be happy and I know what your art means to you."

"Well, it's not that exactly. I mean, I don't want to quit drawing. I've been thinking lately about maybe doing more with it. But, of course, I couldn't because I had to work eight hours a day and there wasn't a lot of time or money left over."

"You mean, maybe go back to school? That's great, if that's what you want." He bit into his sandwich and nodded at her. "You know, if we got married this summer like we talked about yesterday, then you could start this fall at the beginning of the school year."

"But what about money?"

"Well, it'll depend on where you want to go, but we should be able to manage. We might get a loan or something, then when you start using what you've learned, we can pay it back."

"I won't exactly be earning my keep."

"But we'll be married." He frowned at her. "My check will be yours as much as mine. I mean, I hope that's how you'll feel about it."

She nodded slowly, surprised at the sudden tears on her face. She rummaged in the glove box for a tissue.

He drew her toward him, almost upsetting the hamburger in her lap. She lifted it onto the dash and snuggled into his side.

"Did you really think I was going to demand that you earn your keep?"

She shrugged. "Well, you know. You read about how people get married but everything's divided between them."

"I'm not that liberated." He put his face in her hair and she closed her eyes. He chuckled. "On the other hand, you were half afraid I'd ask you to stay home and keep house all day long, weren't you?"

"Well, some people do, you know. My father'd have fits if my mother even thought about working. Not that she would. Woman's place is in the home and all that stuff."

"I may be old-fashioned about some things, but I believe in that kind of arrangement about as much as you do." He squeezed her to him. "But you know that."

She pulled away, staring into the grayness. "I guess. Yes, I did. But sometimes— There are so many kinds of things that people believe now and anything is possible and here I'd gone and said I'd marry you without finding out how we would actually work things and I was afraid maybe I'd made another mistake." She turned her head, watching the windshield wipers on a passing car try futilely to clear the glass.

He handed her her hamburger. "Make no mistake, my dear. You're stuck with me and I'm stuck with you and I'm so glad about it that you could ask me to walk across Lake Washington and I'd do it."

She laughed through her tears and moved away to bite into her sandwich. "I hope I'd have more sense than to ask that!"

"You would." He kissed her cheek. He started the engine and grinned at her. "That's why I said it." He flipped the turn signal on and swung the wheel slightly. "Now let's go see about getting a ring and making this official."

The next morning there was the problem of breakfast. Lawrence slipped out while Jack was dressing. He wanted to see what he could find in the garbage cans behind the grocery.

His foraging was successful and he hid in an alley nearby until he saw Jack leave the building. Then he bounded quickly in and up the stairs before anyone else could see him.

There had been food enough for a meal. A loaf of stale bread and some half-rotten apples. Lawrence had learned the hard way about apples and he nibbled around the bad spots like a finicky rabbit. He forced the bread down with water from the bathroom tap. Then it was time to write.

This was going to work better than he'd thought, if only Jack would leave him alone.

There was no question in Lawrence's mind that the guy was at least slightly crazy. Positive thinking could get you into the unemployment line just as fast as negative thinking. You might not be admitting to yourself that was where you were going, but that's still where you'd be.

But if he was busy chasing contacts he would be leaving Lawrence in peace. Lawrence settled onto the cot with his papers spread out onto a book large and smooth enough to write on. He rubbed his face with his hand and picked up his pen. Now. Where was he, anyway?

He wrote for a few hours, forced down more of the bread, and went back to work. The warmth of the house crept into the attic and made his mind buzz. He'd spent too many nights hunched into corners, always half-awake, and his body craved rest. He drifted into a deep sleep.

Suddenly the door crashed open. The alarm clock on the other side of the room said five o'clock. Jack bounced in.

"Hiya buddy! How're you doing this very fine day? Do you know, the sun's even out, in a manner of speaking. Haven't seen that in a while, now have we?"

He flung his jacket and a brown paper sack on the bed and went to look out the window. He came back, arranged the jacket carefully on a wire hanger and hung the hanger on one of the two nails near his cot. They were pounded into the sloping ceiling and the jacket dangled out at an angle, blocking the little light that filtered through the window.

He sat down on his cot and beamed at Lawrence. Lawrence rubbed his face with his hands. He smoothed out the paper that had fallen beside him and added it to the others. He folded them carefully. Jack watched him.

"So what new and exciting things have been happening to you?" he asked.

Lawrence looked up. "Oh, not much. How are you?" He put the papers and his pen into his overcoat pocket. He laid the overcoat on the cot and reached for his shoes.

"Well now, I may have found the absolutely perfect position!" Jack said. "Gotta go down and see a man about it tomorrow. Got the application right here. It's a humdinger, in a manner of speaking. They give you five hundred a week, can you beat that? Five hundred! And that's take-home, in a manner of speaking!"

Lawrence pulled a sweater over his head and pushed the hair from his face. Jack was watching him. "Doing what?" he asked.

"Sales," he said. "Selling the sweetest little hot tubs you ever did see. Pure luxury items they are, and people snapping 'em up like hot cakes, as you might say. Best way to be cool is to get a hot tub!" He laughed. "Hafta remember that one. Try it on the man I'm talking to tomorrow. Couldn't see me today. Too busy counting his money, in a manner of speaking."

Lawrence pulled on his overcoat.

"You going out huh? What kind of work you lookin' for in the evenings?"

Lawrence patted his pocket. The paper and pen were still there. "I'm going to get some food," he said.

"Ah, you don't want to do that." Jack held up the sack he'd brought in. He shook it. "I've got some cheese and some crackers and—" He lowered his voice. "A touch of some wine. Celebration, in a manner of speaking. Might as well start early, don't you think? You're welcome to join me."

Lawrence shook his head. He opened the door. Jack spilled the sack's contents onto his cot. There were three large hunks of cheese. One was pale gold, one a shade darker and one a creamy white. They lay beside a box of cheap crackers and a large glowing bottle of Port.

"There's more than enough for the two of us!" Jack said. "No point in going out, if it's only food you were looking for." He began to paw through the things in the box over his bed. Lawrence watched him. Jack pulled out two small water glasses. He reached for the wine.

"Go ahead," he said, gesturing with the bottle. "Open the crackers. Do you have a knife? Mine's pretty dull. Don't know if it'll cut hot butter, much less cheese, in a manner of speaking."

Lawrence went to his suitcase. He brought out his heavy kitchen knife. Jack beamed at him.

Jack dug into the food, stuffing cheese, then cracker, then wine, into his always-opening mouth. When he wasn't actually swallowing, he talked.

Lawrence had eaten well that day, by his standards, and the cheese and crackers were filling enough for the wine to only produce a good glow. He leaned back and listened to Jack.

"Saw a Rolls Royce today. A sleek gray with a chauffeur driving it and a man and woman in the back seat. She was all furs. From head to toe, as you might say." He shook his head, spattering cracker crumbs. He swiped at his mouth with his hand.

He gulped down his wine and filled the glass again from the jug. "This stuff ain't so bad if you keep drinking it, huh? Gonna have me a Rolls one of these days. A gray-silver one, just like the one I saw, with a lady beside me all rigged out in furs and diamonds, going someplace fancy to eat. Yessir, I'm gonna have it all, one of these days. Just gotta keep waiting and working, as you might say. Gotta keep moving ahead, in a manner of speaking."

He looked at Lawrence. "What did you say your book was about again? Maybe I could help. Do the promotion and the sales end and stuff. Get you into the movies, man, that's the way to make money. Gotta think Hollywood, you wanta strike it rich with the books! Gotta think movies, if you know what I mean! Here, have some more wine. There's plenty for everyone, in a manner of speaking."

He filled Lawrence's glass again, unsteadily. He lifted the bottle to eye level and looked at the deep red of its color. He set it back down on the floor. "Sure is pretty," he sighed.

He looked at Lawrence. "What'd ya say your book was about? History? Ideas?" He shook his head sadly. "Don't see how you can do much with that." He bent down toward the bottle again. "That sure is pretty," he muttered.

Lawrence looked at the wine in his glass. His brain was working slowly but the wine made everything seem clearer. No, there probably wasn't a whole lot of commercial possibility in what he was doing. But it was an important idea. He knew it in his bones, felt it in the air that he breathed.

Though putting the concepts into words was the most difficult thing he'd ever done. And most fascinating. Better than sex for absorbing every ounce of physical and emotional energy. Surely something that important to him would matter to other people. It would be important with or without him.

"You never can tell," he said to his glass.

"Huh?" Jack's head came up from the side of the bed. "Whew, that was a little too fast." He moved his forefinger back and forth slowly. "Gotta slow down or my head'll pop off, if you know what I mean."

He leaned back against the wall. He blinked slowly. "You know, the idea of history isn't a very good selling point. Not 'less you dress it up with lots of scandal and sex and good stuff like that." He put his head forward to look into Lawrence's face. "Somehow you don't seem the type, in a manner of speaking."

Lawrence smiled, thinking about the arguments he'd worked on so hard. The view of the Church during the Renaissance about Greece and Rome. The feelings in America about England's expansionism and the result: Monroe and his doctrine.

"Not scandal or sex," he said slowly. The wine was beginning to work on his tongue. He touched the knife, its edge smudged with cheese. "Things better than that. Sharper and cleaner and more to the point."

Jack laughed and slapped at his knee. "More to the point than sex, huh? That's a good one. I'd like to see that! Hey, why don't you let me read it, anyways. Get an idea if what you've got has any hope, in a manner of speaking. So you'd know if you had anything worth going on with, if you know what I mean."

Lawrence picked up the knife. "You leave it be," he said quietly. There was a tension in his voice that even Jack couldn't miss.

Lawrence began to clean the cheese from the knife's blade with his thumbnail. Jack edged away from him and watched. Lawrence slid off the cot. He carried the knife to his bed and bent over his suitcase, muttering.

"What'd you say?" Jack got up. Lawrence turned around, still holding the knife.

"You leave it alone," he said. "You'd better leave it alone." Jack shrank back melodramatically. He sat down on his cot without taking his eyes from Lawrence's face and hands.

Lawrence put the knife in the suitcase and began getting ready for bed. He was asleep before Jack had turned off the light.

19

If the weeks of courtship had gone by in a whirl, the weeks of engagement seemed even more kaleidoscopic.

The ring on her finger was both a promise and a pledge already spoken and binding. Deborah found herself watching it while she worked. No matter how often it caught her eye, she was always a little startled at the glint of the stone in the light.

Actually, they were seeing even less of each other. Randy was swamped with a court case that had come up after Easter and he was working nights to gather material and meet clients.

"It's just as well," his voice murmured over the phone that afternoon as she leaned on her drawing board and tried to look relaxed. "I can't seem to keep my hands off you!"

She laughed shakily. "I don't want you to."

"But if we're going to wait—"

"Yes."

She drooped over the board even more after they had finally said their good-byes.

They had decided, in the first triumphant flush of their love, that they would wait until their wedding night to fully consummate it. They were strong and their love was pure. Higher than mere lust. They would prove its goodness by following the old-fashioned rules.

Deborah's lips came together, remembering the salt taste of his mouth. Her hand touched her upper arm and she could feel his arms around her shoulders. The smooth warmth of his skin—

She forced herself to reach for a pencil, breaking the spell. But when Ev came back into the room her face was still flushed, her legs prim on the stool as she tried not to feel the warm tightness between them. She erased the line she'd just drawn. The feel of his hands—

She ripped the paper off the board. She threw it at the trash can and it bounced off the edge. Her stool scraped on the floor as she got down to pick up the paper.

Ev looked up from her board. "That's the third sheet in an hour," she said.

Deb sat back down on her stool. "Never mind," she said. Her throat was dry. She picked up her pencil and tossed it into the container at the top of her board.

"And I thought you said you were happy in love."

"Very funny." Deb reached for another sheet of paper.

"Try not to ruin that one too."

Deb looked at her.

"Hey, I'm kidding, I'm kidding."

"I'm sorry, Ev," she said. "It's not you. It's just everything else."

"Want to tell me about it?"

"There's nothing to tell." It would sound so silly. Who had a problem anymore with whether or not they should go to bed with the man that they loved? Were going to marry? If you went by the magazines, "my fiancée" was another way of saying "the person I'm living with."

Deb shook her head. "I'll be okay." She smoothed the paper onto her board and smiled at her through damp eyelashes. "It's nothing that can't be lived with."

"Anytime you need to talk about it, just say so."

She nodded and tried to work. But her pencil kept wandering off, into lines which turned into Randy's eyes or his hair or his hands. Such nice hands, smooth but not soft, strong but not rough and work-hardened. She forced herself back to the work on her board.

The effort was exhausting and she walked wearily home through the rain, hardly noticing the dripping at her umbrella's edge. It was late April now and they had decided to be married in August in the country church her mother attended so faithfully.

And what would her mother say if she knew of her yearnings? Her wild wish to just get it over with, her most secret fear that he somehow didn't want her, and that that was the real reason they waited. That was ridiculous, she told herself as she went up the stairs. She opened the door and dropped her coat, hat and purse on the table. She flopped down on the couch and stared at the plants in the window.

Her mother would be horrified. She'd had enough things to say about "immoral" magazines when Deb had been living at home. And then it had only been Seventeen and Vogue. What would her mother think about the magazines she'd been looking at last night?

They preached sex as if it were almost a cure-all. An ideal way to get rid of nervous tension. The thing to be practiced until your technique was perfected, like yoga. They talked about intimacy, about love, as if they were secondary to the great act itself. Even AIDS was only something to protect yourself from. Not anything to keep sex from taking place.

Yet her mother ignored it. Deb had learned "the facts" in junior high health class. All she'd had were those facts and her mother's assertion, like a physical law, that one couldn't have babies unless married. That and the awful fumbling in a parked car the night she thought Andrew's insistence meant he loved and would marry her.

For all her reading, haircut and clothing, she was as innocent as any third-grader about love, sex and the magical way they drew themselves into each other. All she had were facts, assumptions and reading. And her own feelings.

It was her feelings that were the trouble. The physical inability to think about anything except him. The frightening way each thought became physical. The strange ache in her bowels and the dampness between her legs, throbbing for she hardly knew what.

So she lay on the couch, with a ring on her finger, a wedding and all its details to plan, the promise of school and security in the fall, and was miserable.

It wasn't something she could share. Ev would know. Deb knew that she would. But how could she admit to the way she felt? To say she didn't have control of her desires, that she hardly knew what to call them, would be admitting she wasn't as liberated as any decent young woman should be.

She looked at the magazines stacked beside the couch. Some help they'd been. They only told her about mechanics. Or nonsense about "talking it out."

They had talked. And they had decided. The problem was that she wasn't sure anymore if she wanted to hold to that decision. That's what it amounted to. She ran her hand through her hair. Randy. She just wanted Randy. Was that wrong? And she wanted him now, not in late August. Three or four months. Oh God, how could she stand it?

But to tell him she wanted to discuss their decision— It wasn't just modesty. Somewhere inside her was a deep fear. Two fears, when she thought about it.

"Andy," she said bitterly. Funny that the names could be so similar, the people so different. "But if I tell him I want—that— then aren't I saying I want only that? I just need it and not him?" She sat up.

"But that's not true!" she cried to the plants in the window. "It's not! I don't feel the same way toward Randy as I did about him. I don't think I felt anything about him, really. I just wanted love and escape from the farm."

She chuckled. What was it Bobby had said about Andrew and his new bride? They were living with his parents in the old farm house until their new place was ready on the back forty. He was going to continue helping his dad for a share of the profits and try to find logging work to supplement it. His wife was already pregnant. Some escape that would have been.

Oh, Randy was better in every way. But the fear rose again. Was she just aching so hard herself that she couldn't tell if he needed her as she needed him?

And maybe he didn't. She bit the back of her hand. To begin the long searching all over again— And he kept saying things like he had this afternoon. "I can't keep my hands off you." Wasn't that a declaration of need?

She fell asleep on the couch with her clothes on, remembering his words and his voice, comforting herself with the promise of his desire.

Jack didn't offer food to Lawrence again. His cheeriness had a wary edge to it and he stayed away longer. His own job search wasn't going well and his money was running low.

One evening he came back even later than usual. "Hiya!" he said. He thumped down on his cot and pulled off his shoes. He leaned against the wall and looped his hands behind his head. Lawrence nodded at him and began folding his papers away.

"Went down to the soup kitchen at that mission in Pioneer Square today," Jack said.

Lawrence pressed a crease in a piece of paper, making sure the edges were together evenly.

"Getting low on my money," Jack said. "Thought I'd save a few pennies and see how the volunteer services provided, in a manner of speaking."

Lawrence reached for his suitcase. He lifted out his knife and began making small changes in the way his clothes were arranged.

"Saw a friend of yours there," Jack continued. "Said he was, anyway. The guy he described sounded like you, that's for sure."

Lawrence slid his papers into the suitcase. He patted the clothing around the manuscript into position and laid the knife carefully on top. The earth is the Lord's and the fullness thereof, he said to himself. The earth is the Lord's and the fullness thereof. He would drown out the crazy voice across the room if he said it enough.

Almost drown it, anyway. It seemed as if it had always been there, pounding at him. He was hearing it at night now, in his sleep, and he had to repeat his charm several times to get its spurious cheerfulness out of his head. The earth is the Lord's and the fullness thereof. The earth is the Lord's and the fullness thereof— He shook his head as if there were a fly in his face.

"—in a manner of speaking," Jack said. "Anyway, this old codger— That's what he called himself. That sound familiar to you? He says to say hi and come see him sometime. He's at the usual place and Mother's been asking about you. That's what he said."

Lawrence snapped the suitcase shut. The earth is the Lord's and the fullness thereof. The earth— He rubbed his hand over his face.

"Who's Mother, anyway? Don't tell me your mother is here and you've been ignoring her?" Jack laughed. "That's not a good way to stay in her will, in a manner of speaking."

Lawrence gripped the handle of the suitcase. His mother? No, she wasn't here. He hadn't thought about her in weeks. That was one load of guilt he'd learned how to handle. He wasn't going to take it up again, either. But the old codger didn't know her, anyway. He must have meant Sister Ann.

"No," he said. He slid the suitcase under the bed.

"But the soup there ain't too bad, if you can stand the smell— 'No' what?" Jack demanded.

"She isn't my mother."

"The woman at the mission? Didn't say she was!" He looked at Lawrence. "Oh you mean the one the old codger was talking about? He was calling her mother too, or it sounded like it. You related or something?"

"No."

Suddenly Lawrence pulled the suitcase out from under the cot and undid the latches. He held up the kitchen knife, ran his finger along the blade and turned to look at the murky light from the window. "No," he said again.

Jack fell silent.

Lawrence replaced the knife, refastened the case and put it back under the bed. Jack slid off his cot and began laying out his clothes for the next day and getting ready for bed. He lay down facing the room, his eyes opening every few minutes to gaze at Lawrence. Finally Lawrence lay down. Jack rolled to the wall and began breathing rhythmically.

Lawrence looked at the sloping ceiling. The earth is the Lord's and the fullness thereof. The earth is the Lord's and— He stared up at the bare boards. The old codger was asking for him. What had Jack told him? Sister Ann was asking too. Did she know he had failed? That he was simply living on the streets in a different section of the city?

After all, that was what he was doing. He rubbed his hand over his face. The square jaw of Sister Ann wouldn't leave his mind. She'd tried to give him a chance. But it had been her kind of chance, not his. Manual labor, not that of the mind.

Not that there had been any manual labor, even if he had wanted it. But to be honest, he hadn't, and the guilt descended again. The pain in the gut he'd become so familiar with those first days in the city. Guilt for not really wanting the jobs advertised. Anger that he wasn't qualified for work that he felt was beneath his abilities. And then guilt again because somewhere a voice murmured that if he'd really tried he could have found something.

And here it came once again. The writing and thinking had pushed it into a corner but it had only festered, not disappeared.

No reasoning would rid him of it. Here was Jack, trying with all he had and not getting anywhere. He was eating in soup kitchens this week. Who knew what next week would bring? Especially if he listened to the old codger's blandishments about "the good life."

But Lawrence knew it was no one's weakness but his own. If he could have known what he wanted and gone for it from the beginning— He'd only known what he didn't want. No teaching. No straightjacket of squeezing the mind into small enough portions for unwilling brains to swallow without nourishment.

And no selling. That was only a different kind of straightjacket. Yanking every stray thought into subservience to the great god of public relations and positive thinking.

But the casual life of the laborer wasn't allowed. No responsibilities but lifting a few boxes a few hours a day. That was as difficult to achieve as the others.

And only a different type of confinement, in the end. A narrowing of focus that the people who hired laborers knew someone with a few years of college wasn't fit for. He was trained to think and they didn't want people who might be distracted by what was going on in their brains. But then, that seemed to be true everywhere he had looked.

And then there were the janitor and security guard companies. The rub-your-face-in-the-dirt jobs. He had cringed at the thought of them but after a few weeks of silence would have begged on his knees for a few hours a week.

But there were more than enough people willing to be walked on for a few dollars an hour. By the time he'd been interested, the labor rolls were more than full. The great god of commerce replete, chewing his victims mercilessly, telling those begging for his mouth's carnivorous warmth that he was full. He wasn't interested in eating them, too.

The earth is the Lord's— No. There was no magic in the words now. Lawrence recognized the sentence bleakly for what it was. An incantation.

He turned his head. He did have this room. The mouth on the other cot made it unbearable, but still he did have it. How long? His mind fumbled back through the days, trying to remember. How long had he been here and how long could he stay?

And then on the street again. He shivered in the room's stuffy heat. Out on the street, his work still not finished.

It wouldn't be so bad if that were done. At least he'd have accomplished something. It wasn't right that they should control him like this. He did know what he wanted to do. Somehow, some way, the book. To pull hazy almost-nothing concepts from his brain and form them into concrete ideas. To put the ideas into words and the words onto paper in forms clear and worthy of being quoted. That's what he wanted.

But it wouldn't sell, as Jack had pointed out so helpfully. Couldn't or wouldn't, because they wouldn't listen. Jack and the rest of the world so much like him.

Lawrence lay in his sleeping bag, his fingers pulling at each other angrily. So much power, so much energy, flowing through him and nowhere to turn it. Unqualified. No experience. The one thing he was qualified for nobody cared about. A book about ideas, about history? No salability, in a manner of speaking.

And there was Jack's voice again, getting into his head, shutting out the sounds of his own thoughts. "Shut up!" he said sharply, into the darkness.

Jack's cot creaked. "Who's there?" he asked.

"Nothing," Lawrence said.

"Mmmm." The cot creaked again.

"Nothing at all," Lawrence muttered. "That's what I am. Sister Ann says she wants to know. But she knows. She's just gloating, like all of the others. Another one not conformable. Not necessary.

Send them into the streets. Let them think they're being taken care of, with a few bowls of soup every week. Really, let them disappear into the grates on the sidewalks. Let them drown in the Sound or freeze on a bench. It doesn't matter. Not really. They're not conformable."

He stayed awake, muttering, in the long night. At last, as dawn broke, he slept.

20

Deb woke to a clear day and her fears the night before evaporated in the sunlight. She showered, ate and watered her plants. Randy and she needed each other. Maybe she would talk to him and maybe she wouldn't. It didn't seem as urgent this morning. Though who knew what would happen the next time she saw or spoke to him.

She found herself watching the telephone at work, willing it to ring. He'd had a late meeting last night, she reminded herself. She wouldn't be surprised if he got in late this morning.

The meeting was to have been an intense one, its end resulting in an out of court settlement. If it had worked they'd be able to see each other more than a few snatched moments a week. Though those few minutes were precious and she'd take them over nothing. Still, it would be nice—

He'd warned her that this kind of thing would happen. Too busy for even a phone call, he'd said, looking at her worriedly. "You will understand? You'll know that I still love you, even if I can't call?"

She'd nodded with tenderness at his fears, but now her stomach cramped viciously when the phone rang again. Ev answered it and shook her head at Deb as she spoke into the receiver.

"Sorry, wrong number," she quipped as she put it down. "You and Randy at odds about something?"

"He's real involved in a case, so he can't call." Deb grinned. "There's nothing wrong with hoping, though."

"He gets so involved that he forgets to call?"

"He gets busy and has to keep his mind focused on what he's doing. Keep all the pieces of the puzzle in his head, is how he puts it."

"Ummm. That makes sense. Still, I can see why you're antsy. Either all kinds of attention, or none at all. Lots of time or no time to turn around in. You both better have a lot of understanding about each other's schedules, or you're going to have problems."

"Why?"

"Well, art is the same way. Deadlines up to your neck or lots of time on your hands."

"Commercial art will be steadier."

Ev gestured at her desk. "Steady boredom you mean. For me, anyway. I'd go crazy if this was my whole purpose in life." She grinned. "Though there are those who tell me I'm crazy, as it is."

"Why crazy?"

"Oh, the painting." Ev waved her hand at the window. "That's what I'm doing when I look at my plants, you know. Figuring out what to do with my latest piece. Mental painting, I guess."

"You paint? I mean, outside of work?"

"'Work' is a word that does not apply to this job." Ev leaned back and pointed her pencil at her board. "That's a job. My painting is my real work."

Deb dropped her pencil and leaned forward. "What do you do? I mean, medium and subject and all that?"

"Oils, when I can buy them." She waved at the window again. "Buying them is the other thing I'm thinking about when I stare out the window. Mostly it's watercolor." She went on, explaining coloring and technical problems she was working on. Deb, her chin on her hand, elbow against the drawing table, listened carefully, trying to ask the right questions. Finally someone came in with an urgent project and they bent over their boards again.

Deb drew slowly. Why had Ev told her all this, when she'd never mentioned it before? Maybe just to show her there were other things she could do besides commercial art?

But there was too much pain and frustration in the other. Ev certainly sounded pained and frustrated enough. And you couldn't do it completely. You had to find time for a job. You couldn't give yourself totally to what you loved.

That kind of divided life wasn't for her. Not that kind of drivenness. As much as she loved art, she liked the commercial part more than the adventurous. She didn't want to wander into the regions of fear Ev travelled each month, scrounging money for canvas and oil.

The same thinking had driven Randy, in his law work, to get involved in the arts issues he took on. It was a kind of outlet. A way of caring without being eaten alive. It was another bond between them. Deb felt her fingers firm into a more comfortable grip on the french curve she was using to get the right sweep into the hood of the car in her sketch. She began shading it in.

Still, she wished he would call. She looked at the phone. She also wished she had the nerve to dial his number, but she was afraid she'd interrupt a meeting or something and only cause problems.

At four thirty she was still listening for its ring. It was usual for employees to leave between four thirty and five, depending on when they'd arrived. She dawdled over her board until there was nothing left to do, short of starting a new project.

She walked slowly home, hardly aware of the air's soft springiness after yesterday's rain. What would she do with herself while she put in another evening of waiting? She could sketch, she supposed. The leaves on her coleus offered some tricky problems in shading and she'd been trying her hand at them off and on.

But the thought made her more listless. She'd rather see Randy. There were her magazines. She didn't really feel like looking at them either. She could read art books. The trouble was, all she really wanted was to see Randy.

And then there he was, standing beside the iron gate at the foot of the stairs, smiling his warm smile at her. The shock took her voice away.

She walked to him and put her face against his shoulder. His hand curved around her neck as he kissed her.

She unlocked the gate and he followed her up. He lifted the purse from her shoulder as they went in the door and helped her out of her coat. It fell to the floor as he reached for her, arms around her shoulders and waist, legs firm against hers, chest pushing against her breasts hungrily.

She pushed herself away from him shakily. She had to work to make her voice light and teasing. "Miss me?" she asked.

He kissed her again, his lips hard and hungry. "Any more questions?" he asked into her hair. He held her away, at arm's length, and looked at her. She moved back into his arms, holding herself against him tightly. "What a nice way to come home," she said into his shoulder.

His arms tightened. "I think we had better get out of here," he said. She looked up at him.

He kissed her forehead, deliberately light. "I have to buy a present for my client. Sort of an appreciation gift for not going to court. She was so mad, she's dying to tell the world all her problems. Really messy, if she'd had her way." He grinned at her. "Ex-client, that is. It would have been extremely time consuming if she'd had her way and we may not even have won. Thank God that case is closed."

She laughed. "I thought it must be, since you've come back to the land of the living."

His hand touched her cheek. "Yes, this is living."

She picked up her coat. "What kind of gift is appropriate for an ex-client, anyway? Do you have certain standards and price ranges and such?"

They went down the stairs discussing gifts and clients. Her face still tingled from his kisses.

~~~

Jack's cot was empty when Lawrence woke the next morning. There was a vindictive relief in knowing he didn't have to endure any chatter today. For a while, anyway. He could work in peace.

But maybe Jack would come back. Lawrence looked at the other cot. It wasn't usual for him to leave it rumpled like that. Normally it was made, then covered with scraps of clothing left over from getting just the right look for whatever business Jack was trying that day. What you were selling made a difference in what you wore. What you were cleaning or hauling did too. Lawrence had been informed of these basic clothing principles every morning for the past several weeks.

And he'd been so quiet. Jack always made a lot of racket, burrowing about, muttering to himself as he tried first one tie, then another. Lawrence was usually awake long before he left. This morning there'd been no noise at all, as far as Lawrence knew.

He slipped down the stairs for his morning browse through the garbage cans. When he came back the cots were the way he'd left them. He munched on the good parts of the moldy doughnuts he'd found and went downstairs to get water. No sign of Jack.

He came back to the room and looked around irritably. Jack's noise was a nuisance, but at least Lawrence knew what he was doing and when he'd be back. Some kind of schedule to fit his writing into. This way, he had no idea what was happening.

"Leave it to Jack," he muttered. He rubbed his hand over his face. "Leave it to any of them. Just keep the pressure on, keep it steady,
~~~

keep it coming, never let up. The minute you get used to the way things are, get to doing it differently. It's another trick, that's what it is."

He walked back and forth the length of the room. He looked at the door. "Damn it, I almost wish he'd come back." He rubbed his face with his hand and went to the window.

He leaned against the piece of wood separating the panes and looked down. The street was empty. The window moved under his weight and he pulled back. If he'd pressed much harder, the wood would have given way completely.

On the other hand, you couldn't force the window up. It was too warped by the weather. This place might be a roof over his head but that was about all it was. "The earth is the Lord's and the fullness— Oh hell!"

He turned and kicked at Jack's cot. Where had he gone, the sneaking bastard? He had no business creeping off, making trouble. It was going to be impossible to get anything done, not knowing when he'd show up. And being Jack, he'd appear just when Lawrence had got a sentence formed but not yet written down. He'd come barging in and Lawrence would lose the whole thing.

He was such a nuisance, getting in the way like he did. His idiot hopes and stupid false cheeriness. The least he could do was tell the truth— He hadn't got work yet and probably wouldn't. There wasn't any to get. He didn't have to pretend the whole world was brimming with opportunities waiting to fall into his hands like rotten berries.

But then, they always did. They were all Jacks. The old codger. The manager. His wife. Sneaking around, making you do things you didn't want to. Sending you places you didn't want to go and didn't have time to waste on. He looked at the door. If there were only some way he could know Jack wouldn't come bursting in ten minutes after he began writing.

His cot. That was it. And the suitcases. They were pretty heavy. He pushed the cot down the wall until it was against the door. He piled Jack's suitcase, then his own, on top of it. He shoved the two chairs side by side between Jack's cot and the end of his own. They made a kind of wedge. The door could only be opened a few inches now.

He looked at it, nodded and opened his suitcase for his paper and pen. Then he stopped and looked at the door again. He pulled his kitchen knife out of the suitcase and laid it on the cot.

The blocked door gave him a sense of solitude he hadn't had in months. He sat cross-legged on Jack's rumpled blankets and began reading through the seventy-odd pages he'd written.

He read slowly, absorbed in the flow of words and ideas, correcting a misspelling here, adding or deleting a word or two there. His excitement grew steadily.

He was on his feet with the last sentence, pacing the floor between the window and chairs. He clutched his papers triumphantly. He really had it. This was good. He stopped and looked down at the pages. Had he really written them? It was hard to believe.

But it still wasn't finished. It wasn't, but it would be. He paced back and forth, his legs searching for more floor space, unsteady with sheer excitement. He'd finish it now. This was good and this would do it. This would make him a name. This would get him somewhere. The small room seemed to open around him into unlimited, free-flying space.

He turned and looked at the door and its barricade. If he could just finish now, in peace and in quiet. This was the first chance he'd had to sit and read the whole thing completely through. Now he knew where he'd been and where he was going. He could finish it now, if they'd only leave him alone long enough.

He was back on the cot, writing firmly and swiftly, when the door's knob turned and its edge cracked sharply against the side of the other cot.

"Hey!" The door closed and Lawrence looked up. He was thinking out another sentence and his eyes didn't see the cot and suitcase in front of him.

The knob turned again, this time more slowly. The door opened its few inches. "Hey Lawrence, you in there?" Jack's false energy brought Lawrence irritably out of his trance. Damn. And there went his sentence. He tried again. "This historical viewpoint of any particular group—"

"Hey Lawrence, old buddy, what's happening? You gotta be in there, the light's on!"

"—will lead them to make assumptions about current events, hence narrowing their perspective and options—"

There was a shout of laughter from the door. ""Hey friend, is this a joke? What've you got in there anyway? Your cot? Sure does work to keep people out, in a manner of speaking!"

"—thus constricting the decision-making process." Lawrence wrote it out and then read it over. He rubbed a hand over his face. Next sentence. "However—"

"Hey Lawrence! Look man, I know you're in there. Why don't you say so and open up and we'll forget all about it, okay?"

Lawrence's hand tightened on the book his paper was on. There was a pressure building inside his head. He gritted his teeth. "However, the narrowing of options creates a state of mind which may be hazardous to the continuation of the power or status of the group—"

There was a melodramatic sigh behind the door. "Okay buddy. You win. I'll go get the manager." The door shut.

Lawrence looked up. The pressure eased. He looked back down at the pages and the warm glow of words flowing smoothly filled him. He reread the last sentence. Now, his argument being the way it was, he'd have to point out the positive aspects in his next paragraph. He rubbed a hand over his face. Balancing it would be tricky. How did he want to say this?

He had another sentence in his head and his pen was poised over the paper again when there was another rap on the door. This was a more polite knock than Jack's banging. The knob turned slowly and the door opened the few inches the cot allowed. Lawrence looked up.

"Yes?" he said sharply.

"Lawrence? That you?"

Who did he think it was? Lawrence began writing his sentence out.

"This room Jack too. You have to share."

Lawrence frowned at the last word he'd written. "Go away," he said without looking up.

"You let in."

His pen hovered over the last word he'd written. He glanced up at the door. "He'll have to wait until I've finished," he said.

"How long you be?"

He looked at the paper again. How long? How could he know how long? How long had it taken him this far and how long to finish with these fools bothering him? "Forever," he said. "Go away."

"You no can do that."

"You're right. I can do it and I am doing it." He was off the cot now, striding back and forth in the small space that was left. "I have work to do. Leave me alone and I'll finish it. But you keep harassing me and I'll make you sorry, understand?"

As he moved from the window to the cot he saw the knife on the bed. He picked it up and looked at the door. He went back to the window and put his back to it. He faced the door.

"See this?" He held the handle up so that the blade showed clearly in the dim light from the window. "See this? You can't understand words but I'll bet you understand this. Illiterate fools!" His voice rose and he raised the knife too, higher, against the window, to make sure they could see it.

There was a sharp intake of breath beyond the dark crack in the doorway. A hand yanked violently at the knob and the door banged shut.

There. Maybe they'd leave him alone. He tossed the knife onto the cot and sat down again. He had work to do.

~~~

Perfume was the thing to get an ex-client, they decided. A female one, anyway. Chanel 22 or something like that. Something classic and expensive without being gaudy.

They found what they needed at Nordstrom's and were edging their way through the crowd to the door. Deb was in front of Randy. Suddenly she stopped short. Her head turned, following someone on the short side of the store. Randy turned too.

She started away from the main aisle.

"Where are you going?" he asked.

"That was Bobby. I'm sure it was."

"Bobby?"

"You know. My brother Bobby. Nobody has red hair like his and I saw a head of red hair moving down—" She stopped and looked around carefully. "This way. I'm sure it was over here." She turned completely around, studying the crowd. "And now I don't see him."

"You're sure it was him?"

"Nobody else has hair like that. It's not just red, it's bright orange."

"True. But—"

"And it was cut like his. I mean short, like a man's cut would be, but real bushy. Like it needed combing."

"Did you see the rest of whoever it was?"
~~~

"Just the head."

"Wait a minute. Look there, straight ahead and then over a little. That counter near where the purses are hanging. Is that who you saw?"

"Why would he— That's him, though." She maneuvered through the other shoppers to get closer. She went more slowly now. Would Bobby be here in Seattle without her knowing about it? And why would he be looking at purses at Nordstrom's?

The figure at the counter was stocky and wore blue jeans and a heavy wool sweater. From the back, it looked like Bobby. Deb moved to the other side of the counter. The figure's head turned.

It was a woman. Stocky, in heavy sweater and jeans and with bright short-cropped red hair. But a woman. Deb opened her mouth, then closed it again, and turned to Randy.

"Nothing here!" she said. She tried to shrug casually. She turned and hurried toward the entrance, with Randy behind her.

He didn't catch up until she'd gotten outdoors. She stood on the corner, watching the lights change color, and kept her face straight, trying to hold herself in.

"Remind me to tell Bobby next time I talk to him that you saw him at Nordstrom's," he murmured into her ear.

She turned, her eyes dancing. "Don't you dare!" She collapsed against his shoulder. "It's a good thing you warned me. I'd have felt like an idiot. And can you imagine that woman's face when I explained I thought she was my brother?"

He was still threatening to tell Bobby she'd mistaken a woman for him when they'd found a restaurant.

They ordered and he grinned at her. "You know, for a sophisticated, experienced woman of the world, you certainly are innocent. You can't even tell a man from a woman!"

She laughed at him, then her face changed. "I don't like the word experienced."

He looked at her. She lowered her eyes. "It makes me think of—You know. Andrew. That guy in high school."

"That didn't sound like much of an experience to me."

"More than you've had."

But there was the waitress. They were silent as she put down their plates and Randy went through the wine-checking ritual.

Deb picked at her food.

"It really does bother you, doesn't it?" Randy put down his fork.

She nodded at him. "Silly, isn't it? Guilt or something, I suppose. Not exactly sophisticated."

"I could go out and do something. Would that make you feel better?"

Her eyes widened and she started to put her fork down.

"Good Lord, I'm kidding. Don't you know that?" He reached for her hand. "Is it really guilt, though?"

She picked up her knife and cut sharply into her steak. "I don't know what it is, really."

He sat for a moment, watching her eat. "Deb—" His voice dropped and looked around at the tables near them. No one paid any attention. "Deb— Are you worried because I haven't?"

She stopped chewing. Her eyes met his, then flickered away. "I know that you love me," she said to her steak.

"Only you? Nobody else, ever? Ever?"

She nodded wordlessly and again he reached for her hand. "Deborah, look at me."

She put down her fork, closed her eyes for a moment, then looked into his face. "I have had all sorts of weird doubts and thoughts lately," she said. Her hand tightened on his.

"I— I love you." She lowered her eyes. "The things I feel about you...or for you— Whatever. I've never felt this way before and it's scary. I— I guess maybe I just worry too much, but I don't want anything to happen between us that's not right. Right for us, I mean. And then there's the moral thing and what would Mom say and—"

"Deb."

She looked up.

"I— I've been thinking a lot about us the last couple of days. I mean, not getting to see you and not daring to call because it would make me ache for you more. Just the thought of you was bad enough and— Well, everything about you is good, and I can't think about anything else because I'm thinking about you and— I love you," he ended.

"I know. I'm that way too." She grinned at him. "About you, I mean. Ev understands and she puts up with me, but I know my work has gone down since we've gotten engaged." She frowned at him. "It wasn't so hard before that. Why is it so difficult to be away from each other now?"

He shook his head. "It was hard before. I just about went nuts at your parents' because I couldn't touch you whenever I wanted to." His fingers moved over her hand. "And all I want to do is touch you."

Their eyes held until she had to pull away from the dizziness. She looked at the untouched food on her plate.

"Randy, I know this is ridiculous, but are you really hungry?"

He looked down. "This doesn't look good to me," he admitted. He smiled at her. "What sounds good is a cup of coffee at your place."

She squeezed his hand between trembling fingers. "Let's go home."

<h1 style="text-align:center">21</h1>

There was an hour of silence. Lawrence stretched into it like a cat. He mulled each sentence carefully before crafting it onto the paper.

And now for the final argument. He counted through the pages again, reread the last one and began to form the summarizing paragraphs in his head. But the tension of being at the end was so great that he couldn't think. Almost finished. The adrenalin pounded through his head until he could hardly see. The end. The end!

He rubbed his face with his hands. He got up, moving restlessly from the cot to the window, and then went back to the cot. He took a deep breath of the thick attic air, willed himself calm with the last bit of psychic energy he had left, and began forming the first sentence of his conclusion. A police siren wailed from a nearby street.

"Thus we see that the view of the past held by those in the present affects their future, both by supplying them with preconceived notions of—"

As he wrote in the next word, there was a sharp echoing bang on the attic door. His hand jerked. The pen skidded across the paper.

"Damn!" He thrust the pages to one side and jumped off the cot. He took the knife from the other bed. "I told you to leave me alone!"

"This is the police." A hand moved cautiously through the few inches of open door and a badge flashed in the light.

"Sure," Lawrence said. "Sure Jack. You're a salesman too, aren't you? And a steel worker." He tightened his grip on the knife. "I told you to leave me alone. I've got work to do. You don't have anything in here you can't live without."

"How long do you plan on making us wait?"

"Fool. I told you that, too." He moved to the window. The crack of the open door was nothing but blackness. "Forever, if you want to. I don't care. Just leave me alone, understand?" There was someone there, though. He could feel them.

Feel them waiting. He rubbed his face with his free hand. "I've got work to do," he muttered. "And I have a right to finish it!" he said to the door. "You hear me? I'm going to do it!"

"Okay, okay," the voice said soothingly. "We'll give you three hours and then you can come out. How's that? But remember," the voice sounded stern. "You have to come out sooner or later and it would be better if it was sooner. Less trouble all around, if you know what I mean."

A spring broke inside Lawrence's head. "If you know what I mean!" he yelled. "In a manner of speaking! I know you Jack and I'm through with your mouth. Understand? Understand?"

He was screaming now. The door remained open. Lawrence moved toward it but he could see only the faint outline of a man's head. There was no sound but his own breathing. It filled the room, the whole world. The noise was unbearable.

"You think you're so smart and you talk and you talk and I can't think!" He was at the end of the cot now. Still no sound but himself. "I can't think and you're talking and talking and I can't hear anything anymore. Don't you understand?" His voice was rasped with strain and the breathing was tearing at his insides. His hand was tight on the knife, but he didn't feel it.

All the tensions that had been building inside him for the last six months were coming out now and he didn't know anything but the need for release.

"Understand?" he screamed at the figure behind the door. It was silent.

He was on the cot now, crouching on it with his knife raised to his shoulder and back beyond it. His voice rose higher, more shrill with each word. "Get away from me! Understand? Leave me alone! Understand?"

His arm came forward, all his tensions released into the working of his taut muscles, and the knife went through the opening in the doorway and into flesh. Lawrence felt it for only a moment, because the body fell away from him and he let go of the knife.

The lunge to the door had made him lose his balance and he fell onto the cot as the door was wrenched violently shut. There were voices and stumbling footsteps down the stairs.

Again there was silence. Lawrence got up from the cot and went to the window. His breath came more easily. His hand clenched and unclenched as if he still held the knife. He pushed his hair away from his face.

"I hit him," he muttered. He grinned. "That'll keep his mouth shut for a while. That'll make them leave me alone."

He walked back and forth in the cramped space between the window and the beds. His leg muscles weren't as tight now.

The walking felt good. "I'll finish you now," he said to the papers and pen on the cot. "I'll finish you perfectly now."

His hand clenched. There was still anger there, if he went into himself far enough. "They know they can't play with me now."

He went to the window again, then turned to pace back. Suddenly he stopped. He turned and looked through the dirt-covered panes. There were spotlights below.

This street didn't have lights lining it. It didn't get enough traffic. He put his head against the glass and cupped his hands around his eyes, to see out.

The voice really had been police. There were patrol cars and flashing red lights at each end of the block. Three more were parked opposite his window. People from the surrounding houses and apartment buildings stood in groups on the sidewalk.

As he watched, a square white van with a red cross painted on its side drove around a barricade. Two men jumped out. They pulled a stretcher from the doors at the back and hurried toward the old house he was in. Lawrence looked at his door and the cot where the knife had been lying all afternoon.

So he'd really hit him enough to shut him up. To call a medical unit, anyway. His eyes glittered.

But the voice had said he was police. Maybe it really hadn't been Jack. It hadn't been as good buddy buoyant, but some of the words were the same. The important ones.

His hand tightened onto itself. Those were policemen down there. Jack or no Jack, they'd be coming. He walked back and forth, to the cots, then to the window. To the cots, then to the window again.

Time. They'd said they'd give him time. But what now, with a knife in somebody's chest? His hands clenched again.

But still there was time. Thinking it made him stand still. He had what he'd wanted. If it gave him enough space to finish in, then he didn't care who he'd hurt. He went to the edge of the cot. The pages were scattered across the rumpled and ragged blankets and pillow.

As long as he could finish it, that was all. There was nothing else anyway. He pushed the despair away. There wasn't time for self-pity. He'd sit here and he'd finish and they could come after him if they wanted to. He had work to do before they did, that was all.

He lifted his head from his pages. Someone below was speaking thickly through a megaphone. He moved impatiently. Someone else boomed shrilly into the air. He knew Jack's voice instantly.

He rubbed his face with his hands. His fist worked convulsively and he picked up his pen. His arm stabbed down at the blankets, making large inky holes. "Quiet!" he muttered. "Fool! Just be quiet!" His arm jerked again and again. At last the voice stopped. Then another voice started talking. It wasn't Jack, though, so it didn't bother him so much.

He picked up his papers. Trying to make him stop, were they? Wouldn't let him finish. Couldn't bear to see him accomplish a single thing. Well, he'd do it. No matter how much they bellowed down there. He'd beat them at their own game. He'd finish, no matter what.

The megaphone ran down after a while and he settled cross-legged onto the cot. The city quieted around him as he wrote. Even the sirens were muted in the silence of the dark sky.

~~~

Deborah made the coffee carefully, trying not to think about what was ahead, Randy a while in the bathroom and coming out to hold her wordlessly. She handed him his cup, got her robe from the closet and kissed him with cold lips. Then she closed the door of the bathroom behind her.

As she tested the shower water for warmth she heard the clock radio beside the couch clicking on. Her face relaxed. The everyday sound of the radio, filling in the spaces of waiting, promised that though this was the first time, there would be more.

She showered slowly, careful to keep her makeup in place, and dried shivering in the sudden cold. She found her fingers dabbing perfume in places she'd never touched with it before.

They were giving the hourly news report when she came out. The voice crackled with static. "—waiting to see what will happen next. From where I stand now—" Randy saw her, switched it off and put his coffee cup on the end table. He had taken off his jacket and tie.

"What was all that about?" she asked.

"Some man barricaded himself in a room at the free housing project on Capitol Hill. The people there called the police and
~~~

when they came and tried to talk him out, he stabbed one of them. He's still holed up in there, I guess. They're talking about going in with a SWAT team in the morning."

She sat down on the opposite end of the couch. He reached for her hand.

"Did he kill him?" she asked.

He put her hand to his face. "Don't you use warm water when you shower? Your hands are like ice." He slid down to her end of the couch. "They said the officer he stabbed was in serious condition. They've got him in surgery at Harborview."

She nodded. She could feel the warmth of his arms and his thigh through her robe.

"Your face is cold too," he said. He kissed her forehead.

"You're nice and warm," she murmured. She moved closer to him. Her lips found his neck.

"Why don't we make out the bed?"

They made it together more quickly than she'd ever done by herself. She undid her robe and slide between the sheets without looking at him.

At the first feel of his body next to hers, she gasped from the shock and then gave in to the sensations which crowded in.

He touched her gingerly at first, then with growing strength, firmly inside her and deft. She could feel the warm tensions building within her like nothing she'd ever dreamed of. Building and building until a sudden exquisite collapse into warm and honey-gold peace. She lay under him, feeling the thrust of his body. She'd come. Wasn't that the word for it? A faraway part of her brain thought it out lazily.

There were tears on her cheeks. He lay on top of her, breathing quickly, then propped his elbows onto the bed to take his weight off her chest. He kissed her face and tasted the tears.

"Deb'rah, you're crying."

She nodded, her eyes closed.

"Deb? Deb'rah, I'm sorry. I thought it was what you wanted. I should have asked you directly, but you seemed so willing and it seemed so unromantic to just say it. I'm sorry, Deb. I—"

Her eyes opened. She smiled at him and touched his chest. "It was so beautiful." She sniffed. "I didn't mean to cry."

He pulled her closer and they lay, thighs touching, between the cool sheets. There was a long moment of silence, then he stirred as if to get closer than he already was. Their bodies curved into each other and he kissed her neck. "Hello wife," he said.

She smiled into his bare shoulder. "We haven't had the ceremony yet."

"For me this was the ceremony, the coming together," he said.

She pulled her head back. "What do you mean?"

"Don't move. It feels too good." He pulled her against him again.

"It feels good to be here," she said. She rubbed her cheek on his shoulder.

"You know, they're right about marriage not being a mere piece of paper," he said. "No, don't pull away. Or am I crushing you?"

She shook her head against the sweet smell of his skin.

"I mean, I want the piece of paper," he said. "I want you in every sense of the word. But if there were no such thing—if marriage in legality didn't exist—I'd still feel married to you." He touched her cheek with his hand. "Hello wife," he whispered.

She blinked back the tears.

~~~

The inhabitants of the house had been evacuated quickly. Most had no relatives to go to. They stood on the sidewalk opposite and watched. The manager had convinced his wife to stay indoors with the children. He and Jack were the only people allowed between the squad cars and the house.
~~~

He stood among the weeds at the edge of the cracked sidewalk and looked up at the small window between the eaves. His anxiety for his home and livelihood was obvious. No one spoke to him.

Jack was sitting in the back of one of the cars, giving his statement. "Personally, I thought the guy was crazy from the start, if you know what I mean. Loco, in a manner of speaking. Always writing. He never looked for work, even though that's the only way you're allowed to stay here, if you know what I mean. He's been here before, from what they tell me. Sounds like he was loco then too, in a manner of speaking." He winked at the officer in the front seat.

"And he gets dirtier and weirder every day. It got so I was afraid to talk to him, if you know what I mean. All he wanted to do was scribble on his little pieces of paper. Thought he was writing a great book or so he told me. You know, that's not the only weapon he had," he added, as if he'd been talking about the knife all along.

The officer looked up from his notebook. "Did you see anything else?"

"Well now, I don't say that I saw it. But he told me he had other stuff. More important and bigger. That's what he said and I quote him exactly, if you know what I mean. Bigger and more important. That's what he said." Jack's eyes were big and his voice solemn. The officer flipped his book shut. He nodded at Jack and climbed stiffly out of the car. "Hey man, I'm not through," Jack called after him.

The officer moved across the street and spoke to one of the officers watching the house. This one had a bull horn dangling from his arm. He listened impassively. The officer Jack had been talking to went to the other patrol car and leaned over the window.

Everything was silent. Suddenly a man's form was silhouetted against the attic window. Then the light went out. Somebody on the sidewalk said "Shit!" in a loud voice. The man with the bull horn raised his other hand. He spoke into a walky-talky.

They waited. Gradually the light began to change. At four o'clock a few birds twittered on the roof tops. At four thirty, a message came that the officer who had been stabbed was out of the operating room but still in danger. At five o'clock the sky lightened enough to see figures in gray-green clothing grouped around the door of the house.

There were automatic rifles in their hands and tear gas grenades clipped to their belts. The people on the sidewalk were told to move to the other end of the block, behind the barricades. Everyone watched the upper window. He had more weapons than the knife.

The megaphone went into action again. "This is the police speaking. Do you hear me up there?"

No answer.

"Hello, the fourth floor. Hello, the attic. Can you hear me?"

No answer.

They looked at each other. Surely he hadn't slept, knowing he'd stabbed a man. A good chance of survival, the hospital said, though still in a critical state.

"Hello the attic!"

No answer, but then the light flashed on. A dark shape moved across the window. The watchers stiffened.

"Hello the attic! Can you hear me?"

The officer licked his lips. He lifted the megaphone again. "You have ten minutes. Ten minutes, do you hear me? If you don't come out in ten minutes, we're coming in. Come out with your hands up within ten minutes and you'll be safe. Do you hear me?"

Silence. The light went out. The window glinted dully against the morning light.

Lawrence wearily paced the narrow space he'd left for himself. The writing was done. The pages lay neatly numbered on top of the cot.

At least he had finished that. They couldn't say he hadn't accomplished something. This was what he had come here for and now it was finished. It was all that mattered, anyway.

But now that it was done— He knew he was going to jail. At the end of the long night of work, now that the manuscript was finished, he didn't care. That's what they did to people who stabbed police officers. It didn't matter. He'd finished what he'd begun.

But what should he do with the manuscript? He couldn't take it with him to prison. He paced the room carefully, feeling his way in the dark. They didn't need to see what he was doing. They'd be here soon enough. In the meantime he had to decide.

He rubbed his hands over his face. If only there was someone he could trust. Sister Ann. Would she remember? Or care? But it was the only route he had open. He pulled the string to the light bulb again. Down below, the SWAT team shifted nervously. They had two more minutes by the lead officer's watch.

Lawrence rummaged in his suitcase, found the piece of paper which Sister Ann had written her address on and some rubber bands. He took out several sheets of the paper he had left. He wrapped them around the manuscript and then carefully wrote her name and address on the outside sheets.

There was a dollar bill left in his wallet. He'd saved it to buy a new pen when this one ran out. He would put the bill under the rubber bands and the postal people could have what was left. It should be more than enough. It was only going across the city.

As he got up from the cot, there was a sudden banging at the door and the wood splintered under the weight of a rifle butt. Lawrence, reaching for his hip pocket and wallet, started and half turned.

The door hadn't been forced further open, but there was a gun barrel in the hole the butt had made and it turned on him as he felt for his wallet.

The impact of the bullets stopped his hand. Their force pushed him back and then slumped him forward onto the cot and smeared the packaged manuscript with his blood. The address was illegible by the time they found the papers beneath him.

22

Deborah and Randy cooked breakfast together, then walked to the store. They bought a Saturday paper along with the special weekend edition. "There isn't any real news in the weekend one," Randy explained on their way back. "Besides, this way we don't have to fight over which sections we want to read."

"You're going to read most of them anyway," Deb told him. "I want to work on my sketching. The light this morning is perfect for trying the shadows on those coleus leaves."

They settled onto the couch, thighs touching, coleus positioned on the floor to get the leaves just right, papers piled onto the glass topped table.

Randy went through the front pages of both papers before he turned to the inside of the Saturday edition. Deb looked up from her work and leaned across him to look at a composite drawing of a man at the top of the page. "Who's that?" she asked.

"That's the guy I was telling you about," he said. "The one who stabbed that officer at the free housing place."

"That's funny," she said. She put her hand under the paper and lifted the picture toward her from the opposite side. "He looks familiar."

He grinned. "The way that woman at Nordstrom's looked familiar?"

She made a face at him. "The hair was the same, you have to admit. There aren't a whole lot of people in this world with that shade of orange."

"True." He kissed her cheek.

She looked at the picture again. "I could swear that I know him from somewhere," she said under her breath.

Randy dropped the corner he held with his left hand and put his arm around her shoulders.

She snuggled in next to him and lifted her sketch pad from her lap. "Not that it matters," she said.

She yawned and studied the shadows on the coleus plant. "You know, if I can get these leaves simple enough, they'd make a great illustration of summer house plants for an ad." She bit the end of her pencil, watching the light on the leaves.

Randy patted her shoulder and pulled her still closer against him.

The End